AZABU GETAWAY

Azabu Getaway

By Michael Pronko

Copyright © 2022 Michael Pronko

ISBN 978-1-942410-26-3

Also available in Paperback 978-1-942410-28-7

First English Edition, Raked Gravel Press

Cover Design © 2022 Marco Mancini, www.magnetjazz.net

Layout and backcover design by BEAUTeBOOK www.beautebook.com

For more about the Detective Hiroshi series and Pronko's other writing: www.michaelpronko.com

Follow Michael on Twitter:
@pronkomichael

Michael's Facebook page:
@pronkoauthor

ALSO AVAILABLE BY MICHAEL PRONKO

Memoirs on Tokyo Life

Beauty and Chaos: Slices and Morsels of Tokyo Life (2014)
Tokyo's Mystery Deepens: Essays on Tokyo (2014)
Motions and Moments: More Essays on Tokyo (2015)

The Detective Hiroshi Series

The Last Train (2017)
The Moving Blade (2018)
Tokyo Traffic (2020)
Tokyo Zangyo (2021)

AZABU GETAWAY

by Michael Pronko

Raked Gravel Press 2022

"Everything a *sokaiya* does has meaning."

—Kenneth Szymkowiak, *Sokaiya*

"Whenever a person says to you that they are as innocent as lambs in all concerning money, look well after your own money, for they are dead certain to collar it, if they can. Whenever a person proclaims to you 'In worldly matters I'm a child,' you consider that that person is only a crying off from being held accountable, and that you have got that person's number, and it's Number One."

— Charles Dickens, *Bleak House*

List of Characters

<u>Hiroshi</u>
    Hiroshi, Forensic accountant, main detective
    Ayana, Hiroshi's girlfriend

<u>Detectives</u>
    Sakaguchi, Chief of homicide, ex-sumo wrestler
    Takamatsu, Old-school detective, smokes
    Ishii, New female detective
    Akiko, Detective staff, Hiroshi's assistant
    Sugamo, Detective, ex-sumo wrestler
    Osaki, Detective, ex-rugby player
    Ueno, Detective injured by gunshot, stays in office
    Ota, Deaf private investigator
    Shibutani, Old-school private investigator, Ota's boss,
        Takamatsu's friend

<u>Walsh Family and Friends</u>
    Patrick, Investment whiz, father, husband
    Miyuki, Bank account manager, mother, wife
    Jenna, Older daughter
    Kiri, Younger daughter
    Grandmother, Miyuki's mother
    Kyle, Patrick's best friend
    Miki, Kyle's girlfriend
    Taiga, Babysitter for Walsh family
    Reon, Taiga's brother

Nine Dragons
- **Leung,** Head CEO
- **Arisa,** Former office manager
- **Mehta,** New office manager
- **Tran,** Head of security

Other characters
- **Watanabe,** Bureaucrat at National Tax Agency
- **Kosugi,** Old-school yakuza and investor
- **Nozaki,** Chasing his money down
- **Tim,** Helps Patrick, arrested
- **Tamura,** Miyuki's divorce lawyer
- **Kamiya,** Head of Pacific Investment
- **Daisuke and hosts,** Host club hosts

Chapter 1

Patrick Walsh waited outside, tired of the cold, of the dark, thinking it through, worried that the key wouldn't work.

In case it didn't, he'd brought along a mini cordless drill, three sizes of drill bits, a screwdriver, a pick, and needle-nose pliers packed into a drawstring bag. He'd watched a few online videos on how to ream out a lock.

He keyed in the passcode at the entrance of his Azabu apartment building—it still worked—and rode the elevator to his floor. He kept his head down under a cap and resettled his mask, protection against cameras, as much as against viruses.

He'd almost never met anyone in the hallway and no one was there now. That's what you paid more for in the middle of Tokyo—few neighbors, silent hallways, extra rooms.

And cleaners. There were always cleaners. The hallways gleamed.

He slipped the key in, held his breath as he twisted, and the deadbolt fell to the side. With the drawstring bag back over his shoulder, he twisted the door handle, stepped in, and toed off his shoes in the *genkan*.

In the room to the left, his mother-in-law was sprawled in her regular spot on her tatami chair in front of the TV. She kept the TV blaring 24/7, but she was out cold, as usual, stoned on a mix of sleeping pills and glasses of *shochu* she hid on a shelf above the refrigerator.

He tiptoed over and turned off the TV. Her cosmetic-smeared wrinkles and thinning hair were just the same, but she was a bit pudgier, eating well on the money he sent while she filled Miyuki's ears with invective against him. She must have smoked inside too, or the smell just oozed out of her.

Patrick turned off the lights in the small tatami room and slid the door shut. She was supposed to be at her weekly mahjong game, but maybe the others had kicked her out for cheating.

After Miyuki's father died and her mother and multiple TVs moved in, the house resonated with the inane patter and forced laughter of quiz shows, travelogues, comedy routines, and program after program about food. Everything was *oishii, sugoi, or yabaii*, the exclamations silly and senseless. She demanded the most expensive tatami mats, but filled their home with drivel.

The living room looked smaller than he remembered, but that was because the rooms in Wyoming were so large. For Tokyo, their place was huge for a family of four, plus grandmother. Until Wyoming, it was the largest place he ever lived in. Miyuki had been overwhelmed to silence when they first looked at it. The living room alone was bigger than their entire former apartment in Monzen-Nakacho.

They'd paid for it in cash, so much cash even Miyuki had been startled when they hauled it to the realtor. After they paid, she collapsed weeping in his arms, surprised at how their happy their life had turned out.

Patrick had just started at Nine Dragons and Miyuki had been promoted after her bank merged with two others. They set up savings, investments, even college funds, and still had more than they knew what to do with. But it wasn't just the money then. It was being together about everything.

The sofa was where they'd curled up every night during her pregnancy, both of them worn out from work, Miyuki doubly tired with the pregnancy. She took leave as late as she could before Jenna arrived, and again, a couple of years later, when Kiri arrived. Miyuki had kept working at the same bank as accounts manager even while taking most of the burden for the girls.

Through it all, their large multisectional sofa served as nursery, game room, study center, work station, bed, table, and, occasionally after the girls went to sleep, the spot for a quick one. He called it "the whale," as it became piled with games, toys, study books, sports equipment, cats, caged bugs, and work files that Miyuki and Patrick carried home to finish up side-by-side.

After nine months away in Wyoming, those times seemed farther away than ever. Patrick looked down the hallway toward the bedrooms.

The cats came out and eyed him suspiciously, but he was too tired from the long flight to re-friend them. The support group advised staying flexible and flowing, without getting stuck on any one task. Now, all he needed to do was gather the girls and get out of there. The support group advised him on all the details of what to do, since they'd been through it all before.

Behind him, the front door creaked open and a man's voice echoed into the entryway. "*Dare desu-ka*? Miyuki? *Ano, dareka iru no?* Miyuki?"

Patrick tiptoed back to the front wall half-expecting to see Miyuki's next conquest. Was this the next one? What man would be coming into the apartment?

He waited behind the wall.

The soft thud of shoes being removed and the crinkle of a plastic bag was followed by silence. Patrick knew this was what the support group meant when they said, "Remain flexible."

A young man, twenty-something, gangly and tall in loose clothes, stepped into the living room. He was carrying a plastic bag weighed down with small cartons.

Patrick stepped out. "Who are you?"

The boy's handsomely chiseled face looked half Japanese, half Western. His hair was longish and dyed in streaks.

"I'm Taiga...the...the babysitter..." he sputtered, in English. "Who are you?"

If he was the babysitter, why was he calling Miyuki by her first name? He was a decade younger, more, and an employee. Babysitter? Did he mean home tutor? What was he doing here this late?

Instead of asking, Patrick swung the drawstring bag full of tools.

The kid ducked but slipped. His head hit the edge of the sideboard and his body crumpled to the heated flooring.

Patrick waited for him to get up, but he didn't. A trickle of urine spread from his crotch and blood oozed from below his spiky, streaked hair. That was a bad sign. A very bad sign. He'd swung the tool bag too hard.

Patrick slung the bag over his shoulder and leaned over to pick the scrawny kid up from under his arms and drag him to the tatami room. He slid open the door at the opposite end from where his mother-in-law slept and wrestled him inside as quietly as he could. Blood dribbled out and quickly soaked into the finely woven *igusa* rush straw of the tatami.

"Remain on task and in motion," the support group had advised. They had done all the recon for him, after he told them the details of their daily life. They were good at what they did. They found the right time, and helped plan it all. All except the babysitter.

He followed the rest of their advice and pulled out two plastic ties for the boy's wrists and ankles. He went for towels from the kitchen, set one under his head where it was bleeding and tied the other across his mouth. The wound didn't look too bad, just a scratch.

He stared at his mother-in-law, stepped back, and slid the door shut. He got some paper towels and wiped the drips of blood from the floor. He rinsed the towels out, threw them away, and washed his hands.

He hurried into Jenna's room and tears sprang to his eyes. Draped in Disney princess pajamas, her limbs were splayed out in all directions, half in and half out of the covers. She'd grown and her hair was longer.

Beside her, Kiri slept in a fetal ball with her fists on her cheeks. She slept that way when she crawled into bed with Miyuki and him. When he left for Wyoming, he'd told her she had to start sleeping alone. At the time, she'd nodded seriously, but she must have started sleeping with her older sister instead.

Their hair was strewn in long tangles over the menagerie of stuffed animals sleeping beside them. He could smell the warm scent of their bodies and hear the little snuffles of their breathing, soft as waves. Watching them sleep was the most beautiful experience in the world. Now, he'd have them every day, and they'd be safe.

He sat down on the bed and jiggled Jenna's leg, but Kiri opened her eyes first.

"Daddy? Is that you?" Kiri wrapped her arms around his neck.

Jenna rubbed her eyes, startled, and sat up before burrowing in beside Kiri, pulling on his shirt and hugging him and trying to wake up all at the same time. "Is this a dream?"

"The best one ever." Patrick held them against his chest, looked at Jenna's mirror, and choked back tears. "Can you two get up and get dressed?"

"Is it morning?" Jenna asked. Her voice had become a little husky.

"We have a plane to catch. To America. We're going to ride horses."

"Horses?" Jenna's face lit up with excitement.

"Where the wild things are?" Kiri asked.

"No, the wild things are here. We're going where they aren't." Patrick hugged them tight for a minute and then set them loose to fill the fold-out vinyl bags he brought for them. They started snatching up their favorite clothes and dolls, and everything they loved so far in their short lives, everything they couldn't live without, and put it in the bags.

"Isn't Mom coming?" Jenna asked.

"Of course she is, but it's a surprise."

Jenna and Kiri looked at each other. "Like a surprise party?" Jenna asked.

"Exactly."

Kiri set one of her dolls back. "Is Taiga coming too?"

"He's coming later with Mom, if he can get away."

"And what about school?" Jenna put her clothes into her bag. She seemed very awake. Patrick wasn't sure if that was good.

"Just a short vacation. Mom will call the school. You'll be back before you know it."

"Before I know what?" Kiri asked.

"Before you know where the wild things are." He checked his watch. They could still make it to the airport, get checked in, and be gone, if they hurried.

Kiri giggled. She was on the borderline of believing in impossible things. But then again, so was he, things like getting away safely.

Chapter 2

The glass doors of Nine Dragons Wealth Management slid open with a soft whoosh. Sanjay Mehta, office manager, put away his passcard and reminded himself to change his key code for that week, as required by the security director.

Mehta grumbled to himself about forgetting to take home the new accounts, but he only had himself to blame. He'd forgotten to upload the new ones.

As office manager, his main responsibility was to keep such things in order. Nine Dragons had become the fastest-growing wealth management firm in Tokyo, and he wanted to keep it that way. If that took a little extra effort at times, so be it.

His apartment was only a short walk from the office along a raised walkway over the roads, shops, and ground floor sidewalks of Shinagawa. Coming back in the middle of the night still meant getting dressed. With all the surveillance cameras, it wasn't a good look if someone decided to check. At least he could dress nicely.

The doors shut behind him and Mehta turned toward his space at the back of the twentieth floor. The office design featured waist-high walls with glass dividers to the ceiling so everyone could see everyone else. Everyone used tables, desks had no drawers, files were online, so the space felt uncluttered and orderly.

The building was located in a prime spot near Shinagawa Station, an area where the post-war tangle of old-style drinking spaces and pipe-frame eateries had been transformed into a hub for high-end tourists and international business. The station marked the southern tip of the Yamanote Line that circled the interior of Tokyo. An express train ran directly to Haneda Airport and high-speed Shinkansen trains left every fifteen minutes.The whole Shinagawa area had become as clearly marked and easy to get around as an airport.

For Mehta, it was the first time to live outside Hong Kong where he grew up and Singapore where he got his MBA. He had settled in quickly to Shinagawa's globalized familiarity, its predictable conveniences.

Since he moved to Tokyo, he hadn't seen much of the city other than the Nine Dragons office. A few weekend outings to temples and tourist sites had broken the routine, along with once-a-week dinners at Michelin-starred restaurants, for which he hired a companion who spoke enough English to avoid confusion during dinner, and after.

But mostly what he'd done was keep things running smoothly as the company expanded. As soon as the deluge of new clients eased up, he promised himself more nights out. Tokyo felt like a city set up for adventures. He wasn't going to miss that.

Nine Dragons had set up its offices in Shinagawa because of Joseph Leung, its CEO. For most of the company's mission, Mehta considered him visionary, but questioned the high outlay for office space. Leung had just smiled and explained his idea of *feng shui*. The right geographic location tapped into earth's energy forces and stimulated the currents of monetary value.

The *feng shui* worked. Overseas investment and wealth management had taken off. Nine Dragons had a waiting list of moneyed Japanese unused to waiting for anything. Some called daily and others gave up angrily, but high-end investors, trust funds, and surprisingly flush pension plans kept coming. Mehta was just glad to be on board the team helping make Leung's vision a reality.

Inside the office, it was quiet. It was true that in the daytime, the office felt cheery and bright, but at night, the ambient glow from the streets and shops below, and from nearby buildings, ricocheted through the glass dividers at distorted angles.

A faint bluish light trickled from Leung's office, the

commanding space where he met clients and planned strategy. Leung's desk faced inward from his slice of the oval. The glass gave the feeling of everyone being on the same team, and Leung could see the whole team at once.

Mehta stepped into his office at the other end from Leung's and clicked on his desk light. He was in the job of a lifetime, and he was lucky to have it, so he wanted to make it work. Attention to detail, he reminded himself, was key. Practiced habits were key too. He'd read all the books on business, leadership, and productivity he had time for. Sometimes he read abridged versions with basic summaries because he wanted the main points quickly.

Mehta spun his ergonomic chair around and sat down to upload the files on new clients to access outside the office. The new security system would record his login, though, which he would have to explain at the morning meeting. All the info was on a flash drive, the one by his headphones. That was less secure, but OK this one time. He wanted to prep for Leung's daily morning meeting.

He tossed the flash drive up, caught it in his other hand, and headed back toward the elevators.

The outer doors to the elevator area glided open. Before he could press the elevator button, though, he noticed something wrong with the long ceramic mural, the proud symbol of Nine Dragons that dominated the entryway wall. The nine differently colored dragons writhing in fierce flight with poised talons and menacing eyes always impressed clients.

But now, the head of the dragon closest to the elevator had been knocked to the floor. Heaps of chips were strewn across the carpeting.

Why hadn't he seen that on the way in? Because he was looking at his cellphone?

Mehta leaned down and picked up the chunk of heavy, glazed ceramic. The thin whiskers and square jaw were intact. One eye

19

stared up at him. He held the dark blue dragon head up to its place on the wall at the end. Maybe the night-time cleaners accidentally knocked it off and fled, or didn't even see it. No one else could get into the office.

He turned it over in his hands. Where would he put the head until morning?

Strictly speaking, vandalism was a security issue, which was the domain of James Tran, the security specialist. But larger problems were all his, as office manager. A broken mural was serious.

He should notify Tran, but he'd never really bonded with Tran. They rarely even spoke. Tran's English wasn't too good, even though the official language of the company was supposed to be English. He spoke some dialect of Chinese with Leung, but Tran's communicative competence was entirely in the realm of computer code. He ran security with strict efficiency.

So, where should he put the dragon head until morning? He couldn't leave it on the floor. He hovered his passcard over the reader, keyed in his code, and the doors whooshed open again.

He stepped inside with the head in both hands. From the far office, a steady glow of bluish light came from Leung's computer. Mehta hesitated to interrupt him, but it was maybe best to take this in to Leung right away. If he wasn't there, he could set the dragon on his desk and leave a note of explanation.

A few steps away from Leung's office, he stopped and stared at the front glass of his workspace. The blue light from the two computer monitors outlined a dark splash across the glass.

Not only had the cleaning crew bashed the expensive dragon mural, but they had somehow not cleaned a stain from the window—the window of the head of the company.

Granted, there were a lot of windows to clean, but leaving the boss's office messy like that was a serious oversight. Tran had vetted the cleaning company as part of his security update, but Mehta would get this issue on that morning's agenda.

Mehta turned from the glass to Leung's black lacquer desk and closed his eyes.

He looked back at the glass again and blinked. The splatter was not cleaning fluid.

Leung's tall, thin body was slumped in his chair, his face badly smashed. One arm dangled limp by his side.

Mehta backed toward the door, but the raw, stagnant air followed him.

Two meeting chairs rested on their sides. The single, locked cabinet Leung kept in his otherwise pristine office had been ransacked. Papers spilled out from Leung's briefcase, crumpled and stained brownish-red. The screens of both monitors were cracked and his cellphone screen was in shards.

Mehta shook his head and walked back to the desk. He set the dragon head down and placed his hand on Leung's neck and then held it over his nose which had been smashed flat into his face.

No pulse and no breath.

Mehta backed to the door and pulled out his cellphone. He called the security office of the building.

None of the internal security guards spoke English, but he managed "*Kite kudasai. Ni-ju-kai*" three times to get them to come to the twentieth floor.

He stepped away from the office into the glass hallway. The reflection of the grisly scene on the windows started to fade, and the reality of it sharpened.

Chapter 3

To stop the buzzing, Detective Hiroshi Shimizu grabbed his cellphone, swiped it on, and fumbled it to his ear. He listened to Sakaguchi, head of homicide, and managed to mumble, "*Hai, hai,*" a couple of times before he realized Sakaguchi had already hung up. He had not been called out to a murder scene for several months, so there wasn't much he could say. Sakaguchi said this case had his name on it, financial crimes and in English. He repeated the address three times.

As he swung his legs out of bed, he felt his heart pumping. Hiroshi hated crime scenes. He preferred his work as a forensic accountant. Numbers didn't bleed. Or smell. Even seeing the spot where a dead body had been made him queasy. He visited the pathology lab once, and nearly fainted.

He set his cellphone back on the bedside table and reached behind him for Ayana, but she wasn't there. It was the middle of the night, but when she worked late, she often fell asleep on the sofa. He lumbered into the shower and jazzed himself with hot water.

He usually told the other detectives he was too busy tracking down the money angle on cases to go to crime scenes, but refusing Sakaguchi was hard. He only asked when needed.

Hiroshi's best argument against crime scene work was reminding them that he was the only person in the department who understod Excel or English, so they should let him focus on that, preferably from his office. It usually worked.

Hiroshi turned the water temperature down to cool off before getting out and toweling off. His current case was the murder of a fish company owner squeezed by the yakuza. His wife had stabbed him while he slept. That much was clear. In the gray zone were his high-interest loans, gambling losses, and total lack of business acumen.

That was the kind of case he liked. Contracts in English with foreign companies and a visible trail of accounting crumbs. He could work those from the safety of his office. He would have to put that case off now that Sakaguchi had called. Maybe the new case would be clean, white-collar crime so he could leave the physical forensics for everyone else in the department.

Were that the case, though, Sakaguchi would have called at a reasonable hour.

Hiroshi dressed and walked out to the kitchen. Ayana was right where he suspected—on the sofa in a tumble of papers, computers, blankets, and long black hair. An empty glass of wine rested by her laptop. He didn't want to wake her. He'd grab coffee and calories at one of the carryout places for harried businesspeople in Shinagawa.

He picked up his coat from the back of the stool and tiptoed out.

"Don't forget," Ayana muttered.

"I won't," he said. "Go back to sleep." He walked over and leaned down to kiss her. He pulled the wool comforter over her shoulders. He loved her shoulders. He let her burrow back to sleep and hurried out.

It wasn't until he hailed a taxi at the large street near their apartment in Kagurazaka that he realized he didn't know what not to forget.

Outside, most cars still had their headlights on. With no traffic, the taxi zipped past Ayana's workplace at the National Archives, the Imperial Palace and the Nagatacho Ministries, and then south to Shinagawa.

Hiroshi got out in front of the office-residence-retail tower near the station. The office complex stretched to the sky, its green glass reflecting images of the canyon of new buildings. Apparently, the urban plan was to continue developing both sides of the Yamanote Line until the entire inner circle of Tokyo was one solid loop of unending skyscrapers.

He got out of the taxi, rode the street-to-walkway escalator, and headed for the entrance to the building. The lobby's coffee stand was not yet open. He stared at it for a minute in the echo-y lobby, trapped by the desire for caffeine and the desire to get the crime scene over with.

His espresso machine waited back in his office. Waving his badge to the police guard, he headed to the elevator.

On the twentieth floor, the doors opened onto an entryway lined by a mural of nine dragons. The sprawling ceramic work must have cost a fortune. The colors were muted but it was impossible not to stare at the menacing claws, sinuous curves, and rough scales. Their eyes glared with courage and control. Dragon-like success waited at the end of the right investment plan.

The head of the last dragon, though, was chipped off, leaving dust and chunks on the carpet below. The other dragons' eyes, large and black, seemed to follow him, questioning him, as he ducked under the yellow tape stretched across the propped-open doors.

Inside, the tech staff bustled around in all directions. The office was orderly, untouched, and ready for a day of work, with a panoramic view of the sky and neighboring buildings through the multiple glass dividers. No wealth would be managed there today, though.

Hiroshi fastened on to Sakaguchi's huge hulking figure at the far end of the space. His ex-sumo wrestler's size stuck out through the glass. He towered over most of the other detectives.

Was that the room where it happened? The thought of a body—mangled, contorted, bloody—made his eyes throb. If he had secured coffee and a pastry downstairs, he would at least have something to throw up.

Most of the other detectives, he suspected, enjoyed the gruesome side of their work. Takamatsu, his mentor, said as much. He lingered over the smallest bloodstain with an old-school glee that Hiroshi couldn't fathom. They tossed around details about corpses that made Hiroshi shudder. Takamatsu had told him that violence was part of life and the human body was vulnerable to violence. The best detectives, he claimed, thought and felt like criminals did.

Paint, or something, was splattered across the window of the office where Sakaguchi stood giving orders. A technician in a white bodysuit knelt on the floor. Another bent over splotches of blood on the carpet tiles. The paint splashed across the window was blood. The victim slumped over with his head facedown on the desk. The room stank of shit, ammonia, and sanitized equipment.

The flash from the photographers made Hiroshi blink. One of the technicians held up the head of the victim for another photo. The victim's face was smashed and the nose crushed level with his cheeks.

Hiroshi looked away, his chest thumping so hard it turned all sound into a loud whisper. He wiped his forehead and directed his gaze outside. The crime scene crew was talking loudly, asking questions, clicking photographs, opening equipment, all of it a mush in Hiroshi's mind.

"Can everyone shut up!" Sakaguchi shouted, something he never did. Sakaguchi had been promoted to provisional head of the homicide division a year before. His position did the actual work and handed the results to the chief, who took the credit. Unlike the chief, though, Sakaguchi had earned the trust of every detective in the squad. His manner was slow and steady, thoughtful and powerful. Behind that manner was the explosive force of his years in sumo, a combined mental and physical force that could be focused where and when he wanted. "Can we work more quietly, please?"

The technicians hushed and bowed their heads. The photographers stood back. Sakaguchi reverted to his usual calm voice and the crew busied themselves with their tasks in a quieter mode. The techs drifted off to examine the rest of the office.

Hiroshi was tall compared to most Japanese but he still had to look up to Sakaguchi's full moon of a face.

Sakaguchi shook his head. "They don't have a body bag long enough for him."

Hiroshi shifted his gaze outside the windows. He didn't want to think about that.

"They'll have to cut one open for his feet, and then slip a second one over, tape it all up."

"Body bags come in sizes?"

"I better get mine pre-ordered." Sakaguchi pulled at his mask. "These damn masks barely cover my mouth and nose."

The crime scene crew assembled two body bags for the victim, but his feet still dangled over the end of the gurney.

Hiroshi turned his gaze to the desk. Below the transparent top spread an all-black wood carving of mountains, streams, paths, itinerant monks, and boats in a harbor. The details were finely done. In the sky, magnificent dragons soared through thick clouds. Hiroshi counted nine of the beasts. The top was cracked and a thick pool of blood was drying, blocking the traditional scene below.

Sakaguchi took a phone call and signed papers from a young detective Hiroshi didn't recognize. He hung up, and turned to Hiroshi. "Can you talk to that guy over there? Name's Mehta or something. He's the one who found the body. Looks as weak-kneed as you and he doesn't speak Japanese."

Through the blood-splattered glass, he saw a young Indian man standing anxiously in a space a couple of glass dividers away.

Osaki and Sugamo hurried in, blocking his way. Both detectives worked hard with no fuss and little comment. They stood as tall and wide as Sakaguchi, but were younger and more fit. Their size drew joking from the older, smaller detectives, though no one joked about Sakaguchi. Hiroshi trusted them completely. Whenever Osaki and Sugamo were there, things went more smoothly.

"Where were you guys?" Hiroshi asked.

Sugamo slipped around him into the office. "We went downstairs to check the video footage from security."

Hiroshi stepped outside the door to let Osaki in.

Osaki shook his head. "One guy in a black mask. That's it. Could be anybody. With a mask on, they can evade any face recognition software."

Hiroshi frowned. "What about their car?"

"Parked outside, so they never entered the garage."

"No cameras on the streets outside?"

"Black sedan, but they covered their license plate. They've done this kind of thing before."

"Did you see the victim?" Sugamo reached for his nose. "I had mine broken once. Took forever to heal."

Osaki nodded at the body. "His nose is broken for good now."

The technicians raised up the gurney and wheeled the body out of the office.

Everyone stopped talking and put their hands together as the body passed, standing with their heads bowed until the body was gone.

Hiroshi wanted to unsee all he'd just seen. He studied the Indian employee from a distance, sighed, and walked off to talk with him. Maybe the guy even had something to say.

Chapter 4

Miyuki Nakano Walsh sighed with relief and fatigue as she walked through the lobby of her building in Azabu. It had been a long day of meetings about new projects at the bank, an early evening workshop on security procedures, and then late dinner with clients.

She drank too much at dinner, and had two more at the *nijikai*, but begged off staying out later. Everyone else, all men, were probably happy to go drinking at a hostess club, where she'd be less than welcome.

It was later than she'd been out in years. She rode up in the elevator, tipsy, but sober enough to get her daughters' stuff ready for their "enjoy nature" field trip. She needed to run down the school's checklist carefully. Their requirements were more exacting than bank compliance measures. Maybe she could get a few hours of sleep too.

She kicked her low heels off in the *genkan*. She didn't hear Taiga, the babysitter, but his shoes were there. Maybe he'd slipped into the outdoor sandals and gone out for ice cream. He was addicted to the stuff, and so was she now, and so were the girls.

Miyuki slung her bag on the kitchen island, checked her two cellphones, set her iPad to silent mode, and tucked them all into her bag. She threw out her mask, she was so sick of wearing one, and washed her hands. The checklist was right where she left it. She got some water from the in-wall fridge. But where was Taiga?

She walked back to the *genkan*, Taiga's designer high-tops were in their usual place to the left, but a plastic bag of cartons dripped onto the tile beside them. Strange. He sometimes forgot the girls' appointments, homework, or bath time, but dropping ice cream on the floor was a new one. She picked up the plastic bag and walked it to the sink cupping her hand to catch the drips.

She started on the checklist for the "enjoy nature" school trip—*bento* lunchbox, outdoor clothes, butterfly nets, bug boxes, sketch pads, and mosquito spray. She couldn't trust Taiga with all that and her mother was next to worthless for anything other than complaining or watching TV.

If Jenna and Kiri woke up sleepy, it would be torture to get them moving. Once they got cranked up by videos and lit up with sugar, it could take half the night for them to get to sleep. Two weeks ago, the teacher called her to come get Jenna after she fell asleep in class. With the tuition they paid, surely there should be someplace for the girls to rest during the day. She couldn't leave work because her daughter was sleepy.

Miyuki went into the bathroom and flopped down for a much-needed pee. She pulled on shorts and washed her face. Where were the cats brushing against her to reprimand her for coming home so late?

She went to Jenna's room. Socks, shorts, and T's were tossed everywhere, but no Jenna. After Patrick left, they often migrated to one or the other room during the night, or to hers.

Stepping across the hall, Miyuki pushed open Kiri's door. The girls were not there, either. She tried her own room, but the bed wasn't touched.

They must be with Grandma in the tatami room. They stopped sleeping with her years ago, complaining of the cigarette smell, but maybe they fell asleep watching TV, which was supposed to be against the rules.

She slid open the door to her mother's room beside the living room.

Taiga lay twisted with his hands tied behind him, blood wetting his hair, his face horribly smashed. Her mother was under her futon with a sheet tied around her. Miyuki slipped the knot and pulled the futon cover back. Her mother's head flopped to the side.

She shook her, checked for a pulse and breathing, closed her eyes, tried again, and sank to the tatami. Her mother's face was haggard and pale, nearly white, the wrinkles smooth again like when she was young.

She crawled to Taiga to make sure he had a pulse. Bubbles of blood popped from his nose and she could feel his pulse.

Miyuki ran to the kitchen for her phone and called 110. She got scissors to clip the plastic ties around Taiga's wrists and ankles, setting the phone down on speaker. The dispatcher said an officer would be there right away and she hung up.

Was this a break-in? A kidnapping? The building was supposed to have good security. Did someone push in behind Taiga? Did her mother let someone in?

A call came from Taiga's phone, which was wedged in the pocket of his jeans. She took the phone, but didn't know his passcode. A call came on her cellphone, but she ignored it. The police would be there soon.

After she filed for divorce, her lawyer advised her to change the locks, but she never got around to it. There was nothing else amiss. The girls would go willingly with Patrick, but would have fought anyone else, little as they were. Patrick wouldn't do this and besides, he was in Wyoming.

Her filing for divorce, after photos of him cheating on her were sent to her anonymously, must have been a blow. They talked about it in tight, angry phone calls, but Patrick had never been violent and in his few messages had said nothing about coming back to Tokyo.

They argued like any couple, and he used strong, angry language during their worst shouting matches, but he had never been physically violent. They didn't fight often, but when they did, she exploded first. She cried, he stormed around, and then they made up. She missed that catharsis.

She closed her eyes, one hand on her mother and the other on Taiga, rocking gently, waiting for the police and the ambulance.

Where were they? She picked up her phone to call Patrick, but set it down again on the tatami.

When they decided to get married, Patrick came to her family's home in Tochigi. She coached him for weeks on how to act and what to say. They rode the Shinkansen Line to her hometown, nibbling on *bento* lunchboxes from the station. Patrick loved the small local lines they transferred to.

The valley around her small hometown stretched over level fields below a range of steep, rocky mountains. Her home was a long walk from the bus stop with manicured rice fields on either side of the simple blacktop road. Her father made the best tatami in the entire region and his attached workshop made the entire house smell like *igusa* and rice straw.

She made a reservation at a nearby *onsen* hot springs resort to celebrate after Patrick asked her parents for her hand in marriage. Her father spoiled her when he had money and no one ever expected her to marry a local boy. She was too pretty, too driven, and too Tokyo.

The plan was for Patrick to ask her father for her hand, a quaint but common custom. She told him it wasn't necessary, but Patrick insisted. Even though his Japanese was weak, he took it as a point of pride.

She helped Patrick memorize the long, complex phrases and demonstrated how to kneel and bow and avoid eye contact. He stumbled over the humble phrases of polite *keigo*, and she'd laughed as they practiced in their apartment in Tokyo.

In the small tatami room at the front of her childhood home, Patrick knelt down and recited the memorized speech. Patrick, usually so calm, was very nervous. His nervousness seemed a cute expression of his true feelings, in contrast to his usual joking around about "getting hitched" or "living in sin," as they had been for a year.

Her father sat in a tatami chair across a low table from Patrick and listened quietly. Her mother bustled in with tea and *senbei* rice crackers before kneeling at the table. Miyuki sat to the side, a little behind Patrick.

After Patrick stumbled through his request, getting most of it right, they both waited for her father to speak. There in front of her father, Miyuki felt proud at Patrick's efforts. After going to a woman's college in Tokyo, finding a job in a bank, and living on her own, she knew she didn't have to beg for her parents' approval. She just wanted her father to be pleased, and her mother too, if that was possible. She wanted to give them one last gesture of respect before she started her new life.

Her father's response was as flat and tight-woven as a tatami mat: "My daughter will never marry a foreigner."

Miyuki got up and gathered their things without another word. She whisked Patrick out the door without translating or explaining. She dragged him down the steps. She was too angry to speak. She waved a car down, an old neighbor, and they rode in silence to the station.

The *onsen* wasn't the celebration they planned, but making love with Patrick on the wood platform beside the private *rotenburo* bath, she realized that she had to make a choice—and she chose Patrick.

They made love outside in the cool mountain air that night, the steam rising off their bodies from the private outdoor bath, and she felt at home for the first time. It was a new feeling, one she never had at her parents' place, nor at any of the apartments she shared with college friends.

She didn't talk with her parents again until she was pregnant with Jenna three years later. She sent a birth announcement to them by mail and her father called, secretly, wanting to see his grandchild.

With a granddaughter on the way, her father forgave her. He came twice to Tokyo to see Jenna, then died of a heart attack in Tochigi before her first birthday. He had always smoked as much as her mother, but it got him quicker.

It wasn't until Kiri was born that her mother moved in with them. As they talked in the new big apartment, Miyuki realized it was her mother, not her father, who had opposed her. She never said it directly. She was too clever for that. But it became clear she was the one against every decision in Miyuki's life going back to joining the English club in junior high.

She let her mother stay with them in Azabu anyway. And now she was dead. So it didn't matter anymore. It was just sad. She hoped Taiga would be all right. It looked like a lot of blood. The police were on their way. She should call Patrick, but she didn't.

It was the girls that panicked her. It had better turn out to be Patrick who took them or she didn't know how she could survive until they were in her arms again.

She would have to stop crying when the police arrived. The tatami was already wet with her tears.

Chapter 5

Patrick had snuck his daughters past the security cameras with his cap down and mask tight. When they got out of the building, the car was waiting right where the support group said it would be. They'd sent the key to him in Wyoming. They were very prepared, or maybe very experienced. Aside from the babysitter, everything was going as planned.

Jenna and Kiri soon fell asleep in the back seat and flopped over their bags. When he was sure they were asleep, he reached back and lifted their cellphones from their hands. Jenna's phone was more adult, but Kiri's was basically an emergency call with a GPS tracker. She could talk on it, but only to three numbers—Patrick, Miyuki, and the school.

After zigzagging several streets, he stopped on a bridge over a canal, stepped out, and dropped the phones into the dark water below.

Tim, the head of the so-called reunion group for foreigners in custody battles had been right about all the small details so far. Cellphone apps would ruin the whole plan. Tim had assured him it had happened more than once.

Patrick made quick turns, slowed down, sped up, and kept one eye on the rear view mirror. The ramp for the Shuto Expressway south to Haneda Airport was halfway there. He could park in the lot where the group told him and waltz through priority boarding in no time.

As Patrick pulled onto the expressway, the cellphone Tim sent him rang. Patrick slipped the Bluetooth headset into his ear.

"Change of plans. Don't go to the airport," the voice said.

"Is this Tim? Where am I supposed to go?"

"No names, as we discussed. How far are you from Ueno?"

"It's in the other direction."

"Turn around and go to Ueno Station. Take the first Shinkansen going north."

"Next one's probably early morning. What am I supposed to do until then, keep driving around?"

"See if you can catch the last train."

"Where are you? Haneda?"

"One of our guys is there. He's been stopped."

"Stopped?"

"They questioned him, but let him go. Airport security was somehow alerted. I don't know how they got on it so quickly. Other times there's been a half day leeway, or longer, to get out."

"How could they already know I've taken the girls?"

"Listen, we've done this many times. Plan B works just as well."

Patrick slowed into the left-hand lane and looked for an exit. "Won't they be watching all the Shinkansen stations?"

"I'll send someone to check and call you back in ten minutes. There's underground parking near there."

Patrick dealt with Tim by encrypted email to set all this up. The group provided support for divorce cases, ones where a spouse refused joint custody or visitation rights. In Japan, custody almost always went to the mother, especially if she was Japanese. Patrick felt his case was a bit different, but then everyone probably felt that way.

In addition to "reunions," the group spoke to politicians, reached out to the media, and filed lawsuits for parental rights. If Miyuki had not filed for divorce while he was in Wyoming, he would never have even thought of googling that kind of help.

He found a place to turn around for the expressway north. So much for the business class plane tickets and ocean-view suite at the hotel in Honolulu. Patrick hadn't even brought a suitcase. He'd left everything checked in at the hotel in Honolulu since he planned to be in and out of Tokyo in a day.

His phone rang and he tapped on the headset.

It was Tim. "The next train won't be until morning. You'd better dump the car."

"What am I supposed to do, walk? I've got the girls and their luggage and…"

"OK, keep the car for now, but if you leave it somewhere, be sure to remember. We have extra sets of keys, so you can toss the ones you have."

This was getting screwed up. He wasn't sure he wanted to keep taking orders from this guy, as efficient and experienced as he seemed to be.

They could stay in a capsule hotel, or an internet cafe, but such places always asked for ID. Maybe heading out of the city and finding a highway rest stop to sleep in the car would be best. The girls were already asleep and jet lag meant he wouldn't sleep anywhere.

"You still there?" Tim's voice sounded distant.

"I'll go to a friend's place. Drop the car off near there."

"How close a friend is he?"

"He wouldn't turn me in, if that's what you mean."

"I meant is he someone the cops would figure out to check on?"

"Not unless my wife tells them."

"Would she do that?"

"Not sure."

"You could contact her to let her know the girls are all right. That might buy you time."

"It might get me arrested." Patrick hung up. He got off the expressway and turned back south. There was only one place to go—Kyle's.

The first years in Tokyo, he and Kyle had worked together at Pacific Investments, a very old-school firm with decent pay and little overtime. Two Americans out on the town made for many wild nights. Tokyo life became a never-ending tour of new restaurants, cool bars, music clubs, art openings, and film festivals. They double-dated, single-dated, triple-dated, and stayed out until dawn. What better place in the world to spend their bachelor twenties than Tokyo, they agreed.

Patrick thought he'd be a condom-carrying bachelor forever—until he fell in love with Miyuki. That stopped the boys' night outings, slow braking at first, and then altogether. Miyuki checked all the boxes, and he didn't even know he had boxes. She was a rising star at the bank where she worked, smarter than any woman he'd ever dated, bilingual, and gorgeous. Within a few months, they were living together.

Kyle was best man at their wedding, though he passed out after starting on Bellinis at breakfast after no sleep. The nonstop bottles of champagne and prosecco the night before didn't help. When it came time to say, "I do," Kyle was still out. Another friend pulled the ring from Kyle's pocket and stood in for him. When Kyle roused himself during the after-party, they restaged the ring bestowal a second time. "Married twice," people shouted, and the party raged on to morning.

After that, Kyle kept up the bachelor lifestyle while Patrick settled down. Kyle had always been able to sleep odd hours and still function. Hungover or not, he went jogging every morning along the shored-up canals and straightened-out rivers around his apartment. The upper-floor apartment on reclaimed land offered a spectacular view, which he claimed was the best aphrodisiac.

It was a short drive to Kyle's place. Patrick found a lot nearby, parked, paid, and sent Tim directions to the car. Patrick hoped he would be home, or that he still kept a spare key under a potted plant down the hallway.

He woke the girls. They flopped around, but didn't complain when he told them they were going to Uncle Kyle's because they missed their flight.

He pulled their bags over his shoulders and started toward the apartment. As they passed over a canal, he stopped to toss in the car keys and the drawstring bag with the tools.

Jenna watched him, but she was too tired to ask what he was doing. "We haven't seen Uncle Kyle for a long time."

"He wanted to see you before you left," Patrick lied. Kyle didn't even know they were coming, but he'd be cool with it, the only person Patrick knew who would be.

Struggling with one of the bags, Kiri said, "What about Hello and Goodbye?"

"Your cats? Mom will take care of them."

"Is she coming?"

"Later. She has to take care of Grandma." Patrick promised himself to never lie to his daughters, unlike his father, but a few small ones wouldn't hurt. "Actually, I bought us a house. In Wyoming. With a huge field. It's a surprise for Mom, so we're going there first, and then she'll come. So, can you keep a secret?" He stopped and squatted down, looking into their faces. "Can you?"

Jenna nodded, and yawned.

Kiri looked unsure, but when Jenna nodded, she did, too. "Are we really going to ride horses?"

"I promise. But you have to be good and not worry about anything, OK? Promise?"

Jenna and Kiri nodded in unison.

Patrick stood up and walked to the apartment door, waiting until someone came out. Before the doors shut, he pushed the girls forward into the large lobby.

"Do you remember which floor?" Patrick quizzed them.

"Wait," Jenna said. "Twenty maybe?"

"You're a smart girl."

"I got an A in math."

"This is about your good memory, not math. But that's a great grade."

They got in the elevator and rode up in silence, their images reflecting back from the polished brass of the walls, yawning and blinking. He told them what troopers they were and how proud he was of them.

They walked quietly past a bank of windows along the hallway. Tokyo would soon be transitioning to daytime mode so they had to get out of sight. He rang the doorbell.

No answer.

He was about to go for the extra key under the flower pot when the door opened. Kyle stood there in a black kimono with a shock of red hair hanging to his shoulders, more frat boy stoner than investment advisor. "Booster? Dude, what are you doing here? Why didn't you tell me you were coming?"

"Horndog. I should have. Kind of a last-minute thing." Patrick leaned forward for a bro-hug.

Seeing the girls, Kyle did a jaw drop and eyebrow wiggle. "And you brought my two favorite girls." Kyle leaned down and Jenna and Kiri did little dances of happiness before Kyle wrapped them in a hug.

"What's 'Horndog'?" Kiri frowned at Kyle.

Kyle laughed. "I'll explain later." A woman's voice called from inside the apartment. Kyle smiled.

"We need a place to crash." Patrick tried to stifle the urgency in his voice. He didn't want the girls to hear it, or Kyle, either.

Kyle nodded, serious, and waved them in.

"Uncle Kyle, we missed you," Jenna said.

"I missed you girls too. You are top of my list for Thanksgiving. And Christmas, too."

"Did you buy a turkey?" Kiri giggled.

"I'm feeding one on the roof." Kyle put his finger to his lips to keep it a secret and took their bags.

"Can we see it?" Kiri asked.

"After you get some sleep," Kyle said.

The woman's voice called out from the bedroom again. "*Kai-ru?*"

"Do you have company?" Jenna looked around Kyle.

"I do and she's very nice." Kyle wiggled his eyebrows up and down.

"*Kai-ru*? Is she calling you 'frog?'" Jenna giggled.

Kyle laughed. "Yes, I am a big frog, but a beautiful princess kissed me."

"Uncle *Kaeru*, Uncle Frog!" Kiri said, and the girls giggled, and it was all right.

Over the top of the girls' heads, Patrick gave Kyle a serious look that said thanks, I owe you one.

Kyle raised one eyebrow. It held all the questions he would ask in the morning.

Chapter 6

The trip from the Nine Dragons office in Shinagawa to the second crime scene didn't take long. Sakaguchi sent Osaki and Sugamo ahead in their own car while Hiroshi informed the early-arriving employees that their workplace would remain a crime scene for as long as it took.

Sakaguchi talked on the phone almost the entire way, telling Hiroshi only that there was another murder scene and that yes, it involved English, since one of the persons of interest was American. And yes it involved money, since it was in Azabu, a well-off neighborhood in central Tokyo.

A new young detective, whose name Hiroshi had forgotten, drove them. Hiroshi noticed her in the meetings, but he didn't know anything about her, not even her name. She let Hiroshi and Sakaguchi out in front of the apartment building.

Inside the spacious lobby, a nervous-looking local cop checked their badges and a thin-faced apartment manager escorted them across the marble floor peppering them with questions. They ignored him and got on the elevator with a terse bow.

On the eighth floor, the door to the apartment was open. The *genkan* was crowded with detectives' shoes, so Hiroshi left his outside in the hallway and followed Sakaguchi into the large LDK, living-dining-kitchen, area. The crime scene crew finally had enough space to work without bumping into each other. Ayana's entire apartment would have fit in the living room.

Ueno had been the first detective at the scene after the local police. He had already finished the preliminaries of contacting the airports and train stations and was instructing the younger detectives from where he sat on the multisectional sofa. Ueno's leg was still healing from a gunshot wound, the repeated infections confining him to headquarters or easy-to-work scenes like this. Hiroshi wondered if he could ever return to the field full-time again.

Sakaguchi's knee wasn't any better. Multiple knee surgeries and a brace kept him away from arrests, chases, or the rare shooting. Sakaguchi plopped down next to Ueno on the sofa, a piece of furniture that fit his size. Everyone told Sakaguchi to stay off his knee, but he came from a working-class area of Osaka where people took national holidays as the only rest. For Sakaguchi, hard work was basic, but working his way up from beat cop also meant being easy to get along with while almost no one else was.

Ueno pointed Hiroshi toward the tatami mat room. Double the standard six-mat size, the room was lined by sliding doors that granted privacy when shut and enlarged the living room when open. At one end, a head-sized bloodstain blotted the tatami. Even the tatami was high quality, golden, and smoothly woven. A floor chair and *zabuton* pillows were tossed around. A small panel TV rested off-center on an antique *tansu* chest. Hiroshi said a prayer of thanks the bodies had been taken away.

Sugamo and Osaki were supervising the detectives in the bedrooms from the back hallway. The two of them, despite Sugamo doing sumo and Osaki playing rugby in the police league, didn't appear quite as massive in the spaciousness of this apartment.

The open kitchen held a recessed refrigerator, a freezer, and a glass-fronted wine cellar with a stack of wine crates. The kitchen island was too wide to reach across, with a built-in flat grill, double sink, and plenty of space to eat. Tall stools held two schoolgirls' backpacks.

Sakaguchi was reading something on a clipboard from one of the medical staff. When he finished, he waved Hiroshi over. "Can you go talk to the mother? I can't speak English."

"Isn't she...?"

"She's Japanese, but she married a foreigner, so there's a batch of stuff in English." Sakaguchi handed a printout from the portable printer Ueno had in front of him. "The daughters are gone. Her mother is dead. The babysitter is in a coma. Husband left a year ago. Apparently she filed for divorce."

"How old are the daughters?"

Ueno read from the printout. "Nine and five."

Sakaguchi stretched his leg, the knee brace visible under the billow of his pants. "And see if she knows anything about the babysitter's cellphone. We couldn't find it."

Hiroshi turned to go.

"And get a description of the cats."

"Cats?"

"Their cats are gone. She's concerned."

"Now it's cat abduction," Hiroshi mumbled as he walked past the kitchen to the bedrooms.

Like the living room and kitchen, the bedroom was larger than any Hiroshi had seen. An attractive woman with thick hair bunched in barrettes sat on the end of the bed, folding clothes. The room was decorated in pink and white with a vanity mirror, a study desk, bookshelves with books in English and Japanese, and stuffed animals on every surface.

Hiroshi held out his *meishi*. "Are you Miyuki Nakano Walsh?"

Miyuki took his name card and nodded absently, maybe still in shock.

"I'm Detective Hiroshi Shimizu. I'm sure you've been barraged with questions, but could I ask you just a couple more? We want to find your girls as soon as possible."

Miyuki kept folding the clothes, taking them from one side, shaking them straight, rolling them up, and nestling them against her thigh. She was dressed in loose-fitting workout clothes, some designer brand.

Hiroshi pulled the pink chair from the desk and sat down in front of her. "So, Walsh-san…"

"Miyuki is fine. I'm used to the foreign first name custom."

"Miyuki-san, then."

"It was my husband. I can't imagine anyone else." Miyuki nodded as she rolled up another shirt.

"When did you see him last?"

"He hasn't been here for nine months. I filed for divorce while he was gone."

"Gone where?"

"Wyoming. For work. At least at first, for work."

"Do you have any sense he was somewhere else?"

"The girls are gone." She acted like that would be evidence enough.

Hiroshi wasn't sure she understood the question. Shock did odd things to people.

Miyuki looked up at Hiroshi. "Other than that, no, I don't, no. I just hope it was him who took them. I can't think of what it might be otherwise."

"Could you tell me why you were divorcing? Did you fight or...?"

"No more than most couples."

"Most couples don't get divorced."

"Most do, I'm told by my lawyer. I suspected Patrick was having an affair. Or multiple affairs."

"Did you have any evidence of that?"

Miyuki refolded the small T-shirt in her hand. "He said Wyoming was for a short time. He wanted us to go, but I couldn't leave my job. And the girls like their school. His work there kept getting extended."

"He extended it or his company did?"

Miyuki shook her head. "I was so busy with work and taking care of the girls."

"Why would he take them?"

"To punish me for the divorce, I guess." Miyuki crumpled a baby blue pajama top in her hands, then flapped it out straight and folded it.

"Where was he working?"

"Nine Dragons Wealth Management."

"Where?" Hiroshi turned over the sheet Sakaguchi handed him, but there was nothing about Nine Dragons.

"Nine Dragons? In Shinagawa?" Hiroshi took a minute. Sakaguchi must have known this, but he didn't say anything. Or maybe he didn't know, but that was unlike him. The distance between the two crime scenes would be easy to figure out.

"And where do you work?"

"At MizuTNG Bank, accounts manager. Toranomon office."

"It must be difficult working full-time and taking care of two daughters."

Miyuki started folding bright-colored tights. "People always say that, but we manage. I manage."

"This is your oldest daughter's room? Your younger daughter sleeps where?"

"They sometimes sleep together. Her bedroom's over there, and our bedroom, I mean, my husband's and mine, or what used to be ours, is at the end of the hall."

Add on the tatami room where the grandmother died and that made a 4LDK, in real estate parlance, four bedrooms, and a living-dining-kitchen. The mortgage probably ran one to two million yen a month, maybe more.

"Did they take a lot of clothes?"

"Yes. And toothbrushes, hairbrushes. And the cats, it seems."

"Maybe the cats escaped? Did you leave the door open?"

"They're supposed to have an 'enjoy nature' outing tomorrow." She stared at the clothes beside her as if noticing them for the first time. "What am I supposed to tell the school?"

"When did you get the last message from your husband?"

She shook her head and shrugged. "Last week. I didn't write back."

"Why not? Were you...?"

"My lawyer said I should wait until we got the divorce settled.

47

It didn't seem like he was coming back to sort it out."

"He received the paperwork?"

She nodded. "I'd hired a detective—"

"To find proof of infidelity?"

Miyuki unrolled and rerolled another shirt without answering.

"Can you give me the name of the detective?"

"I have it somewhere." Miyuki pulled out her phone, and, after scrolling for a long time, held out the information to Hiroshi.

He took a quick photo of the info.

"And can you tell me about the babysitter?"

"The girls love him."

"Could you start with his name?"

"Taiga Smith Sato. Is he OK?" Miyuki looked up, her face tight.

"Head wounds always look worse than they are. Three names?"

"He's half. Like my daughters."

"Did you see Taiga's cellphone? It's important."

Miyuki shook her head.

Hiroshi nodded. "When did you hire him?"

"At the start of the semester. Taiga's great with the girls. He really connected with them. Takes them from school to soccer to cram school. Out to dinner if I'm late. My mother—" Miyuki choked up. She took a breath, glanced at Hiroshi, and then stared at the mirror.

"I'm sorry for your loss."

Miyuki recomposed herself. "Is that all you need from me?"

"Is there anyone else other than your husband you can think of who might be involved? From your work, or his work, or...?"

Miyuki shook her head more slowly. "I've been over every possibility in my head since I found my mother and Taiga." She looked up. "If you have more questions, could we talk at my lawyer's office tomorrow? I mean, this afternoon."

"Yes, of course. You need some sleep. We'll leave detectives in the living room and monitor your calls." Hiroshi wished Takamatsu were there to ask more questions in his inimitable, irritating way. But instead of asking a Takamatsu-type question, Hiroshi let it go. "As for your cats, do you have a photo or—?"

"Fuck the cats!" Miyuki shouted in English, rising up red-faced, her eyes full of tears. "I don't care about the goddamn cats." She let out a scream as tears poured from her eyes. She snatched a handful of the just-folded clothes and buried her face in them.

Chapter 7

Sakaguchi left in a rush for a meeting before Hiroshi had a chance to ask him about Nine Dragons. So, Hiroshi caught a ride back to headquarters with the same young detective who'd driven him to the apartment in Azabu. Hiroshi had seen her in meetings, but never spoken to her. He was supposed to know her name.

It was good to see one of the female detectives out in the field. Most were still young, and hired recently, so they ended up making calls, reviewing video, compiling data, and redoing forms instead of gaining hands-on experience.

This case looked like a matter of catching the husband. An American with two little girls should be easy to spot. Still, with the kind of money that size of an apartment meant, there might be more to it. Was he making that much money? Or were they the kind of couple that did everything on credit? An embezzlement case gone wrong?

"What do you think about this case?" she asked, looking over at Hiroshi.

Hiroshi cleared his throat. "Which case?"

"Weren't we just at a crime scene?" She looked at Hiroshi again.

"We were. Two of them. I'm sorry, but I forgot your name."

"Ishii," she said. "No one seems to know it."

"I don't pay attention in meetings."

"I don't either. Except for people's names."

Hiroshi smiled. "When the chief starts talking, I tune out."

"That Borsalino hat?" Ishii made a gesture with her hands mimicking the chief putting on a hat.

"Some of the things he's said and done over the years..."

"Not much we can do about it." Ishii raised up to see why traffic was slowing down.

"Wait him out is the best we can hope for."

"The Japanese solution to everything. I heard you lived overseas?"

"I did, but maybe I should have stayed longer."

Ishii chuckled. "Me too. I never re-adapted."

"Did you live outside Japan?"

"I did. America. For grad school and a bit after. So, what about these cases?" She braked to avoid running into the back of a truck that stopped suddenly. One brake light was out.

Takamatsu would have leapt out and terrorized the driver, but Hiroshi patted the dash and ignored it. "If it's the father, I guess the guy abducted his daughters to teach his soon-to-be ex-wife a lesson. But the murders are confusing. Anyway, he'll get caught at the airport or train station soon enough."

"There's a lot more ways out of Japan than that."

"If he knows them."

"Looks like he could pay for anything."

Hiroshi stole a glance at Ishii. Her square jaw was handsome and her high cheekbones framed her deep-set eyes. Her face and her manner was as calm as the way she drove.

She was right. If the father was working at a high-end wealth management company, his compensation must be generous. "I'll be able to tell once we crack open the Nine Dragons' accounts."

"How long will that take?" Ishii leaned to the side as the truck pulled off.

"Depends. Have to get into them first."

"What do you think about Nine Dragons?"

"It's a short drive from there to Azabu."

"So if the victim was a Chinese national and the company was Chinese—?"

"We'll let the chief sort out the embassy stuff. He loves that kind of thing."

"He's got the hat for it." Ishii made the hat gesture again and both of them laughed. "I wish he'd make the meetings more efficient."

"Don't you like to listen to him hold forth, to show his vast knowledge of...well..."

"It ends up just the opposite, doesn't it?" Ishii stopped herself. "I shouldn't say that."

"You've got it figured out. Don't worry. Everyone else feels the same."

Ishii chuckled and drove the rest of the way quietly. She let Hiroshi out at the entrance to the annex near his office by the back parking lot.

Hiroshi got out, but leaned back inside. "Come in for an espresso?"

Ishii leaned across the front seat. "I have to pick up Detective Takamatsu in Enoshima."

"That's where he is?"

"A family suicide. Out of our jurisdiction, but he handled those before."

"How did he get down there?"

Ishii shook her head.

"Well, drive safely. You must be tired."

"I'm sure Detective Takamatsu's commentary on the return trip will keep me wide awake."

"You know him."

"I worked with him on a case when I first arrived two months ago."

"Tell him to call me when he gets done beachcombing down there."

Ishii smiled. Hiroshi closed the door and watched as she pulled off.

Everything in headquarters was getting up to speed for the day. A few well-rested detectives hustled in the door with a spring in their steps. Hiroshi trudged in. He needed a double espresso.

Hiroshi stretched on the steps and headed inside to his office, a windowless, functional cave, the exact opposite of Nine Dragons where the well-designed space encouraged things like collaboration and productivity. Hiroshi's office gave him privacy and a place to nap. A faint whiff of cleaning solution, a mix of chlorine and floral scents, lingered from when the room served as a cleaning supply storage closet, but the espresso smell was gradually taking over.

Hiroshi's two new computer monitors were waiting on his desk like sentinels. Together, entire real estate scams could be spread out for scrutiny. After Akiko, his invaluable assistant, had managed to requisition two monitors through her mastery of bureaucratic paperwork, his efficiency had increased exponentially.

Having two monitors for Excel spreadsheets, flow charts, faked ledgers, forged documents, and fraudulent bank transfers let him spread it all out and dissect it. The wider visual field helped to untangle and reassemble cases in half the time. Something about being able to see more information in one frame, actually two frames, let him ponder what money did to people.

He hung his coat up on the rack behind the door, tossed his mask in the trash, and doused his hands in sanitizer before turning on the espresso machine. He was going to need a steady stream of espresso to get anything done.

Hiroshi flipped through the sticky notes Akiko had recently started leaving on the back of the monitors. She said the handwritten notes tempered the digital flow on the other side. They certainly saved Hiroshi from calling her when he forgot things. He skimmed the litany of meetings, missed calls, and reminders, and left them where they were. He suspected he'd get a call from the chief interrupting his current case to work on the Nine Dragons killing and the abduction. He wanted to finish as much as he could before then, so he sat down and got to work.

As soon as he reopened the files on the case from the day

before, Sakaguchi called.

"Are you back at headquarters? Why not stop by my office?"

Hiroshi said. His office had become a gathering spot. It was a far enough walk away through an underground tunnel to be a firewall from the unceasing confusion of the main offices.

"Can't. Meetings and more meetings. I'll probably fall asleep." Sakaguchi's sigh was large and loud. "My knee is killing me. When I don't sleep, it swells up."

"You should have it looked at."

"The Chinese Embassy people are stopping by along with bureaucrats from the Ministry of Foreign Affairs. The chief loves that kind of thing. The Chinese want first access to the accounts."

"What? I can find whatever the husband embezzled, or whatever he was up to, if I can get in first. And it won't be hard to find him and his daughters in Tokyo. They'll pop up at some station."

"Every time someone says it won't be hard to do something, my knee hurts worse."

"The company was registered in Singapore, wasn't it?"

"But they're in Shanghai and Hong Kong too. Why not call that guy you know in the tax office?"

"Is this about taxes? Or unpaid taxes?"

"I couldn't care less about taxes, but can't he get us in there before the Chinese?"

"Maybe. I'll call him."

"The medical examiner said her initial thought is that Leung died of brain hemorrhage from repeated trauma."

Hiroshi shivered, thinking of the pathology lab. "It was that bad?"

"It was that easy to see. His head hit the desk, window, files, computer monitors, his own cellphone. She'll know more later."

"What about the grandmother?"

"Lack of oxygen. Fibers in her lungs. Maybe smothered."

"Doesn't seem like something a wealthy investment specialist with an apartment in Azabu would do."

"After killing his boss."

Remembering the scene, Hiroshi closed his eyes. "Can I ask you something? Why didn't you tell me the husband worked at Nine Dragons?"

"I didn't realize it myself until Ueno told me. Ueno didn't go to Shinagawa with us, so the name meant nothing to him. And I didn't even look at the printout I handed you."

"I'll dig into their business setup and then go interview the babysitter in the hospital."

Sakaguchi sighed. "The chief is setting up surveillance at every Shinkansen station, long-distance bus station, and airport in Tokyo."

"That will take people away from—."

"That's what I said." Sakaguchi grunted. "Let's hope the husband turns up at an airport or train station before the day's over."

"A foreigner with two little girls won't be hard to—"

"Kidnappings always end badly."

"Are we sure Patrick Walsh is even inside Japan?"

"Ueno's checking with immigration."

"I'll check on Nine Dragons."

"You keep telling us to follow the money, so follow it."

Sakaguchi hung up and then called right back.

Hiroshi was halfway to the espresso machine.

"And I hate to tell you, but Akiko is going to be pulled away to lead a call-around to all the hotels in Tokyo."

"What? Who decided that? The chief?" Hiroshi couldn't survive a day without her. He already had a list of things for her to check. It would take forever to call all those hotels.

"Want me to tell her?" Sakaguchi asked.

"I'll tell her." Hiroshi sighed.

"Send her over here when she gets to the office. And don't waste any time on the cats."

"They'll have the best garbage in Tokyo to eat in Azabu."
Sakaguchi grunted and hung up.

Akiko bustled in with a smile on her face. "Something wrong?"
she asked.

"Missing cats." Hiroshi went to the machine to make her an
espresso.

Chapter 8

Patrick felt the weight of Kiri on his arm as he struggled awake, though he wasn't sure he'd even slept. Jenna was still asleep against the wall with her hair splayed out and her legs angled like she'd just kicked a soccer ball in her sleep.

The eight-tatami floor was a chaotic jumble of bags, clothes, pillows, futon covers, and blankets. In the corner were meditation cushions, yoga mats, and a compact stereo system with a tower of relaxation CDs. Kyle had been using the tatami room, more of a box than a room, for meditation or yoga. Kyle had always been there for him, but meditation didn't seem like him. Maybe it was his girlfriend.

Like Patrick, Kyle was Boston Irish, from the well-off suburbs of Boston, while Patrick was from the poorer south side. That difference meant little in Tokyo far from the subtle hierarchies of the East Coast, and anyway, they both attended name schools, Kyle at Amherst as a legacy and Patrick squeaking into Northeastern. They both studied economics, hated it, but liked making money.

They became best buds in their first few months in Tokyo, bonding over a shared love of laughing, eating, drinking, and chasing women. They both took their postings to Tokyo as a lark. They went in search of adventure most nights and always found it one way or another.

One night after they sealed a big deal for Pacific Investments, before Patrick had been headhunted to Nine Dragons, they were dancing at a DJ club in Shibuya called "Unicorn." Patrick tried to explain the symbolic meaning of unicorns to one of the two Japanese women they met. The women kept ordering champagne and Patrick kept charging it. He couldn't remember either of their names.

Kyle hoisted a flute of champagne and threw his arm over Patrick's shoulder, spilling his drink on one of the women's shirts. She jumped back, brushed her clingy black midriff top, and giggled. Kyle apologized, Patrick got a towel from the bar, and the two women went to clean up.

After they left, Kyle leaned close and shouted over the pounding throb of the music. "Booster, I want to live here forever."

Patrick cupped his hands over Kyle's ear. "In this club?"

"No, you fool. In Tokyo. Everything's here. Everything."

"Horndog, you're just going through a phase."

"No, man, I'm not. I'm going to die here."

"Not soon, I hope."

"Maybe never. If I'm lucky. That's how I feel tonight—like I'll live forever. In Tokyo." Kyle wrapped Patrick in a bro hug. The women, whatever their names were, came back and threw their arms around them in a hot huddle, jumping up and down and spilling more champagne. As they spun out to the dance floor again, Patrick realized that was how he felt too—that he wanted to live in Tokyo forever.

Patrick felt little fingers tickling him. "Does that tickle?" Kiri asked.

"Not so much." Patrick pulled her close.

"Where's the bathroom?" Kiri sat up.

Patrick rose up on an elbow and pushed the futon aside. "I'll take you, sweetie. I got to pee too."

He pushed himself up and pulled Kiri to her feet. She pushed her hair back just like Miyuki did and started doing a little have-to-pee dance. Patrick hurried with her down the hall.

From inside the bathroom came the sound of running water. That made him want to pee all the more. He knocked.

"Come in!" a woman's voice shouted.

"My daughter has to pee," Patrick shouted.

"That's fine!" Kyle's girlfriend poked her head around the

door. She had dimples, white teeth, and a small tattoo of some mythical bird poking above the towel wrapped around her. She stooped down, smiled, and took Kiri's hand. "I'll show you where."

Kiri let go of his hand and hurried in, immediately chattering away in Japanese. He wondered how long they'd take. He really had to pee. He was about to start looking for a sink when both of them poked their heads out. Kyle's girlfriend said, "We're going to take a shower. Could you get her clothes? I'm Miki, by the way."

"Miki. OK, hi, I'm Patrick. And Kyle...?"

Kiri said, "Tell Jenna to come. It's a super-cool shower."

"I'll get her and some clothes," Patrick said.

Miki shut the door and Patrick could hear Kiri giggling inside.

Jenna was still sleeping, so he pulled her into his arms. She opened her eyes and snuggled into him. "Kiri's taking a shower and you're next. Can you pick out something for her to wear?"

"I have to pee." So did he, thinking of the kitchen sink.

"Let's get a change of clothes for you and Kiri and I'll show you where."

Jenna dug in the bags. "Everything's out of order in here."

"We can repack later. Just pick something you like."

Jenna dragged out two changes of clothes and rolled them neatly. "I really have to pee."

"So do I. Come on."

She got up, clothes in hand, and Patrick led her to the shower. Kyle came out of his bedroom in his black kimono.

Jenna eyed him up and down. "Uncle Kyle, I think that's a woman's kimono."

"I'm a cross-dresser." Kyle laughed, his curly red hair bouncing like a toy lion's mane.

"What's that?"

"Look how pretty you are even with bed hair." Kyle patted Jenna on the head.

Jenna wiggled and smiled and hurried off to shower.

"I'm busting for a piss," Patrick said.

"There's another toilet by the front door, you idiot."

"Oh, I forgot." Patrick sprinted down the hall.

His bladder empty, he strolled back to the kitchen lured by the scent of coffee brewing. Through the sliding glass doors of the balcony, he could see all the way to the Chiba coastline across Tokyo Bay. Rainbow Bridge spanned the water like a science project and planes took off like toys from Haneda Airport to the south. Patrick closed his eyes, imagining the missed plane landing in Honolulu.

Kyle had changed from the kimono into sweats and was putting out breakfast things. "I was going to wake you up for a jog, but it seemed like you and the girls were sleeping."

"You jog in that kimono?"

Kyle laughed. "Maybe on Halloween." Kyle set out fruit and bagels. "These aren't like New York, but they're not bad."

Patrick squeezed a bagel.

Kyle handed him a mug of coffee. "You did a runner. I was really shocked. Miyuki called me, worried. What's going on?"

Patrick sipped his coffee and gestured it was delicious.

Kyle looked at him. "Why didn't you tell me you were coming back? I would've..."

"We missed our plane. We should have been landing in Honolulu just about now."

"Your plane? You came here and... ah, I get it. Custody thing?" Kyle sipped his coffee.

Patrick looked at him. "You don't want to know."

"Did you rebook the flight?" Kyle gestured for Patrick to sit down.

Patrick clutched his mug and surrendered to yesterday's fatigue and the coming day's uncertainty. "I might need your help."

"Why don't you crash out here today and let me arrange it for you. You want to fly out right away?"

"Actually..."

"Actually, you don't want to use your card. Miyuki will trace it, right?"

"Miyuki's the least of it."

Kyle paused. "Use mine. Take however much you need."

Patrick looked him in the eye and didn't say what he was thinking, that that was the problem, knowing how much you needed.

Chapter 9

Akiko fumed as she packed up her things to go to the main building on the chief's orders to call every hotel in Tokyo. She guzzled two more espressos and stormed off. She could handle anything, but it meant she wouldn't be handling everything that would produce results.

After she was gone, the office felt quiet, and not in a good way.

Hiroshi texted Masaharu Watanabe at the National Tax Agency. After Hiroshi's uncle introduced them during a murder embezzlement case, they met for drinks, each delighted to find someone to talk shop with. Watanabe focused on tax evasion from big corporations and the ultra-wealthy, while Hiroshi zeroed in on investment scams, real estate rip-offs, and pension thefts. Watanabe could see him in a couple of hours.

Hiroshi called the lawyer and the judge handling the divorce case Miyuki filed. They would know more about their marriage and finances than was apparent from the little information they had so far. But lawyers and judges were great at evasion too, better than most criminals. The judge's secretary promised to squeeze him in before noon, and the lawyer reserved early afternoon to meet with them and Miyuki.

Maybe the wife, Miyuki, would be forthcoming on the where, when, and how of her husband's work. If she wanted to divorce him and keep the money, she'd have to know most of it. Or maybe she was covering up for him, the divorce a financial scam of some sort.

Hiroshi reviewed what he had, which wasn't much. Murder was almost always connected to money, but the homicide division always started with more on the murder than on the money. Hiroshi wished he had a money crew as professional as the crime scene crew.

On the money side, there wasn't an actual scene to work over. It was forensic, but account information, transfer forms, balances, and numerical abstractions were harder to grasp than physical evidence.

Hiroshi sat down at his monitors and searched online for Nine Dragons. The website came up right away, but before he could navigate to any concrete information, an ancient map of Asia rolled over the screen. He searched for a "skip video" button but couldn't find one. Chinese triple-sail junks arose from the waters of ancient maps and sailed across the waves from the coastline of China past Vietnam into the South China Sea, the Gulf of Thailand and the Java and Flores Seas, and finally to the Strait of Malacca and the Indian Ocean.

Gradually, the old boats morphed into modern ocean-going yachts and docked at harbors. Airplanes took off from major cities, evolving from turboprops to jets, spreading out in all directions with stops in Panama and the Caribbean. Japan figured prominently. Behind this imagined history of global capital, dragons, threatening but protective, writhed and darted, pausing only to stare out with fierce eyes and sharp claws before zipping into the clouds.

When the graphics finished, an image of the Nine Dragons offices appeared. Hard-working, good-looking employees discussed spreadsheets in friendly groups. The numbers whirled by, arrows zigzagged up, dipped down, and headed back up. Rows and columns of numbers faded in and out before turning into dragons—wealth as a primal force of nature, as fluid as ocean currents, as invisible as the wind.

When the video finished, the screen said, "Contact us" with an email and phone number, and nothing else.

He clicked off and went to the police database of articles. In the investing and financial section, he found few articles other than an announcement of registering in Japan and a couple short puff pieces. They didn't do interviews, didn't do press releases, or if they did, he couldn't find them.

Even if they grabbed the husband at a port of entry and interrogated him, they still had the problem of digging deeper into Nine Dragons. The CEO of an investment firm didn't get beaten to death in his office because the accounts were all in order.

He called Akiko to see if she could shake free and help him find more information, her specialty.

"Do you know how many hotels there are in Tokyo?" Akiko yelled in English, so whoever was in the room with her wouldn't understand.

Hiroshi had rarely heard her so impatient. "I can only imagine."

"Would you stay at a hotel if you'd abducted your own daughters?"

"Why don't you ask the chief to at least let you work from here?"

"We skipped the love hotels, *minshuku*, and *ryokan*. Many of those don't ask for identification."

"The love hotels especially."

"So, we focused on the mid- and large-size Western-style hotels. Even those number in the thousands. They all claim to record every guest, but they all do it in a different way. One place has robot check-in, and they weren't sure how to retrieve the information from the robot database."

"Did you check four-star hotels?"

"We saved those for the afternoon. At this rate, I'll be up all night."

"And if they stay on the move, we'll always be a step behind." Hiroshi started looking through the sticky notes on the back of his monitors.

"*If* he even went to a hotel. *If* he's even in Japan."

"Do you know Detective Ishii?"

"Of course. All the women in the homicide division know one

another. Basic self-defense."

"Women never have a hierarchy."

"We're all equal in the women's room. Gossip central." Akiko laughed. "Again, self-defense. Did you see the notes about the investment scam I left on the back of your monitors?"

Hiroshi flipped through them. "Maybe someone will report the missing girls with their father."

"Did they find a lot of cash hidden in the apartment?"

"I didn't think of that. Who would the girls go with willingly?"

"Their mother, the babysitter, or their grandmother. Or their father, if he was back. They might not feel it strange that he came in the middle of the night, but he'd have to tell them some kind of story."

"And if it was the father, where would he go?"

"Not to a hotel where he had to register with ID. To a friend's. That's why calling the hotels is a waste."

Sakaguchi knocked on the doorjamb, his huge body filling the frame.

Hiroshi looked up, pleased to see him. He told Akiko, "I've got to go. Sakaguchi's here."

"Tell him to get me off this hotel thing."

"I will." Hiroshi rolled out his computer chair for Sakaguchi. It was easier to slip into and get out of with his knee bothering him.

Sakaguchi grunted as he sat down. "We got something from the surveillance camera outside the building." Sakaguchi pointed at Akiko's computer. "I just sent it."

"I'll tell her if you ever get her back here. What did you find?"

"Three hundred license plates. Nothing from the parking lot. No other images of anyone, masked or unmasked."

"Nothing then. Can you get Akiko back over here? I need her."

Sakaguchi sighed. "I'll try the chief again later."

"Anything else?"

"They put the babysitter in an induced coma so hold off on that until they call us. What did you find about Nine Dragons?"

"Not much other than a slick video and a contact form. Wealth protection firms don't share much online. You want to see it?"

"After I have some wealth to protect."

"I'm heading out to talk with Watanabe about any tax violations and then the judge and the divorce lawyer."

"Maybe the babysitter will come to and tell us everything we need to know."

"I think we need to find out why Nine Dragons came to Tokyo, and what Patrick was doing for them in Wyoming."

"Couldn't they work from wherever they were, Shanghai or wherever, just as easily?" Sakaguchi asked.

"I would have thought so. So there must be other reasons to come here."

"New client base?"

"It doesn't seem like Tokyo rent is worth it. That space must be outrageous. They could do all this from Hong Kong, Singapore, or Shanghai, and they handle wealth management services in English, Japanese, Chinese, Vietnamese, and Bahasa Malaysian."

"Check into their other customers."

"I'm waiting on client information from Mehta, the office manager."

"Speed him up a bit."

"I'll wait until Takamatsu gets here to do that. I worry the Chinese Embassy will get in ahead of us."

Sakaguchi shook his head. "The chief always wants to talk with those bigwigs, and he always kowtows to them, but he's too indecisive to ever say OK. So, we might have a little time."

"If we can get in there before the embassy does, or some other agency—"

"The tax office guy Watanabe won't tip off other ministries, will he?" Sakaguchi lifted his thick leg with two hands, wincing.

"No, he won't, but they find out things anyway. Another reason to send Akiko back here. I need her."

Sakaguchi pushed himself up from the chair. "When the chief

gets an idea, he has to torture everyone with it. The file Akiko pulled up showed ninety thousand hotels in Japan. More than half of those in Tokyo."

"What about car rental agencies? He's got to move the girls somehow."

Sakaguchi rolled his head around, stretching his neck and shoulders. "We might get lucky there."

Hiroshi sighed. "Add in limousine services, private taxis, and the car agency is as hopeless as the hotel route. Akiko said the hotels will take days."

"And by then they'll be gone. The chief wants to showcase this as a feel-good rescue story, one to boost relations with the Chinese Embassy and the ministries. Which are my next meetings." Sakaguchi put his hands on the doorjamb and leaned back on his leg to stretch his knee. Then he stood up straight, breathing deeply. "The first twenty-four hours are crucial with these kinds of cases. And a quarter of those are already gone."

Chapter 10

Hiroshi took the train to talk with Masaharu Watanabe at the National Tax Agency. The train gave him time to think, the best place for it. With the virus dominating daily life, every train ran at half capacity, about where they should be. Everyone on the train was masked or double-masked, and the open windows let a cool stream of fresh air into the car.

Hiroshi reset his cellphone for both strong vibration and loud ring. He didn't want to miss any incoming calls. The girls, if they were going to be moved, would probably be moved during the day. The police were ready to act instantaneously if a sighting came in, and Hiroshi had to be ready to get to wherever they turned up.

Were the daughters reason enough to come back to Japan? Why would Patrick do that in person? Was he taking them back to Wyoming? Pending divorce and the fear of being denied custody or visitation rights was horrifying, but was that enough? Patrick could have done all of it, but the money, wherever it was, would be telling. The beatings were done by practiced hands, not a sloppy explosion of passion.

At Kasumigaseki Station, police in riot vests with long *keijo* staffs stood at the inside exits, many more than usual. The station, like most in Tokyo, had dozens of entrances to watch when some foreign dignitary, controversial speaker, or the imperial family was visiting nearby.

Hiroshi headed to the Kasumigaseki exit closest to the Ministry of Finance. The wind blew cold as he walked upstairs and along the walkway to the main entrance. Outside, more officers were stationed on every corner. It was a lot of personnel, but it meant they could rapidly descend on any problem with sufficient force.

The National Tax Agency office was housed in one of the squattest and blandest buildings, as if exhorting the bureaucrats and staff who worked there to produce tangible results without being too elegant about it.

Hiroshi's name was on the visitors' list, so they waved him through security.

Watanabe had just been promoted to senior investigator in the National Tax Agency, though he was younger than Hiroshi. He always dressed in a trim three-piece suit with suspenders and a bright red and blue tie over a pinpoint Oxford shirt. He looked like a businessman in the Taisho or Meiji era when men's fashion started to look Western, but still felt Japanese. Hiroshi never wore a tie but thought about it each time he met Watanabe.

The office was small and neatly arranged, with an old wooden desk and folders marked "In" and "Out" in old-style *kanji*. Watanabe used two computer monitors too. Case files towered across his desk in careful columns. Watanabe held out his hand to shake and then corrected himself with an elbow bump and a laugh. He waved Hiroshi into a chair. "So, Nine Dragons? Great name, right?"

"It looks good on the promo video, that's for sure."

Watanabe clicked through files on his computers, looking back and forth at the monitors. "Nine Dragons was one of the fish nibbling off the same hook with another so-called wealth management firm I was tracking. Their so-called 'managing' is draining Japan."

"What kind of tax shelters do they use?"

"Depends on the tax haven. The British Virgin Islands veers one way, Malta another, Nevis and the Bahamas another again. Malta and Luxembourg are the classics—pure bank secrecy. But most are just layers inside layers. What country are we talking about?" Watanabe put his fingers together in front of him and raised an eyebrow.

"The US."

"South Dakota, Delaware, Wyoming. Lots of choices of late, but I'll guess Wyoming?"

"How did you know?"

"I've followed cases up to the state line, but no further. All states recognize trusts, but Wyoming state law allows any LLC to have complete control of a trust through an agent. All anyone needs to be an agent is an address and a heartbeat. The agents often know nothing about the companies. And some act as agents for a couple of hundred companies."

"No way in for us, and lots of ways out for them."

"Precisely. They call it Offshore Wyoming USA. Nice marketing, don't you think?" Watanabe chuckled. "Wyoming now has the strongest privacy laws in the US, maybe in the world. It's outlawed even cursory oversight from regulators."

"I thought America was the land of laws?"

"Except when it's not. And then it's the land of freedom. Financial, in this case. In Wyoming, company owners don't need to identify themselves. The industry is sprawling, growing, becoming even more anonymous. Every state has its own banking laws and Wyoming loosened theirs to bring in as much business as possible. It's the Wild West."

"How does that work?"

"I guess they buy off the state legislators. Once the firms set up LLCs with a registered agent, they can put a private trust company inside that LLC for another layer of protection, add on a second company for assets, and slather the whole thing in misleading information. The agents don't have a clue. The state officials look the other way."

"What do those trust companies start at?"

Watanabe pulled on his suspenders. "Anonymity isn't cheap. Most want a hundred million US to get started. But how much do they funnel through? That's the thing we don't know. What we do know is they are exempt from any periodic examination or state scrutiny, much less tax authority."

Hiroshi hummed. "It feels very Japanese, doesn't it? Wrapping something valuable inside layers inside layers, like a gift or a kimono."

"But a lot less pretty. Maybe that's why you're here, to see what kind of wrapping Nine Dragons likes to use?"

Hiroshi nodded. "And to figure out what kind of client would ask Nine Dragons to wrap up their wealth?"

"Anyone who wants to shield it from taxes."

"That doesn't narrow it down much." Hiroshi sighed. "Do you work with anyone over there about all this?"

"I used to get help from one of the state regulators, but she quit. Blocked from doing her job by privacy laws. She told me some days she did nothing except draw her pay. The Equality State, Wyoming. That used to be a claim for equal rights, but with enough money and the right lawyers..."

"And someone to structure your company..."

"You can have a little more equality." Watanabe chuckled. "So, Nine Dragons was in Wyoming?"

"One of their guys moved there for a year. I don't think he was on vacation."

"Probably not." Watanabe put his hands together and sat quietly. "I'll check into it. Can you give me a few days?"

"That's the one thing I can't give you. He abducted his daughters. We have to find them. I don't think it's just a divorce gone bad."

Watanabe reset his suspenders and leaned forward. "Wealth does strange things to people, and protected wealth even stranger things. Want me to expedite access to their books?"

"I do, but it's tangled up already. Nine Dragons is a Chinese company."

"The Chinese are everywhere. But that won't stop us getting inside the way I do it."

"That'd be helpful." Hiroshi made a few notes. "How would a firm like Nine Dragons get money out of Japan?"

"They move it from big Tokyo banks to regional banks, and then send it along in smaller pieces. The smaller, local banks in the north were hit pretty hard after the Tohoku earthquake. So now they generate income by facilitating capital flight."

"They do it for the transfer fees? That can't be much."

"It adds up. And doesn't take much time."

"Where do the small banks send it?"

"To whatever foreign bank they have connections with."

"Doesn't that generate Suspicious Activity Reports?"

Watanabe leaned back in his chair. "For years, the Ministry of Finance ignored the SARs. And most of the time, the banks file the SARs late, sometimes six months late."

"By which time the money is long gone." Hiroshi tapped the desk. "But it flows along traceable paths at some point."

Watanabe leaned forward. "Of course it does. But when confronted, the banks say they didn't know the company was fake, that it was an oversight, that the other bank accepted it, or whatever excuse comes to mind most quickly. Undelivered goods or the return of a loan are always good excuses. Loans are often in cash. There are plenty of dodges."

"So Nine Dragons could move unlimited amounts if they're clever enough."

"Nine Dragons probably has contacts at banks all through Asia."

"So they came here because it's easy to tap in and siphon off."

"The regional banks in Japan send it to big banks in Hong Kong, New York, London, wherever. Then small regional banks in Panama, Liechtenstein, or the Caribbean receive the deposits from those big banks. And from there, it makes its way piecemeal to Wyoming before being reassembled. Once there, it's given 'Wyoming Home Cooking.'" Watanabe slapped his stomach. "Nice, huh?"

"It sounds like you have it all figured out." Hiroshi sighed.

Watanabe leaned back in his chair. "If I had it figured out, they wouldn't keep getting away with it. The Ministry of Finance is working to close the loopholes, but when it involves other ministries, inertia sets in. Along with jealousy, territoriality, indifference."

"What about the SARs? They seem like the weak point of the whole operation."

"That's the point of the SARs. But there are hundreds, even thousands a day. They deluge the system. You want to check all those? Impossible. The irony is Japan has a good reputation."

Hiroshi sighed. "You mean Japan seems so aboveboard, so no one wastes much time digging below the surface?"

"That's right." Watanabe laughed. "Japanese seem too honest to check up on."

"So, that's why Nine Dragons set up shop in Tokyo."

Watanabe spread his arms. "Plus, in Tokyo, there are so many great places to spend what they rake in. Upscale apartments, luxury goods, high-end restaurants. Tokyo has higher strata of luxury most people never see. And you can pay for anything in cash here. What's not to like?"

Chapter 11

Hiroshi walked out of the Ministry of Finance building thinking over what Watanabe had told him. The appointment with the judge overseeing the divorce was in a half-hour, and the judge's secretary told Hiroshi to be on time or the judge wouldn't see him. The office was not far, near the Tokyo District Court. A short walk through Hibiya Park, one of the first Western-style parks in Japan, would clear his head.

He turned into the side entrance. Even with the sun out, it was cold in the park. He took the path around the copper statue of a crane with open wings, the stream of water shooting up from the crane's mouth toward the sky.

Patrick was managing a lot of wealth in Wyoming, so maybe he got ahead of himself, became involved with someone, or simply needed a change. Sometimes a short time apart was enough to reveal the problems in a marriage. Or in household finances. Or life plans.

Patrick returning to Japan, killing his boss, driving to his apartment, killing his mother-in-law, beating up the babysitter, and taking his daughters was a scenario that connected the ugly dots, but Hiroshi couldn't see it. That was a lot of violence for reasons that were too well hidden. It wasn't coincidence, but it wasn't clearly connected, either.

For that matter, Patrick could hire someone to snatch his girls and sneak them out of the country. They had no proof that he was even in Japan. Ueno was checking with immigration, but getting away with the daughters was too neat of a scenario. Between all the ugly dots in this case would be ugly lines. Or worse, no lines at all.

Hiroshi's cellphone buzzed. It was Takamatsu.

"Aren't you smoking on the beach in Enoshima?" Hiroshi

asked.

"I'm smoking in the car. Much better. The chief's ordered us to help you."

Hiroshi stopped. "Where are Sugamo and Osaki?"

"I thought they were with you."

"I'm in Hibiya Park. Alone."

"We're just pulling off the Shuto Expressway now. We'll be there in fifteen minutes."

"I'll be at the Kasumi Gate."

Several ginkgos with long, straight branches dropped bright yellow fan-shaped leaves that turned the walkways golden. Hiroshi thought of the missed walks under the ginkgos with Ayana. She'd left her camera by the front door, unused for weeks already.

He took photos of the ginkgo trees and sent them to her. Then, he called.

"Wait a minute. Let me sit down." Hiroshi heard her office door click shut. "I'm so tired this morning. You left early."

"You were snoring away on the sofa."

Ayana chuckled. "I don't snore."

"OK, call it purring."

"You called me to talk about my sleeping noises?"

"No, I wanted to share the ginkgos with you. I'm in Hibiya Park, and they are stunning."

"Describe them to me."

"Did you see the photos I sent?"

"Yes."

"Nice?"

"Very nice. But not as good as the real thing."

"We'll go soon. Also, well, I don't know when I'll be home tonight."

"So, you can't help me with my wedding speech." Ayana sounded irritated. "That's why you called."

"I'm calling to apologize."

"I'm going to kendo practice."

"Tell sensei I'll be back soon."

"He won't believe me, you've been away so long."

Hiroshi saw the car at the stoplight, Ishii driving and Takamatsu smoking. "I've got to go."

"Be careful."

"You too. Those dangerous library shelves." Hiroshi hung up and hurried to the front gate. The car pulled up and Hiroshi got in the back.

Takamatsu turned around and rolled his eyes toward Ishii.

Hiroshi ignored him.

Ishii pulled out into traffic and headed toward Uchibori Dori Street, the wide six-lane road that ran by the park. Traffic was light, or seemed so with the well-timed lights and extra wide lanes.

Ishii looked back at Hiroshi in the rearview. "Where's the judge's office?"

"Head straight to the moat and turn left, then left again. On the other side of the Justice Ministry."

"Half a cigarette away." Takamatsu lit up and blew the smoke out the window.

Like the Tax Agency, the office building wouldn't win any architectural design contests. It was bland and functional, its function being to make better designs stand out.

Ishii opted to stay in the car. Hiroshi and Takamatsu hurried in.

The judge's outer office was walled in by gray metal cases lined with brown and maroon law books.

The secretary stood up with a polite bow. "Court is in thirty minutes, so he won't have long to answer your questions." She knocked on the door and slipped inside, leaving the detectives standing.

Takamatsu shook his head. "They know we're coming, and they ask us to wait anyway." He stared at the law books that lined the room. "All these words are not the law."

"What are they then?" Hiroshi frowned. "It's where authority comes from."

"Does it?" Takamatsu tapped on the glass. "Do you use big, fancy, foreign legal words when tracking down someone who's stolen a pensioner's life savings?"

"That doesn't mean it's pointless to write it all down."

Takamatsu growled. "Everyone knows what's right or wrong without it being written down in minute detail."

Hiroshi sniffed. "You smell like tobacco."

"Every time we go into an office, you lecture me. That's what makes me smoke so much."

The secretary stepped out, held the door open, and ushered them inside with a stiff hand.

The office was taken up by a wooden table that could sit a dozen people if they didn't try to go in or out at the same time. Bookcases fronted by locked glass doors lined the walls. Inside, rows of neatly labeled folders for years of cases formed a history of the judge's work.

At the end of the table sat Judge Yamanaka, still talking to three thirty-something law clerks, two men and a woman in crisp white shirts. The judge had a broad face with gray hair that sprang out of control. His chin jutted like the *ukiyo-e* woodblock print of a wild *aragoto* character from kabuki.

The three law clerks finished taking notes. They nodded to Yamanaka before resting their hands on top of their notebooks and turning to the detectives. The room was warm and stuffy, making it harder to breathe through their masks.

Judge Yamanaka invited them to sit down. "You don't mind if my clerks listen in, do you? It can be instructive what detectives ask, and how they ask it."

Takamatsu scooted the chair and dropped down in the same way he did when interrogating a suspect. Hiroshi thought he better take the lead.

Hiroshi looked the judge straight in the eye. "In your decision about Miyuki and Patrick Walsh, you planned on awarding custody of the children to the mother, correct?"

The judge nodded.

"And what about visitation rights for the father?"

The judge folded his arms over his chest. "I didn't decide yet. I wanted to meet him first."

"Under what circumstances do you deny rights to the father?"

"Most circumstances. In cases like this, the father's more likely to remove the children from Japan, where they belong."

"Did he suspect you were going to decide that way?"

Judge Yamanaka cocked his head to the side. He didn't like being questioned. "The possibility was included in some papers sent by the wife's lawyer."

"That may be the provocation."

The judge scowled. "Provocation for what?"

"The father may have abducted the two girls."

"So I was right. He couldn't be trusted."

"Being denied visitation might have encouraged him to take action." Hiroshi waited for an answer.

Judge Yamanaka leaned forward over the table with his hands clasped. "I routinely award custody to the mother in international marriages for this very reason. Japanese mothers take better care of their children. Japan's a safe country. And the husband was absent for nearly a year."

"He was posted abroad for his job. *Tanshin funin* is basic Japanese corporate practice too, isn't it?"

"There were issues of infidelity."

"Another Japanese corporate practice," Takamatsu chimed in.

The judge looked at him.

Hiroshi tried to redirect. "Infidelity?"

"Japanese women have good instincts in that regard."

"But you didn't see proof?"

The judge frowned. "Her lawyer said there was proof."

"Isn't that what lawyers say?"

The judge's square jaw stuck forward.

"Were there other issues in this case, violence, abuse?"

"Not that I recall." Judge Yamanaka nodded the clerks toward the shelves. "C8 or so, custody cases, 'W' something."

One of the male law clerks hopped up, unlocked the case, fingered the files, and handed one to Yamanaka with two hands.

Yamanaka pulled open the file and put on his reading glasses. He flipped through several pages, scanning the text. After a minute or two, he shrugged. "Very straightforward. The American husband left. The wife wanted a divorce and protection for the children. Done." He handed the file back to the clerk.

"Can we get a copy of that?"

Yamanaka nodded for the clerk to take care of it. "I'll have it sent to homicide by the end of the day."

"What about any investigation into where the husband went and why?" Hiroshi could sense Takamatsu fidgeting and didn't want to leave an opening for him to enter in and mess things up.

"Beyond the scope of the filing, there wasn't any need." Yamanaka's grey bushy eyebrows turned to a sharp 'V'. He was used to staring people down.

Hiroshi decided he'd get nothing more from him. "If the husband does ask for custody, what's the likely outcome?"

Yamanaka checked his watch. "In international divorce cases, visitation rights cause confusion. There's the language and cultural differences, and in this case, there's now the abduction."

"That's not confirmed yet."

"I set restrictive conditions for the safety of the children. The problem is typically with the non-Japanese spouse, usually the man."

Takamatsu stood up, his chair scraping the floor.

Judge Yamanaka waved at the other door of his office. "I've got a deposition in ten minutes on a complex case, and we're not finished reviewing the details."

Hiroshi offered his appreciation in polite but curt Japanese.

Takamatsu walked out ahead of Hiroshi. He said nothing until the elevator reached the lobby. "That judge wasn't telling us everything, but I agree with him about the case."

"Didn't she file for divorce a bit too quickly? Hardly a year and he was over there for work. Divorce cases often stretch on for years. Especially if there's enough money to keep everyone happy." Outside the building, they looked for Ishii.

Takamatsu pulled his lighter out. It was a heavy model with an engraving on the side. Some gift from some passing affair, Hiroshi guessed.

Takamatsu flicked the flint wheel, and the flame sprang up. "Unless there isn't as much money as it seems." He blew his smoke straight up into the air like the crane fountain in Hibiya Park. "Or much more money."

Chapter 12

Miyuki woke up covered in sweat. She stumbled to Kiri's room and stared into the emptiness. She closed the door, walked to Jenna's room, and sat down on her bed. She put the T-shirts and sweatpants she had folded into the drawer and listened to the silence. That was why she couldn't sleep.

She kept expecting the detectives to wake her with news. They were in the living room with her cellphone and passcode in case any calls came in. She smoothed the covers and thought about the enjoy nature field trip the two girls wouldn't be on.

She called the school to tell them—in a tight, fake voice—that both girls had a fever and would miss the field trip. She called her boss and told him she had a fever, assuring him she would answer emails all day on her work phone and iPad.

She went to the bathroom, dropped her sweat-drenched clothes in the hamper, and got in the shower. She let the water run until her skin turned red and her fear and fury turned to dry-eyed determination. "God fucking damn you, Patrick!" she screamed in English. Japanese had plenty of swear words, but few things were as satisfying as yelling, "Fuck you!" in English.

She toweled off, blow-dried her hair, careful not to look at herself, and went back to her empty bedroom. She wrote a message to Patrick, then deleted it. Clutching her cellphone, she leaned backwards on the bed, staring at the ceiling. Her eyes closed and she gave up trying to stop her mind spinning.

She hadn't slept until then.

When she woke, she was surprised at the time and rushed to the closet, choosing a plain black skirt and black blouse—mourning clothes—with no makeup, a simple ponytail and a single strand of small pearls.

She found the detectives snoozing on the sofa, her sofa, the family's sofa. Did they think she was going to make them tea? She wasn't. The two detectives stirred at the sound of the door from the bedroom hallway.

Ignoring the detectives, she walked to where her mother had died and stared at the spot. It made her want to cry and curse all over again.

One of the detectives came over and Miyuki spoke to him without turning her head. "I've got to go to my lawyer's office. One of the detectives is meeting me there."

"We heard that. We'll drive you." The detective turned to look for instructions from his superior rousing himself on the sofa.

"Just find my daughters." She checked to be sure Taiga's cellphone and her prayer beads were in her purse next to her iPad and phone. She slipped on her shoes at the *genkan*, and hurried out.

When she got to Tamura Legal Offices, her lawyer, Tamura, came out to the waiting room with a deep bow and formal condolences. He ushered her in to his office. His desk was centered in front of a picture window that looked down the hill toward the new buildings and nightlife streets of Akasaka.

Tamura's bookshelves were half law books and half baseball memorabilia. His team had made it to the high school finals at Koshien Stadium, the sacred ground of baseball. He mentioned this every time she talked to him, but if he mentioned it today, she'd scream.

She settled into the chair and set her plain black purse beside her. Her iPad jiggled and she pulled it out to read the email from the bank. She dropped it back in her purse without answering. "When are the detectives coming?"

Tamura bowed again. "I'm so sorry for your loss. If there's anything I can do, tell me right away."

Miyuki looked away. "Help me with the interview with the detectives."

Tamura nodded.

"And I need you to do a few things about Patrick. Can we get to work?"

"Of course. Let's finish an inning or two before the police get here." Tamura took out a notepad and leaned forward. "If you really think it was Patrick who took the girls, we need to—"

"It was him." It had to be. She refused to think otherwise. "I want to make sure he can't cross any border without being picked up."

"That requires an international red notice from Interpol."

"Well, do that."

Tamura nodded.

"And I want all the credit cards and bank accounts frozen." She dug in her bag for a sheet of paper with all the relevant information.

Tamura took the sheet from her and spread it out on his desk. "The detectives might want those left open to track him."

Miyuki fidgeted. "Well, then, after we find the girls, I want him to live with nothing again. No money, no credit card, no accounts, nothing."

"He'll be in prison." Tamura held his pen over his notepad like a bat over home plate.

Miyuki didn't answer. From the elevation of the hill where his office was, a wide view of Tokyo opened to the horizon. The buildings faded into shades of gray that lightened and darkened as far as she could see.

Miyuki dug in her small black purse for Taiga's cellphone. "I need an address, and can you have this phone unlocked for me?"

Tamura didn't ask whose address or phone it was and called his secretary to take care of both right away. "And what about your mother's funeral arrangements?"

"One of my classmates married the director of a funeral service and crematorium. They divorced, but he, or actually his family, will help. He's an old friend."

His secretary buzzed the intercom, startling them both.

"Show them in," Tamura said into the intercom.

Hiroshi and Takamatsu came in. Miyuki took her bag and set it on Tamura's desk and pulled her chair around to face them, but didn't stand or bow.

Takamatsu took off his camel hair coat and folded it carefully over his arm. Hiroshi kept his coat on, in hopes they'd get done quickly. Hiroshi offered his condolences to Miyuki for losing her mother and sat down.

Takamatsu took the chair opposite Miyuki, from where he could study her.

Tamura pulled his chair from behind his desk after exchanging *meishi* name cards with Hiroshi. Tamura's secretary came in with a notepad and sat on a chair to the side.

Hiroshi started. "We just have a few questions that will hopefully—"

"Did you find anything about my daughters?" Miyuki interrupted.

"We are working on it. There is no way the perpetrator—"

"My husband." Miyuki smoothed her black dress.

"Your husband. All airports and Shinkansen entry points are being watched. We're reviewing surveillance camera footage. Probably the biggest help will come from you."

Miyuki nodded. "There's the credit card and bank account information."

Tamura handed the paper to Hiroshi. He took a photo and handed it back.

Hiroshi looked at Miyuki. "You filed for divorce, but what reasons did you have?"

"Infidelity." Miyuki reached in her bag and pulled out a plain envelope and handed it to Hiroshi.

Tamura got up to see the photos. He sucked air in through his teeth.

Hiroshi and Takamatsu leaned forward.

Miyuki looked away.

In the first photo, Patrick had his arms wrapped around an attractive woman with thick blonde hair and dimples. The next showed Patrick and the same blonde in front of a long bar with a stuffed moose head, a huge mirror, and shelves of bottles. The next one showed them embracing on the porch of a house.

"How did these arrive?" Hiroshi asked.

"The first ones came in the mail in that envelope with no return address." Miyuki pulled out her iPad and scrolled through. "These came to my work email address." Miyuki handed her iPad to Hiroshi. "I hired a private investigator to check on it, but he didn't manage clear photos like these."

Hiroshi handed the paper photos to Takamatsu and forwarded the iPad photos to his own address, and to Akiko in the office. He handed the iPad back."We have just a few more questions."

"What more do you need to know to find my girls?" Her voice came out in a sharp, raised pitch.

Hiroshi thought she was going to continue, but she stopped herself.

Miyuki reached into her purse and pulled out a small set of prayer beads, the kind for funerals and memorial services, red tiger eye beads tied with fine silk thread. "I'm sorry. I'll do anything to get the girls back."

Hiroshi nodded. "Can you tell me where you found your babysitter?"

Miyuki turned the prayer beads in her hand. "Is he going to be all right?"

"He's in the police hospital in Nakano. He's in a coma, an induced one, but he'll recover."

"Um, an agency that specializes in foreign families. Of course. I wanted someone who spoke both English and Japanese."

"What did he do for you exactly?"

"Is he a suspect?"

"We have to ask about everything."

"Taiga picked the girls up at school and stayed with them until I got home from work. He was studying too, so they all three studied together. He helped the girls feel comfortable being half-Japanese, half-not, switching between languages, thinking differently."

"What was the name of the agency?"

"Global Minding, or something like that. I have the number at home."

"Not in your phone?"

"It was on a *meishi* a friend gave me." She flipped the beads around again. They clacked when she got to the end of one count.

"And Taiga had been taking care of them—"

"The same as always." Her beads clacked.

"You didn't notice anything unusual in his behavior?"

Miyuki shook her head and flipped the beads around her wrist.

"Can you tell us about your work at the bank?"

Miyuki twisted the beads and leaned back in her chair. "I'm an account manager."

"What kind of accounts?"

"Mid-size companies and individuals with sufficient-sized accounts."

"Do you facilitate overseas transfers outside Japan?"

"I'm more on the side of domestic accounts, making sure everything's running smoothly." Her tablet buzzed inside her purse and she pointed at it. "Excuse me." She checked her incoming messages, sighed, and dropped it back into her purse.

"And about Patrick, who were his closest friends here in Tokyo?"

Miyuki sat up and fingered the beads, clacking them a bit louder. "Kyle was his best friend."

Hiroshi prompted her after a moment. "What's Kyle's last name?"

"Kyle Shawcross. Best man at our wedding."

"We'll need to talk to him. Can you give us the number?"

She pushed the beads up on her arm and got her phone out, scrolled down until she found it and held out the contact information.

"Is there anyone else Patrick could rely on in Tokyo?"

"Not that I can think of."

"Was there any change in your relationship after your husband left for Wyoming—"

"He got busy with work. Stopped answering calls as quickly. We'd never been apart, and I couldn't get over there with the girls and work. He said it'd just be a month, but it stretched to six, and then I got the photos."

"Were you fighting?"

"We gave up fighting when the girls arrived. That was the problem."

"Was he unhappy here in Tokyo?"

"No more than any foreigner who never learns much Japanese."

"He didn't speak Japanese at all?"

"He could order at a restaurant, but he couldn't read or catch the TV news. But he loved Tokyo, loved the girls. I thought he loved me."

"Was his work mainly with foreigners?"

"Other people at Nine Dragons handled Japanese clients, especially his boss." Miyuki twisted the prayer beads.

"Do you mean his boss, Joseph Leung, handled the Japanese clients?"

"That's what Patrick told me."

Hiroshi leaned forward. "Did you know that Joseph Leung was murdered?"

Miyuki pulled her hands up and the string of prayer beads broke, sending the tiger eye beads exploding over her black dress and onto the floor.

Everyone leaned down to pick them up and the interview was over.

Chapter 13

After more bagels and coffee, Kyle got ready to leave for work. Kiri and Jenna followed him to the door.

"I'll see you girls tonight!" Kyle leaned down to hug them with a tickle in their ribs.

"We want to see the turkey on the roof!" Kiri giggled.

"First thing when I get home."

When Kyle was gone, Patrick got the girls reading. He'd done one thing right with them at least, encourage reading. They took it so seriously it made him laugh, their cute little faces pointed at the page. Without his mother-in-law there, the girls didn't notice the absence of TV.

Once they were lost in their stories, Patrick called Nine Dragons and asked for Leung. A voice he didn't recognize asked him who he was. He tried to identify the voice. It was not a smooth welcoming tone in polite Japanese *keigo*. He asked for Arisa, the office manager. Without her, nothing happened at Nine Dragons.

When he was told she was no longer working there, he couldn't believe it and hung up.

He called Arisa's work phone and was told it was no longer in service. He called her personal cellphone, which went to message. He had her LINE address and sent a message, waiting until he saw the "Read" popup. She was there, someplace. He wrote her again and said they had to meet.

Jenna came in from the tatami room. "I can't find our phones."

"Did you forget them at home?" Patrick looked away. The lies were adding up.

"I had mine last night. Kiri had hers."

"It's probably in the room somewhere. We'll find it when we straighten up."

Jenna made a face, just like Miyuki's. "And what about school?"

"You're on vacation today."

"We were going on an 'enjoy nature' field trip today. I wanted to find a rhinoceros beetle."

"Plenty of beetles in Wyoming. And horses. You can ride horses there. Listen, I need to call about the flight."

"When's Mom coming?"

"If we're flying overseas, you should rest up."

"I want to send messages to my friends. Can't we go back and get our phones?"

"Maybe Mom can bring them with her. But we'll get new ones in Wyoming. I told you it was a surprise."

"Surprise is fine, but Mom and Taiga can't call me, and I had my friends' LINE contacts on there."

Patrick pulled her around by her arms and looked into her face.

"And what about..."

Patrick picked her up and dropped her on his knee. "It's just for a day until we get there. Disconnect. It's healthy. Talk to me. Talk to Kiri. Let's have a spirit of adventure. It's going to be fun." Patrick had to look her in the eye on this one. That was hard. She might never see her friends again.

Jenna wiggled away, put her finger in the air, and danced off singing, "OK, reading time, Kiri!"

"And straighten your things," he called after her.

When he went to Wyoming, he missed the girls so badly he couldn't sleep at first. He missed them even more than Miyuki. They left Zoom or FaceTime running in the morning and at night so he could let the pitter-pat noise of them soothe him from so far away.

The time difference got tiring and they left early for school and work, or went to bed before he could catch them. And he became busy setting up the LLCs in Wyoming. Leung didn't help, so he had to put everything in place by himself.

Wyoming had been a nice change at first. It gave him time to himself, something he missed after the girls were born, even though he loved them more than anything. He loved Miyuki, too, until the photos, and later, the divorce papers.

He never thought of anything other than working hard, providing for the girls, and moving toward financial independence. He wanted his own clients and his own firm. "Someday," he and Kyle sang to each other as a code word for patience. Being alone and looking out on the Grand Tetons from Jackson, he felt marriage and kids and job and apartment had taken something from him. He felt guilty for feeling that way, but he did.

Miyuki was busier than he was at times. Japanese banks didn't let their employees rest. An account manager had to be in touch 24/7. She never missed a call. She took care of the girls too, more than he did. No little help with dishwashing or dry-cleaning pick-up could give her back her life. He didn't know how to make her excited about life again.

Miyuki complained about work, but he knew she loved her job. Her college friends became full-time housewives, flight attendants, or *haken* temp workers. She was proud of her high-flying bank job and delighted in their girls' nights out, but it took something from her, too, the work, the girls, her mother, the fast tempo life had taken.

Together, they acquired a combined income that boggled his mind. And they spent like never before. The apartment, meals out and ordered in, the girls' school fees, clothes, every facet of their lifestyle became astronomical. And still, they saved for the future. It was never enough. And it was way too much.

Once he got to Wyoming, his feeling about their financial situation started to shift. Sums passed through his work day that were staggering, digits larger than he had ever handled.

Now, it was all under siege and he wasn't sure why. He knew it was certain, though. He had to get the girls hidden away and sort things out with Miyuki. He socked away all the money he could and grabbed a plane to Honolulu, dropped his things off there in a reserved suite, and caught the next flight to Tokyo to get the girls.

Patrick checked his LINE app to see if Arisa had written back, but there was no message.

He searched for Tim's number. He should know how to get out of Japan by now. He certainly paid the divorce survivors reunion group enough for their assistance and advice.

Tim picked up on the first ring. "I was going to call you, but I figured you and the girls needed sleep. Where did you end up crashing?" Tim spoke in the short, certain phrases of American confidence.

"A friend's place. Someone I can trust. He won't tell anyone."

"Police will start figuring out your old friends, your workplace. Call your wife and say the girls are safe with you. Hang up quickly."

"How long will it take to get things set up for us to get out of here?"

"I'm working on the options. They might cost extra."

"I've already paid—"

"I know you have. That's why I'm still on this. We'll make sure it gets done."

Patrick took a breath.

"I'm waiting on return calls. But first I'd leave your friend's place. Go to a fancy hotel. Let the money hide you. Rich people are eccentric. Look, I'll come get you."

It made an odd sort of sense. He shouldn't drag Kyle into this. He wondered if Kiri and Jenna could keep from talking too much. They seemed to draw people in wherever they went. He was glad they weren't any older. They'd question things more.

But Kyle couldn't get involved. They'd have to move.

Patrick gave Tim the address and hung up.

The sun had shifted straight in the window, warming the

room. He opened the sliding glass doors and stepped out on the balcony. It was a spectacular view, the exact opposite to how he felt. They would figure out Kyle easily enough. And it wouldn't be long before someone figured out he wasn't in Wyoming.

He thought it best to call Miyuki. They'd barely spoken or messaged after she sent the divorce papers.

Kiri came into the kitchen. "Dad?"

"We're going to a big hotel. We need to pack."

"Big hotel?" she squinted at him.

He picked her up, tickling her, and carried her to the tatami room. "A friend's coming to pick us up. Come on, let's get things packed."

Jenna was putting things in order and he kneeled down to help them, explaining. "We can't stay with Kyle. This room is too small, and we can have a little fun before we catch our flight. I had to change the plane reservation."

"Again?" Jenna frowned but started putting things into the bags. Kiri followed her older sister.

"Yes, again."

"We need a bag for dirty clothes," Jenna said in a bossy tone, the same one Miyuki used.

He hoped that meant they were complying. "Right away." Patrick went to find a big trash bag.

Jenna had folded the dirty clothes as neatly as the clean ones. The two of them pestered him with a hundred questions. As they packed, he answered some, deflected others, and promised they'd be back to see Kyle and Miki soon.

When they were ready, he wrote a note to Kyle and tucked it under a glass on the kitchen table.

His cellphone buzzed. It was a LINE message from Arisa, a short row of question marks.

He set the bags down by the front door and wrote to her. "I have to talk with you."

"I quit."

"That's what I want to ask you about."

"I don't go out."

"I'll go where you are."

Then she didn't write back.

Patrick kept an eye on his phone as he checked the tatami room. He pulled his cap low over his face, but there was no way to hide Kiri and Jenna. Tim was probably right. They needed to be in a conspicuous place to be less conspicuous.

He waited for an answer from Arisa while herding the girls out of Kyle's and down the hall to the lobby with soothing fatherly directions.

Tim was already waiting in front of the building in the same model car they loaned him for the failed airport run, a Toyota...something...Harrier maybe. Patrick didn't know cars. Tim got out to help. He was as big as a linebacker. His hooded sweatshirt, shirt jacket, jeans, and baseball cap made him seem like he was heading to work on a construction site.

Tim stood on the sidewalk and folded his arms, looking at the girls with one eye closed. He pointed at them in turn. "Hmmm, you must be Kiri, and you must be Jenna. Am I right?"

"You're right." Kiri laughed. "How did you know?"

"Lucky guess. Let's get this show on the road." Tim waved them into the car with reassuring movements. Patrick put the bags in, and got in the front seat.

Tim pulled out, watching the rearview mirrors carefully.

Patrick scrolled through hotel options on his cellphone. "It'll be odd if I don't call ahead."

"The bigger and more expensive the better."

"Shinjuku then." Patrick called and asked about a room. They had vacancies. Patrick told them they'd missed their flight and wanted to stay just one night. And of course, at a hotel in that price range, that was fine.

As soon as he hung up, he got a message from Arisa.

Patrick turned to Tim. "How far is it to Kokubunji?"

"It's definitely out of the way."

"This might solve part of the problem."

Tim looked at Patrick, sighed, and said, "OK."

Chapter 14

Tim drove to Kokubunji Station by alternately creeping down back streets and zipping along four-lane roads that flowed quickly. He studied the rearview mirror on both, and at every intersection, and in-between. Patrick started looking behind in the side mirror too.

When Tim pulled into the circular drive of Kokubunji Station, the coffee shop was right where Arisa said it would be next to the station entrance. But right beside it was a *koban* police box with two police officers standing out front.

Tim put the car in park.

When Patrick undid his seat belt, he realized he was going to leave his two girls in the car with someone he only met in person for the last half-hour of driving. And if the info had been distributed at airports, it might be at every police box in the country. He would be walking right in front of them.

But he had to talk to Arisa.

He leaned back toward Jenna and Kiri. "You two need to stay in the car and don't cause any trouble for Tim, OK?"

Tim kept his eyes on the police officers.

Patrick took a deep breath before he got out and closed the door. After looking at Kiri and Jenna once more, he plunged through the flow of people scurrying in and out of the station, keeping his face in the other direction from the police.

The coffee shop was a run-down place with faded lace curtains and a door with window panes, one of them cracked. Above the door, a once-cheery blue coffee cup, big as a barrel, balanced on a saucer, its blue paint chipped and the wood rotted to splinters. When he pulled the door open, cow bells jingled.

The tables and chairs in the shop were made of thick, dark wood. A dull-pink, coin-operated Showa-era telephone was plunked on the counter. Antique coffee cups and sewing machines filled the shelves up to the ceiling. No one shouted, "*Irashaimasse.*"

Patrick glanced out the window again and walked back to where Arisa was sitting at a back table. The chic office wear and neat bob haircut she sported at Nine Dragons were replaced by a sweatshirt several sizes too large and uncombed hair with dark roots below the coloring. He never noticed she wore makeup in the office, but now he noticed she didn't wear any at all.

Patrick sat down. "It's good to see you."

She glanced into his eyes and then looked away at a faded street map of Paris pinned to the wall.

"Are you OK? What happened? Why did you quit?"

Arisa turned back to him and shrugged.

"I need to ask you a few questions."

Arisa fiddled with her empty coffee cup. "I'm not sure I know the answers."

"Do you want another?" Patrick heard someone stirring in the back kitchen, but no one came out. "I need to know what's going on at Nine Dragons. I can't get hold of Leung."

Arisa gnawed the inside of her cheek and kept her eyes on her empty cup. "I don't work there anymore."

"Why did you quit?"

Arisa looked at the map of Paris, the monuments sketched to stand out. "I don't know what to tell you because I don't know what you know."

"Why did Leung insist I set up those LLCs in person? And why did he insist I stay so long?"

Arisa clenched her jaw.

In the office, she sorted out glitches, remembered birthdays, eased new hires into their positions, made sure meetings started and ended on time. At office *nomikai*, Arisa was always the bubbliest, the one who kept the exchanges going, poured drinks, and stayed until everyone headed home.

Arisa picked up her cup and swirled the remaining foam. "I'm not sure why Leung wanted you to stay, but things changed after you left for Wyoming. New people came. It got busy."

"New clients?"

"And new employees."

"Like who?"

"First a man named Tran, and then another named Mehta. Both from the Hong Kong office. Tran ran security and Mehta did my job. Tran went back, but Leung still talked to him every day."

"Your job? But you—"

"New clients arrived, with huge accounts, and Leung told me we needed two office managers to handle it all. However, I stayed with the old clients and Mehta handled the new ones."

"Who brought in those clients?" He had been too busy setting things up in Wyoming to notice.

"Leung did. I didn't see any of their files or any information about them. But you must have seen something in the bank transfers."

"All I saw were new accounts coming in. I was working my ass off getting all the transfers set up for the right accounts and making sure the LLCs and agents were in order."

"You didn't see anything else?"

"Like what? I mean, the transfers were rerouted to other accounts and some came from strange routings, but—"

"The clients who came in after you left were different. It was like Nine Dragons had divided into two." Arisa pulled her sweatshirt tight around her and put her hand on the map of Paris spreading out in boulevards and old lanes, the Seine snaking blue through the middle.

"Arisa, please tell me what's wrong. Why did you quit?"

Arisa picked up the empty cup with her hands inside her sleeves. "One day, I was working late, and Shimada from accounting called me down to the parking lot. He said his car wouldn't start and he needed my help. I don't know a thing about cars, but I went anyway, for hand-holding. When I got there, a car pulled up."

"Where was Shimada?"

"He wasn't there. Two guys got out. They didn't say much, but it was clear I was supposed to get in the car with them."

"You didn't, did you?"

"They were insistent." Arisa put her empty cup down.

"Who were they?"

"I'm still not sure. Maybe new clients. Or they knew the new clients. I thought they might be detectives at first, but they weren't."

"So, who were they?"

"Just three guys. In black suits. Bright ties, orange, purple, maroon. I sat in back with a tall guy who told me that Shimada was going to quit. They drove me around for an hour asking me questions."

"What kind of questions?"

"About accounts, clients, how the office worked, who had access, all kinds of things."

"Things only you would know?"

"Me, or Leung. The new guy, Mehta, and you would know too, except for the newest accounts. I told them some things. I worried what would happen if I didn't say something."

Patrick thought about that. "And then they drove you back?"

"I took the next day off. And then the next. It took me a day or two to realize how scared I was. I thought it was just strange at first, then I realized how serious it was."

"Did you tell Leung?"

"No. I quit."

"Why didn't you tell me all this?"

"How would I have told you?" Arisa finally looked him in the eye. "There was my section and Mehta's section. And you were handling both in Wyoming." Arisa nodded slowly. "Did anything happen while you were over there?"

"Yes, that's why I came back." He didn't want to tell her about the photos, but it was more than that. "I was told by a paralegal at one of the firms that someone had asked about me. A tall Asian guy. Then I got a message about my girls. I ignored it. I got a second message and realized I was being...I don't know...threatened. My girls were being threatened. I came back right away."

Arisa's eyes widened. "Are your girls OK? And your wife?"

"They're fine." Patrick looked at the door of the coffee shop but couldn't see out. "I've got to go." He stood. "Are you going to be OK?"

Arisa looked up at him. "Quit, will you? Stay away from Nine Dragons."

Their eyes met. "There are a couple of things I need to do first."

"Forget those things. It's worse than you think."

Patrick patted the back of the chair, looking at Arisa.

"My girls are waiting."

"Your girls are outside? You really need to get out of Japan and take them with you."

She'd always known everything at Nine Dragons. Now, she didn't know anything. He looked at the map of Paris and hurried outside.

Along the row of cars in the drop-off circle, Tim's car was not there.

A jolt of adrenaline shot through him and he hurried to the curb, glancing at the police, trying not to run.

He looked in both directions while jamming his finger on the callback button for Tim. Two policemen watched him from where they stood by the *koban* police box.

Tim didn't answer, so he redialed as calmly as he could. He had trusted someone and he would not do that again. Patrick stood there watching every car, thinking things he didn't want to think.

He walked to the end of the half-circle and stood beside a line of people waiting to board a bus. Taxis and private cars pulled up, stopped, and then pulled onto the busy street that ran parallel to the train line. Redialing was all he could do.

Finally, Tim answered. "Be there in a minute, buddy."

Patrick stifled a yell. "Where the fuck are you?"

"A cop asked me to move. I couldn't park there any longer without drawing attention. Relax. We're just around the corner."

Patrick saw Tim's black car pull into the opposite side of the drop-off area and circle to where he was.

He yanked the door open, trying not to explode in front of the girls. He got in the front and turned to Kiri and Jenna. "Did you have a nice drive?"

Jenna looked at him. "What about you, Poppa? Did you have a nice talk with your friend?"

"I did, actually. Thank you for asking."

Tim pulled off. Patrick stared out the window, too angry to acknowledge how frightened he'd been.

When the highway noise muffled their conversation, Tim looked over. "You took longer than I thought. We'll be at the hotel in thirty minutes and you can lie low. I got a text about a private yacht that could run you to Korea. I think it'll work."

Patrick nodded. So, maybe they would be out of Japan by tomorrow and the girls would be safe. Once he got them to safety, he'd figure out what to do about Miyuki.

He didn't know what to do other than get them out of Japan safely, and he was failing at that. Watching Tokyo pass by, he reminded himself he'd have to be more careful if any of this was going to work.

Chapter 15

Hiroshi and Takamatsu walked down the steep, narrow lanes from the lawyer's office in Akasaka. Halfway down the slope, Takamatsu stopped to light a cigarette.

Hiroshi kept walking. It was a perfect autumn day, crisp and fresh, except for the tobacco smoke.

"I've been cutting down." Takamatsu held the cigarette at arm's length. His gold watch and cufflinks glistened in the sun. "What did you think of our mourning daughter?"

"More like a frightened mother."

"Her beads kept her busy. At least until they spilled all over the floor."

"Her lawyer's office was expensive. All that baseball memorabilia."

"With clients like that, he can afford it." Takamatsu blew his smoke away from Hiroshi.

"This credit card information should catch him pretty quickly." Hiroshi tapped his pocket.

"The credit card's good if he's here in Japan and if he uses that card. If he's not too smart and if he runs out of cash. That's a lot of ifs."

As they walked down the slope, Hiroshi checked his messages.

"Nothing yet on the father and two daughters?"

"Akiko would have texted if they'd found something at the hotels."

"Hotels?" Takamatsu frowned.

"The chief pulled Akiko over to call every hotel in Japan."

"He *what*?" Takamatsu stopped and took a long last drag on his cigarette before grinding it out underfoot. "The chief's an idiot. There are a lot of ways to hide kids and a lot of ways to get them out of the country."

"Like what?"

"Private boat's the easiest. Private plane's the fastest. Or, he could send them out one by one. Or lie low until we back-burner it. He's rich enough to manage any of them. Those are the options where the girls stay alive."

"If it was the father, he's not going to harm them."

"I thought America was the country where fathers grab a gun, hold the family hostage and—"

"That's a stereotype."

"Makes the mother driving with her kids off the pier yesterday seem civilized in comparison."

Hiroshi called Ishii to meet them at the bottom of the slope where the small streets spilled onto a recently built plaza that conjoined three new office buildings.

Hiroshi called Akiko and gave her the credit card info. She updated him on the hotel call-around. Hiroshi smiled as she gave him the last tidbit.

Hiroshi hung up and looked for the car. "Well, it seems Taiga wasn't always a babysitter of little girls."

"Why am I not surprised?" Takamatsu nodded at Ishii pulling up at the small drop-off circle. "Let me guess. He likes to work at night too?"

After they got in, Hiroshi held out the map on his cellphone and Ishii inputted the address into the GPS on the dashboard. Ishii frowned at the address and frowned at Hiroshi. And then pulled off.

It was a twenty-minute drive past the Akasaka Palace and one of the best ginkgo tree walks in the city. Hiroshi thought of Ayana as he watched the tops of the yellow-leaved trees go by. They zipped past Shinjuku Gyoen Gardens, slowing to walking speed after Ishii turned into the small streets between Kabukicho and Shin-Okubo.

A gaudy jumble of oversized signs covered the decrepit state of the love hotels, spas, karaoke centers, and host and hostess clubs. The signs were trying hard to make everything more appealing, more suggestive. At night in Kabukicho, everything inflated—signs, hairdos, prices, buildings, and desires—but in the pale afternoon light, the area felt ratty and empty.

Takamatsu told Ishii to stop by a chain strung between two poles sunk into concrete blocks. Takamatsu got out and took the plastic "No Parking" sign dangling in the middle, jimmied it free with the multitool he kept in his coat. He set it halfway on the curb, stomped on it, kicked the pieces aside, and waved Ishii into the space.

"What was that?" Ishii asked.

"It wasn't issued by the metropolitan government." Hiroshi explained. "He loves doing that."

Takamatsu smiled. "Best parking spot in Kabukicho."

Hiroshi started up the curving stairs to the second floor. A small brass sign for the club, "Acquire," hung on the wall beside a filthy red carpet hung out to dry. Photos of hosts filled a display board beside the entrance. Their spiky hair, smooth faces, and wide shiny collars in the too-bright flash photo gave them a ghostly appearance. Hiroshi took a photo of the hosts in the display. The edges of the photos were crinkled, unchanged for years.

Hiroshi pulled the brass handle of the door, pushed aside a black curtain, and headed in with Takamatsu and Ishii right behind.

The club smelled of day-old alcohol and aftershave. Low chairs and banquettes on either side of knee-high tables led to a small stage at the far end. Overhead, a row of chandeliers formed a low ceiling of pure glitz.

In the center of the room, a refrigerated case displayed silver, pink, and gold champagne bottles covered in sparkles, ribbons, and bright bows. They glittered, ready for the "champagne calls" the hosts wheedled customers into buying. "Champagne calls" made or broke a host's career.

Takamatsu pulled open his camel hair overcoat and pulled out his friction-lock baton as he moved down the left-hand aisle, with Ishii behind. Hiroshi went down the right. The walls were covered in parallel mirrors that made the club seem bigger than it was and formed infinite reflections of the three detectives as they strode to where three young hosts sat at a circular booth.

The hosts tensed when they noticed the detectives coming at them, but it was too late to do anything more than put on hard, indifferent faces. Their gold necklaces and earrings competed for attention with their designer workout sweats, and their hair hung loose without the mousse and gel they slathered on in the evening. Drinks, coasters, cigarette packs, and lighters littered the table next to their cellphones, two or three each.

The closest host reached for his phone, but Takamatsu flipped out his baton and smacked it on the table. He waved the baton back and forth in the host's face until he set his phone back down.

Takamatsu looked at each of the three in turn without saying anything. "We have a few questions, and if you answer them, you can get back to your important consultations before the start of your working day. But if you hesitate, we will shut this place down and hold you for three weeks minimum."

"For what? Sitting down?" The youngest guy at the table scoffed. He looked barely twenty.

Hiroshi braced for Takamatsu to whack the kid, but instead he laughed. "I haven't been to a club yet that didn't have plenty of violations. It can take a long time to go through all of them. We'll be sure to tell your boss you were the one who provoked us. Who's the spokesperson here?"

The three of them squirmed and scratched the back of their necks. The closest guy nodded his streak-blonde hair. "I'm the manager."

"A position of authority and responsibility. Your mother must be proud."

Hiroshi pulled out his cellphone before Takamatsu got more

sarcastic or more violent. He scrolled for a picture of Taiga. "Here's the before shot. And here's the after." Hiroshi held his cellphone closer.

The three leaned forward and squinted. The "before" photo had a faint smile, but the "after" photo showed Taiga in the hospital, his face a blue puddle of bruises.

Hiroshi took over the questioning. "So, tell us about Taiga."

The guy furthest from them sat back. "He works here, or used to."

"What's his family name?"

The manager picked up his phone, asked for permission, and started scrolling up and down. "Sato. And his English name is Smith."

"How old is he?"

"He told everyone twenty-one, but he could be younger."

"Where's his work application?"

"Application?"

"Address?"

The youngest looking host spoke up. "He lives in a *gaijin* apartment out on the Chuo Line, Asagaya maybe?"

"Ok. Let me explain clearly." Takamatsu tapped his baton on the table. "Whoever was looking for him may come looking for you."

All three hosts nodded, their feigned indifference turning to concern.

Hiroshi interrupted. "Was he a popular host?"

The kid at the back spoke up. "He had a terrible attitude, but the more he ignored customers, the more they adored him. Women showered him with gifts, found him day jobs."

"Day jobs?"

The two hosts in the back of the curved banquette laughed.

"He had the record for the most champagne calls," one of them said.

"I heard he was shacked up with some rich woman in Azabu."

Takamatsu whacked the table. "But he's not shacked up now, is he? He's in the hospital struggling to breathe." Takamatsu pointed his baton at each of them in turn. "So, why don't one of you tell us who put him in the hospital?"

They shook their heads.

"Did he have debts?"

The manager shrugged. "He was making a lot of money here, but he was studying at a *senmon gakko* training school."

"I asked you if he had debts."

"He never had any money. I don't know what he did with it."

"Drugs?"

"I doubt it. Maybe."

"Training school for what?"

"To be an office worker at a city office." All three hosts laughed. "He paid for that by doing porn videos, I heard."

"Easy work."

"No, hard work." They laughed some more.

Takamatsu smacked the table with his baton and they quieted down. "I'm not hearing what I need to know from you."

The manager seemed a dozen years older than the other two. He sighed and sat up. "Some other guys stopped by asking about him. Serious guys."

"How many?"

"One guy with two assistants."

"Assistants?" Takamatsu looked at Ishii, who had taken out her baton and held it by her leg. "Well, what did the serious guy and his assistants look like?"

"Like anybody. Black suits with colored ties. Sunglasses."

Takamatsu reached down and grabbed a handful of the manager's gold chains and yanked him to his feet. "What was his name?"

The manager twisted his head to the side. "Some loan shark, I guess. I never saw him before."

"Loan shark. I thought you didn't know if he owed money."

Takamatsu twisted the gold chains tighter. "His name?"

"I don't know."

"So find it. We know you have good connections. That's why you have this job, right?"

The manager nodded OK.

Takamatsu let go and the host tried to look tough as he rubbed his neck. "If we have to come back here to recheck this, the only thing you'll be manager of is your asshole in the prison yard."

Hiroshi dropped his *meishi* name card on the table. "Call me with the name. Later today."

The three detectives walked out, the parallel wall mirrors turning their images into infinite detectives in infinite clubs, smaller and smaller into the distance.

Chapter 16

Miyuki maintained her composure until she got down the hill from her lawyer's office. She wanted to weep, but instead she bought an *onigiri* rice ball and a can of hot tea from a convenience store and found a bench not far away. In her mourning clothes, people stared at her.

As she ate, she answered messages from her section chief at the bank. Because he didn't really pay attention to the accounts, she worried he'd botch things. It would take more time to undo his damage than to stay on top of it. When she finished damage control, she read Taiga's messages on the phone her lawyer hacked for her.

Taiga was still in touch with the other hosts at his former host club. She thought he'd broken off all contact with them. She searched for any comment about her or the girls, but the messages were mostly banter about the customers, middle-aged women with too much money.

Despite what she'd told the detectives, she met Taiga not through an agency but at his host club. At a bachelorette party for a college friend, she and her girlfriends ended up guzzling champagne at his club. When the cutest host of all—Taiga—appeared by her side, she felt like a college girl again. After he confided he planned to get out of the *mizu shobai* nightlife and go back to school, she invited him to become the girls' babysitter.

Yes, she was drunk, and yes, she was lonely. Patrick was overseas, her mother was no help, and she was exhausted. She wasn't sure why she trusted Taiga, but she did. He started the next day and became part of the family. Her mother liked him, and she didn't like much outside of *shochu* and cigarettes.

One evening when she came back from dinner with clients, she joined him on the couch to watch a film. She was half asleep, so she didn't notice at first when Taiga put his arm around her, and touched her thigh. She didn't stop him. He knew his way around down there and she let him.

The moment he began kissing her neck, though, Kiri came in. "Momma? There are wild things under my bed."

Miyuki clicked into mother mode and sat up. "Kiri-*chan*, that's just a book. There are no wild things."

"Taiga read us the book." Kiri pointed at Taiga, who had moved to the other end of the sofa.

"Let's go back to bed." She took Kiri's hand, put her in bed, snuggled into a pillow beside her, and fell fast asleep.

In the morning, Taiga acted like nothing had happened. And so did she.

She was surprised at herself, didn't think she had that in her. But she realized she was just exhausted by the years of motherhood, work, and resenting Patrick for being gone. Still, she couldn't imagine that Taiga was involved with Kiri and Jenna's abduction and her mother's death. He wasn't like that.

Her lawyer had also found the address of the office manager from Nine Dragons, Arisa. The one time Miyuki met her, she was the epitome of a Tokyo woman, stylish, confident, and ready for something interesting every moment. Patrick said that when he and Kyle started their own investment firm, they'd hire her away. She would know something about Nine Dragons and about Patrick.

Miyuki dug out her mask as she walked to Akasaka-Mitsuke Station. She took the Marunouchi Line to Yotsuya and changed to the Chuo Line going west. She got a seat and reached in her purse for the bag holding the prayer beads, which Tamura's secretary had gathered for her. She'd get them restrung before her mother's funeral.

Her childhood had been a dull procession of her parents' arguments, sports and schoolwork, and nice, plain friends who liked gossip and karaoke. There was only one bus an hour to the shopping mall in the next city. The day she came to Tokyo for university was the day she started living.

She wanted to create a big city life for her daughters. She filled Kiri and Jenna's every moment with piano lessons, soccer, and after-school schools. The girls took to studying, and it was often Miyuki who dragged them out to Tokyo's parade of kid-oriented pleasures—the Ghibli Museum, the Ninja Restaurant, Kiddy Land, Legoland, Disneyland. There were special kids' days at museums and *bunraku* theater workshops, pottery, *ikebana* and calligraphy lessons. Kiri and Jenna became the sisters she never had.

At Kokubunji Station, Miyuki roused herself, promising herself they'd do all that again when the girls were back.

Out the south exit, she followed a winding street of dry-cleaning and flower shops, and an old liquor store with a dusty vending machine that once sold beer. Most of the shopfronts were buried behind sun-faded drapes and rusted pull-down shutters. Along the way, old homes had been torn down and new unit homes installed, as if one or the other was on the wrong street.

Miyuki stopped to check her navigation app. The back lane that branched off the street was crowded by rows of shrubs and shoulder-high walls. The cross lanes had school commute routes painted on the pavement.

At a small parking lot in front of a faded yellow apartment building, a black car, low and lean with tinted windows, angled across the parking spaces. Bicycles and trash cans had been knocked over. On the other side of the car, three men were shouting at someone. Miyuki checked her cellphone app. It was Arisa's apartment.

She walked quickly and cautiously around the car. Sitting on a cinderblock wall, a woman in a big sweatshirt cowered between three men in black suits. They wore long overcoats and sported bright-colored ties.

Miyuki shouted, "Hey, what are you doing?"

One of the three guys turned toward her and thrust his chin out over his dark purple tie. "Get out of here."

From her purse, Miyuki pulled out her rape alarm and yanked the strap. Over 130 decibels of ear-piercing siren shattered the silence of the back street and echoed down the cramped lane. She held the alarm up as she backed away.

Windows slid open in homes. Someone shouted from a second-floor balcony, and a man stepped out from his front door looking in all directions.

The three men stared and the one with the purple tie started for her.

Miyuki dug in her bag for her pepper spray, right next to the bag holding the prayer beads. She held it straight at him.

He stopped and turned back toward the tallest guy, the leader, who was glaring at Miyuki, as if the siren didn't reach his ears. He waved the other two guys into the car.

They slammed the doors and backed over the fallen bicycles, crunching them as they spun into the lane, the engine roaring louder than the rape alarm.

The neighbors who had gathered in the lane leaped aside as the car sped away.

Miyuki wasn't sure how to stop the siren, since she had never used the thing before. A middle-aged man took it from her and slid the pin back in, mercifully stopping the noise. The neighbors gathered around her and barraged her with questions.

Miyuki pointed at the woman in the oversized sweatshirt. She walked over and helped her up. "Arisa? I'm Miyuki, Patrick's wife."

Arisa pulled her sweatshirt tight around herself and stretched her back.

A policeman rode up on a bicycle. He dismounted and talked to the man who'd stopped the siren. Four more policemen arrived from different directions. The neighbor pointed in the direction the car sped off. Two of the policemen rode off in pursuit, but the car had a head start.

Miyuki stood beside Arisa as they answered the policemen's questions. Arisa told them the car pulled up right when she got home. She had no idea what they wanted. She told the police she'd never seen them before.

It was cold, and the neighbors gradually drifted back to their homes. The police wearied of Arisa's unwavering answers and promised to ride by for the next day or two.

Miyuki took Arisa by the arm and helped her up the outside stairs to her apartment on the second floor. The *genkan* was only wide enough for one person at a time. Miyuki followed her inside, turning sideways to scoot by the cardboard shoe box and convenience store umbrellas.

The kitchen was neatly arranged with a small refrigerator, folding table, and a single chair. Beyond the kitchen an eight-mat tatami room was full of clothes drying on laundry racks. The glass door to a unit bath opened to the right. Not one thing in the place had character. Arisa must have had a salary at Nine Dragons that could afford a bigger, better place than this.

Arisa washed her hands at the kitchen sink, wiped them on a towel, and turned to Miyuki. Her mask was torn and she threw it out.

"I'm looking for Patrick and my daughters." Miyuki stood in her socks on the cold kitchen floor.

Arisa pulled her hood back. Her eyes were red, but not crying. "How did you find me?"

"You saw him, didn't you?" Miyuki took a step toward her and Arisa flinched. Miyuki lowered her voice. "My girls are missing."

Arisa looked down. "I saw him today."

"Did you see the girls?"

Arisa shook her head. "He wanted to know about Nine Dragons, but I quit."

"You what?"

121

Arisa shrugged.

"Where did you meet him?"

"At a coffee shop near the station."

"And the girls were with him?"

"He said they were. And they were leaving Japan soon."

Why wouldn't Patrick at least call? She closed her eyes. "Who were those guys just now?"

Arisa put her hand on the chair, her eyes down. "I don't know who they are."

She realized it was worse than she thought. Maybe Patrick was taking care of the girls. But why wouldn't he tell her anything?

"He was back to get the girls, he said. That's all I know."

"Why did you quit?"

Arisa stared at the kitchen floor. Cockroach traps were spaced along the edges. "I don't know how they found me."

"Are those guys connected to Nine Dragons?"

Arisa sat down in the single chair at her half-folded table and stared at the floor.

Miyuki took a step toward her. "They'll be back. You shouldn't stay here."

Arisa raised her head. "You're dressed for a funeral."

"My mother…she…I'm arranging her funeral." The cold seeped from the floor through her socks into her feet.

Arisa looked into Miyuki's eyes. "Patrick needs to get out of Japan. So do you."

Miyuki knew she was right. If Leung had been killed in his office at Nine Dragons, he wouldn't be the last one. Patrick would be next. Or they'd find her to get to him. She didn't want to think about the girls.

Chapter 17

The hotel lobby was huge, with subdued colors, and low lighting that would set most customers at ease. Like most of the fanciest hotels in Tokyo, the lobby was not on the ground floor. The hotel started on the twentieth floor and went up from there. Patrick sat Kiri and Jenna on a cushy bench in the center of the lobby and went to reception.

The concierge, an attractive woman in a tight black skirt, hurried over with kids' bags for Jenna and Kiri. Patrick kept looking back and forth from the girls to the check-in clerk.

He explained that they missed their flight, which was technically true, and that his wife would join them, which was technically untrue, but worth saying for camouflage. The young woman at the counter accepted cash payment and his residence card instead of his passport, a little more camouflage.

The receptionist called a bellhop. The girls tried to help him load the bags. The bellhop and concierge joked with them in Japanese.

"Your girls are so cute!" The concierge brushed the side of Jenna's head. "If we can do anything else—"

"What about a swimming pool?"

The concierge smiled. "On the top floor. Open all day."

"We didn't bring our suits," Jenna said.

Patrick whispered, "We'll buy new ones." Patrick turned to the concierge. "Are there shops close by?"

"We have two floors of shopping on the floors below. And there are department stores at Shinjuku Station a short walk from here."

"And I need to use the business center."

The concierge hurried back to her desk for a small card with an access code. Patrick thanked her and followed the bellhop and luggage cart to the elevator.

The room, on the twenty-third floor, was much larger than he expected. Kiri and Jenna raced over to look out the window before exploring the room, opening everything, Jenna explaining it all in her older sister voice.

Patrick peered at the white-gray tumble below. What he loved about Tokyo from the moment he arrived was its endlessness. He'd tried in those first years to do everything, see everything, visit every place. Parks and temples snuggled into every corner of the city. Restaurants and bars opened and closed before he could even try them. When one art exhibition finished, another started. Miyuki made him love it all the more. And Kiri and Jenna even more.

Now he was worried that he might not ever come back again, that Tokyo was lost to him forever. That would be the least of it.

After they unpacked a few things, he led the girls to the business center one floor down from their room, eyeing the hallways in both directions. The passcode let them into the room. It was empty, and felt unused. The computers, printer and fax machine, still much in use in Japan, were new. The chairs, some European ergonomic design, were pristine, as if they'd never been used. The room smelled new.

Patrick checked the hallway, made sure the door latch worked, and pulled over chairs. "You two will have to wait while I check a couple things."

Jenna bounced against the counter holding the computers. "We want to see what you're doing."

Kiri climbed up on her chair.

He logged in with the code and went to the Nine Dragons access site. The accounts were not frozen. They could be soon, he knew, but not yet. If he stayed on too long, they could find where he logged on from easily enough. "OK, now look at this. These are all the accounts that I handle."

Kiri and Jenna nodded seriously.

"Now, I'm checking a couple of accounts to find out what happened in the last six months."

"What happened?" Jenna looked back and forth between the screen and his face.

"That's what I have to check. See these numbers here?"

The girls squinted at the spreadsheets of balances, withdrawals, deposits, and transfers.

"These are all in order, but let's check another, bigger account."

"How big are the accounts?

"Very big. See this one? It's quite high, and then here, it's quite low. That's unusual. So, to find out why, we check here." The girls stared at the screen from either side of his chair. Patrick opened Leung's main transfer account.

Leung had been withdrawing money and moving it to another account, then transferring it to accounts only Leung could access. He found Tran's master account but couldn't log in. As Arisa had said, the accounts were divided. So busy in Wyoming, he hadn't even noticed.

"Now, we'll check some of the other accounts."

Kiri wiggled. "What's an account?"

"It's like a school bag for money." Patrick pulled up the accounts Leung had accessed most recently.

Jenna wiggled off her chair. "Mom checks the accounts on her cellphone."

"This is like that."

He could see the money spinning through, but he couldn't see why. Leung pulled money from one account, sent it to the main account, then transferred it somewhere else. Within a week, the same amount returned. The amounts didn't line up exactly, but were close enough.

"Is it OK?" Kiri asked.

"It's fine." Patrick patted her arm. "Fine."

But it wasn't. Leung had been toying with the largest clients' accounts. Patrick knew them only by name, but he could tell these clients didn't make their money from selling shoes, running restaurants, or buying real estate. They made large deposits all at once. Most used EMIs, electronic money institutions, which were not quite banks, but not quite cryptocurrency, either.

That would have to be enough for now. He didn't want to be traced through any of his accounts. It would be nice to know if the police had been to the Nine Dragons' office yet or not. He logged out, erased the browser history, restarted the computer, and made sure no trace was left.

He stared at the screen for a minute. "OK, let's go get some bathing suits."

"Yeah, new suits!" Kiri and Jenna skipped toward the door.

In the elevator, he took the girls' hands. They were small and warm. He had missed the girls so much in Wyoming. He missed Miyuki too.

The stores on the shopping mall floor were expensive even by Tokyo standards. The clerks hustled out to help, more out of boredom than duty. They brought out bathing suits for the girls, a suit for him, goggles, and bathing caps. At a men's store, Patrick found a change of pants, a couple of shirts and an autumn weight jacket, underwear, and socks.

Back in their room, they changed quickly and slipped into the hotel slippers and bath robes. He called for a laundry pick-up and was told to leave the bag in the room. They headed for the swimming pool on the top floor.

"Can you two go through the women's side on your own? And rinse off?"

"Of course," Jenna said, taking Kiri's hand. "We're not stupid."

"Be sure to pee while you're in there."

Jenna gave him a look and they disappeared inside.

The muskiness of the men's locker room mingled with the smell of too much cleaning fluid. A man in street clothes came in after him. He was tall with a chiseled face and wore a black outfit.

He sat down and took off his shoes and socks, folded his black coat beside him, and undid his bright-colored tie and rolled it into a pocket.

Patrick washed his hands and walked out to the pool.

The high arched ceiling ran to a giant window. Along the side windows, a row of exercise bikes pointed outward as if you could ride off and hover over Tokyo if you just kept peddling. The water slushing in the drains was the only sound. The air was wet and full of chlorine smell.

The girls came out and hurried over to dump their slippers and bath robes on a deck chair at the shallow end. He helped them get their goggles, caps, and suits adjusted. Jenna jumped right in, but Kiri held his hand and eased in down the steps.

Jenna swam out and back. "Poppa, watch me. I learned how to kick and breathe. Let me show you."

Kiri dunked under the water, but her goggles were too loose and she jumped up spluttering.

Patrick tightened them for her. "I'll catch you if you sink."

Kiri put her hands in front of her, gave a little jump, and started kicking. Patrick slipped his hand under her tummy to keep her up.

"Dad, watch!" Jenna turned and swam off, kicking and stroking strongly.

He marveled at how her teensy little arms could move her at all. It hardly seemed like there were muscles in her body, but she zipped right along.

Jenna stood up. "How was I?"

"You must be part fish."

"We did swimming and water ballet at school."

"Try to swim over there and back."

Jenna did a strong crawl over. When she swam back, he pulled her high up out of the water and held her up for a moment before gently tossing her toward the deep end. She squealed in delight.

Kiri dog-paddled to him. He took her by the wrists and

dragged her in a long sweeping arc through the water like a torpedo and delivered her to the shallow end.

"Shark!" Patrick sank underwater and moved with one elbow angled up like a shark fin. They copied him as best they could, all of them sharks in a shark family.

Kiri got tired first and sat on the top of the steps with her feet in the water, shivering. Patrick got out to help her dry off.

"Why aren't there other people swimming?"

He bundled her into the bathrobe, which engulfed her.

As he watched Jenna go back again, in the windows opposite he saw the reflection of the man he'd seen in the locker room. He was lying on a deck chair with his shoes and socks on a towel and his black coat folded beside him.

Jenna climbed out and wrapped herself in the towel Patrick held for her. She took another towel and leaned to the side drying her hair in exactly the same way Miyuki did. The soft slosh of water echoed against the high ceiling.

Patrick wrapped smaller towels around their heads and tied their bathrobes tight. "Who's hungry?"

The girls put their hands up, shivering.

He walked them toward the changing rooms on the opposite side from where the man sat, and hurried the girls into the women's side.

The man sat up on the edge of the chair gathering his black clothes and shoes.

Patrick hurried through the dressing area.

The girls were waiting in the hallway. He put a hand on their backs. "Let's see who can get to the elevators first."

The girls took off, but Kiri tripped on the too-big bathrobe and Patrick stooped down to sweep her up. He pressed the elevator button and looked back down the hallway.

The man exited the changing room with his shoes on and his black coat over his arm.

The elevator rose slowly. When it arrived, he pushed the girls in, jammed the close door button, and pressed the button for the floor below theirs.

"That's the wrong floor," Jenna said.

"Oh, is it? We can walk up."

"Can't we ride up?"

"We need the exercise."

"We were just swimming."

Patrick gave Jenna the father-said-so stare. When they got to the wrong floor, Patrick punched the lobby button and hurried down the hallway to the stairway. On their floor, he looked back but there was only carpeted silence. He herded them into their room. He put the latch on as quickly as he could, trying to sound like a normal dad. "Let's order food and then you can take a hot shower while we're waiting."

Jenna looked up at him. "I thought when you went shush, Mom would be here."

Patrick patted her head. "Me too honey, me too."

Chapter 18

Back in the car, Takamatsu said, "You must have missed something at the crime scene."

"You're right," Hiroshi said. "We missed figuring out who the murderer was and what the connection to the two missing girls must be."

Takamatsu turned around in the front seat to Hiroshi. "What I meant was, let's go take a look."

"We should talk to Patrick's friend first." Hiroshi scrolled through his phone for the address Miyuki had given them in the lawyer's office.

Takamatsu cracked the window and lit a cigarette.

Surprised Takamatsu gave up so easily, Hiroshi gave the address to Ishii who put it in the GPS and pulled west toward the on-ramp for the Shuto Expressway.

Hiroshi called Akiko back at headquarters.

"Wait a minute." Hiroshi could hear her walking out to the hallway. "There's so much to do to find the girls and calling the hotels won't help."

"I'll call Sakaguchi again, but the chief is adamant. He wants to solve this in the most headline-friendly way."

Overhearing Hiroshi mention "headline-friendly," Takamatsu leaned over to Ishii. "Whatever the chief suggests, do the opposite."

Ishii made the gesture of putting on a Borsalino hat. Takamatsu laughed.

Calling the hotels was wasting time and resources. The girls had to be somewhere else, at the friend, Kyle's place, or on the move through some transportation hub. And Takamatsu was right that the crime scene itself must have something they missed.

When they pulled up at Kyle's apartment in Tsukishima, they looked at the sharp, straight lines of the recently built apartment building, its neatness a sort of emptiness. In the new areas in east Tokyo, residents adapted to the buildings, not the other way around.

In the tangled, mismatched area of Kagurazaka where he and Ayana lived, sidewalks darted in all directions and the old cobblestone stairs were so irregular you couldn't walk without paying attention. Buildings started at mismatched levels along the slopes and rose to their own height.

Takamatsu got out of the car and leaned over again to Ishii. "I don't think we'll have hand-to-hand combat here, so why don't you wait in the car."

"My baton and I will be right here if you need me," she said.

Takamatsu laughed. "Our hero over there always forgets his. He'll get his lesson someday."

"That's not a lesson anyone wants." Ishii smiled and settled in to wait.

They waited nonchalantly for someone to exit, slipped in, and headed for the elevator. Hiroshi promised himself never to live in a place that required an elevator, or a parking garage. Trains and stairs were what kept Tokyo sane.

In the upper hallway, Takamatsu whistled at the view over Tokyo Bay. They found Kyle's apartment, knocked on the door, and rang the bell.

Takamatsu pulled out his multitool, flipping through the choices for the right one to pop the lock.

Hiroshi put out his hand to hold Takamatsu back. "Give them a minute."

Takamatsu stared at him, gesturing with his multitool. "Don't you want to be the one who finds the girls? Let's go in." Takamatsu stepped forward and put it to work.

Hiroshi hammered the door with his fist.

Takamatsu picked a different blade, trying to slip one of the blades into the gap beside the lock, but it wouldn't go in. "It's a damn shame some Japanese company doesn't make these. Japan used to be better than that." Takamatsu wedged a different blade in, moving it back and forth, but it fell out. "This is a country of swords and knives, but lock picks are needed too." Takamatsu smacked the back of the tool with the heel of his palm.

"Looks like the locks are better than they used to be."

"They put a plate inside the door." Takamatsu stared at the lock.

"You've left some nice scratches on the door." Hiroshi pointed at them. "Want to call the superintendent to let us in?"

"Let's come back later. We would have heard movement if they were in there." Takamatsu folded up his multitool and slipped it back in its small leather holder and put it back in his camel hair coat. He eyed the door again, and turned to follow Hiroshi back down the hall to the elevator. They rode down in frustrated silence.

"No luck?" Ishii asked.

"Takamatsu got some lock picking practice." He turned to Ishii. "You remember where Nine Dragons is?"

"Of course." Ishii pulled out and headed west and then south on the expressway.

In Shinagawa, she drove quickly through the streets. The stoplights were few and most pedestrians used the overhead walkways. She pulled into the underground parking lot of the Nine Dragons' office building.

They rode the elevator up and two uniformed officers checked their IDs and stepped aside for them to enter.

The cavernous space was quiet, dark, and empty. Sunset was coming earlier and shadows fell by late afternoon. Takamatsu found the switch and flipped all the lights on. Hiroshi and Ishii winced at the brightness.

"The crime scene's over there." Hiroshi pointed to the half-circle office at the end.

"Who's that?" Takamatsu asked, looking back through the layers of glass dividers.

Mehta stood up and bowed awkwardly. He grimaced, waiting for them to work their way through the maze of glass.

"He doesn't speak Japanese? Let me know what he says." Avoiding English, Takamatsu wandered off to examine the office of Joseph Leung. Ishii went with him.

Hiroshi strode back to Mehta's office. Hiroshi said, "I know something's wrong here at Nine Dragons, and I think you know what it is."

Mehta cocked his head.

"Why did you come here tonight?"

Mehta rocked his head back and forth.

"If they didn't get what they wanted from Leung, they'll come back to get it from you."

"I can't stop thinking that. I am staying in an undisclosed hotel, as you recommended."

"If they killed once over this, it won't be hard to do it again."

Mehta nodded, frowning, moving from foot to foot.

"So, why was business expanding in Tokyo? New clients?"

Mehta slumped. "There were lots of new clients."

"Where did they come from?"

"Leung brought them in."

"What kind of people were they? What kind of wealth?"

Mehta frowned. "Tokyo has loads of underperforming assets. Real estate portfolios, unused business lines, treasury shares, cross-held portfolios, that kind of thing. In the old economy, before globalization, those were part of building relationships. One company held assets of another. That might be good for old-school connections, but not for growth."

"Growth?"

"Many individuals and companies in Tokyo fell behind the curve. Some of them wanted to catch up to world standards but didn't know how. That's where Nine Dragons comes in. We help our Japanese clients find the hidden value in their holdings and put that to work."

"In so-called offshore accounts. That's what Patrick Walsh was doing in Wyoming?"

Mehta continued. "If the Japanese government won't help with reinvesting Japan's wealth, someone has to. The government encouraged it, but we actually did it. Patrick was a genius at finding what could be developed inside a portfolio—"

"Personal portfolios or business portfolios?" Hiroshi asked.

"Both. In Japan, many small and mid-sized businesses are single owner. They let everything sit earning nothing. They're often too busy to take care of what money they do have. It's a real pity."

"What did Patrick do for these accounts?"

Mehta clasped his hands together and cocked his head. "He would find foreign bond issues and mortgage-backed securities, anything really. Leung told me Patrick had the knack of finding the safest and most lucrative investments. That appealed to Japanese customers. He was a whiz with all that. His shell companies in Wyoming were airtight."

Mehta's phrases echoed those on the Nine Dragons' website video. Hiroshi peered through the glass at Takamatsu and Ishii in Leung's office. Takamatsu was surveying the scene from every angle. Ishii was asking questions. He turned back to Mehta. "You promised to give me a list of your clients."

"I believe I am ahead of you on that one, sir." Mehta fidgeted and tapped the top of his computer. "It is in the secure file I was just opening when you detectives arrived. I need to restart the security procedure since it timed out. I was only half finished when you came in." Mehta sat down at his computer. "May I?"

Hiroshi nodded OK. "What kind of security procedure?"

"We have a complicated verification system." Mehta typed in codes and checked his cellphone, then inputted the code.

"Complicated like what?"

"Very complicated." Mehta breathed deeply and verified it on his phone before confirming again. "There were leaks."

"What leaks?"

"Passcodes, server information, account numbers."

"So your system had holes in it?"

"Or someone made holes. We couldn't decide." Mehta nodded at the screen, sat forward and scrolled, the blue and white from the computer lighting his face from below. "That is what Tran, the security specialist, and I were trying to find out."

"I should talk to Tran."

"Unfortunately, he's in Shanghai."

"Can you get that set up?"

"I can try. I'm not sure if he knows, though. Client information was compromised, which would have ruined our reputation. So, we're trying to figure out what happened."

"Nine Dragons was hacked?"

"Hacking is from outside, this was from inside."

"And was any money moved?"

Mehta shook his head. His printer lit up and started printing. "We changed all the passwords, made our clients change their passwords. Clients complained, but we insisted. Even employees complained. I, too, got tired of using three devices every time I needed some information. We set up encrypted vaults to protect the passwords and added on a program to match passwords with URLs. We set up multifactor verification. And then we restricted full verification credentials to just five people—Leung, Tran, myself, Patrick and the office manager, Arisa. Arisa quit, so we took her out of the system, redid all settings, and waited."

Hiroshi looked at him. "And...?"

"And then Leung was killed." Mehta picked up the printout, stapled it, and handed it to Hiroshi. "Here's our client list."

Hiroshi took it and left him to whatever he was doing when they arrived. It would be better to get into the accounts himself, but Sakaguchi, or the chief, was working on that.

Takamatsu turned off the lights and he and Ishii walked back to where Hiroshi stood in the dim light of the office holding a dozen sheets of paper with Nine Dragons' client list.

Takamatsu nodded at the list. "At least you got something. We found nothing."

Takamatsu walked over to the ceramic wall mural of Nine Dragons, flipping his lighter, examining the remaining eight dragons.

Chapter 19

Hiroshi called for two detectives to take Mehta back to his hotel to gather his things and move to a new place. Mehta was not pleased when Hiroshi confiscated his passport, but he set up a rotating schedule to guard Mehta, and that seemed to pacify him.

Hiroshi, Takamatsu, and Ishii rode the elevator down to the parking garage. Takamatsu fiddled with his cigarettes and lighter as they walked past the empty parking spots.

Hiroshi got in back. "The next crime scene might well be his."

Takamatsu pulled out his cellphone. "That's why we'll call Shibutani and Ota."

"To watch him?"

"No, to speed things up."

Hiroshi leaned across the hood of the car. "You want to outsource this?"

"If Shibutani puts Ota on this, he'll turn something up faster than we would." Takamatsu called Shibutani.

Shibutani was a private investigator who worked with Takamatsu in homicide until he retired to start his own office, mostly handling divorces. The two had repaid favors to each other for years. When Takamatsu was suspended, he worked for Shibutani.

Ota was Shibutani's employee, a small bowling ball of a guy who had taken over the office when Shibutani was in the hospital after a bad beating. Ota was deaf, which had surprised Hiroshi, but the lack of hearing didn't impede his endurance, competence, and follow-through.

Takamatsu hung up and smiled. "Shibutani and Ota are on it."

"On what?" Hiroshi asked.

Takamatsu didn't answer. Ishii got into the driver's seat and Hiroshi started taking photos of the client list pages and sending them to Akiko. He'd take them to Watanabe at the Tax Agency in the morning.

"All this corporate stuff has me thinking about *sokaiya*." Takamatsu blew his smoke out the window.

Ishii pulled to a stop at a light. "Corporate blackmailers? They're long gone, aren't they? When the Japanese economic bubble burst."

"Extortion didn't disappear."

Takamatsu rambled, but Hiroshi knew him well enough to wait.

"The easiest companies to extort were the dishonest ones. The more corrupt they were, the quicker they paid off the *sokaiya*." Takamatsu laughed. "The murder of a company executive was the first real murder case I worked on. Shibutani was on that one too. Everyone was surprised the *sokaiya* actually followed through on their threats. It wasn't all bluff."

Takamatsu got a phone call. He listened without a word and hung up. "Sakaguchi's joining us."

"Joining us for what?" Hiroshi growled. He knew what he meant.

Takamatsu put his hand up. "Look, every Japanese needs several things before sleep—food, drink, discussion, and a hot bath."

"You're forgetting sex." Hiroshi sent all the info to Akiko. He hoped she'd have time to back it up.

"Your girlfriend will wait. Women are good at that."

Ishii leaned over. "Some are good at waiting, others not."

"That's what I meant." Takamatsu chuckled. "Nearly all cases are solved while sleeping. Didn't you learn that working at the *koban*, Ishii?"

Ishii smiled. "I just learned to stay awake all night. I wouldn't mind a drink, though. I'm driving, so just one. Or maybe two."

Takamatsu smiled at Ishii's enthusiasm. "There's a place in Takadanobaba. Halfway home for you, Hiroshi."

Hiroshi sighed and sent Ayana a text message.

Ayana wrote back and reminded him not to drink too much.

Hiroshi promised he wouldn't, a promise more aspiration than certainty.

They were at a parking lot down Waseda Dori from Takadanobaba Station in a few minutes.

The *izakaya's* front window held three rows of empty sake bottles, green, brown, and clear. A spotlight hit them and the light refracted through the glass, a poor man's chandelier.

"*Irashaimasse!*" the wait staff sang out as the detectives entered.

They pressed sanitizer onto their hands from the bottle by the door, trying not to crowd the people at tables next to the refrigerated cases holding all the bottles of sake.

One of the chefs hurried out with greetings and led them to the back wall where a sliding door opened to a private tatami room up two steps. He turned on the overhead light, pushed the low tables together, pulled out *zabuton* floor cushions. Handwritten menu items and beer girl ads were thumbtacked to the walls in neat rows.

The detectives toed off their shoes and climbed into the room. Before they sat down, Sugamo, Osaki, and Sakaguchi arrived. They made it past the front tables without bumping anyone, turning sideways down the aisle. When they climbed up the two steps and ducked inside, the room seemed to shrink.

With the table tight against their bellies, there was just enough room for Ishii, Hiroshi, and Takamatsu on the other side. Everyone hung their coats from hooks on the wall and settled onto the *zabuton*.

The base straw of the tatami poked through the top *omote* weave here and there. Spilled sauce and oil left curved, dotted stains in places. The patterned *heri* borders of all the mats had lost their shine. The tatami felt worn and comfortable, support to unwind.

The chef came in with *oshibori,* cracked the plastic from the hot towels, and held them out steaming for the detectives.

A waiter brought out draft beer in big mugs. Everyone toasted, trying to summon the energy to relax. Ishii took a polite sip, and set it aside to nurse slowly. Takamatsu belted his down, and Hiroshi, despite his email to Ayana, finished half the mug in one gratifying guzzle. Sugamo's and Osaki's hands made their mugs seem small.

Takamatsu read the list of daily specials from a printout and Hiroshi scanned the menu options pinned to the wall.

Takamatsu called out orders and the waiter shouted the orders to the kitchen staff. The aroma of grilled vegetables, smoking fish, and deep-fried chicken *karaage* began to feel real.

When the beers were finished, Takamatsu ordered sake for everyone. The waiter came back with two large bottles of *nigori* sake and hand-sized cups. After stirring the rice lees with a deft twist of the bottle, he poured out six glasses of the cloudy-white, bubbly sake.

They toasted and took the first sip.

"I love this sparkling sake," Ishii said. "A hint of sweetness at the edges, and goes down easy."

Takamatsu smiled. "It's better than champagne. Fuller flavor and the bubbles are more refined."

Sakaguchi finished his sake. "Takamatsu, you didn't tell me about Enoshima."

Ishii winced and looked away.

Takamatsu frowned. "Two girls and a boy, the oldest was six." Takamatsu took almost every death as part of work, but he shook his head and frowned at this one. "Their mother drove them right off the end of the pier into the water."

"Did she leave a note?" Hiroshi asked.

"Mailed it to her mother-in-law. Her husband gambled away all the money. She didn't want the kids growing up with such shame." Takamatsu reached for his cigarettes in his camel hair coat. "They owned a yacht berth, but hadn't paid fees for a year. She drove off there."

"Certainly made her point," Ishii said.

Takamatsu pulled over an ashtray from a stack at the end of the table. "The father was a typical rich kid. He just sat there on the sofa with his head in his hands. Made me want to punch him."

Plates of sashimi arrived, five kinds neatly arranged on a bed of daikon. Sakaguchi, Osaki, and Sugamo started in on one plate. Hiroshi, Takamatsu, and Ishii shared the other. Bowls of cold tofu with ginger and small dishes with pickled vegetables arrived.

Takamatsu held up his sake. "I left it with the Shonan police. As soon as they find who the husband owes money to, they'll find who's really responsible. Loan sharks don't mind destroying families."

Sakaguchi looked at Hiroshi. "What did you find out today?"

Hiroshi shrugged. "Seems like the babysitter, Taiga, lived a double life."

"And?" Sakaguchi took a breath and bent his knee up.

"We met his colleagues," Ishii said. "But they weren't too helpful."

Sakaguchi nodded. "Make them help."

"After he gets out of the coma, we'll talk to the babysitter directly to find out who he knew. He must have been involved somehow." Hiroshi finished his sake more quickly than he planned. "Speaking of knowing people." Hiroshi pulled out the client list. "I've got this list from Nine Dragons to check tomorrow."

Takamatsu drained the rest of his sake. "Why'd this guy come to take the kids anyway? If he had enough money for a 4LDK apartment in Azabu, you'd think he'd leave the dirty work to someone else."

Ishii nodded. "You can't get that rich without cutting a few corners."

"And how do the two scenes connect?" Sakaguchi straightened

his knee.

Hiroshi shrugged. "Something was off at Nine Dragons and something was off in their marriage."

"Something was off? That's all we have?" Sakaguchi stared through his thin eyes at Hiroshi and Takamatsu.

Takamatsu smiled and Hiroshi waved for another drink.

Ishii spoke up. "No news on the girls?"

Sakaguchi shook his head.

Two plates of deep-fried eggplant bathed in *ponzu* sauce arrived and two more of pumpkin, the orange meat grilled brown on both sides.

Akiko arrived, walking down the aisle rubbing sanitizer in her hands. She straightened everyone's shoes facing outward and stepped up into the tatami room and peeled off her mask.

The waiter brought a beer for her and everyone toasted again.

Takamatsu called the waiter over and started to order more food. A waiter brought a beer for Akiko.

"I have news." Akiko settled in, held up her mug, and looked at everyone with her eyebrows raised. "The chief is retiring."

Everyone stopped.

"He has some heart thing."

None of them really liked the chief, but he was still the chief.

Takamatsu was the first to pick up his sake cup. "To the chief. I won't be sorry to see him retire. But he's done his part."

Everyone toasted the chief and drank silently.

Hiroshi wondered about the reshuffle. Sakaguchi would make a good chief and his leg was slowing him down in the field anyway. He just hoped he wouldn't take Akiko away to be his assistant.

After everyone sat quietly for a few minutes, Takamatsu spoke first. "So, what about the abduction? It's going to be twenty-four hours pretty soon. Those girls are either well hidden or already gone."

Sakaguchi leaned back and straightened his knee. "Tomorrow,

we go back over everything we did today."

Osaki and Sugamo groaned.

Hiroshi turned to Akiko. "Did you find anything on the guy's credit card or the hotels?"

"Nothing on the cards or accounts." Akiko took a steadying sip. "We narrowed the three thousand hotels down to the most likely half. And we finished half of those. But not a single one had an American with two little girls. There were Americans, couples with kids, couples without kids, or single travelers."

Sakaguchi set his chopsticks down. "I'll figure out something to tell the chief. He called me all day."

The waiter moved dishes around for space to set down plates of deep-fried chicken *karaage,* roasted ginkgo nuts, and *shumai* dumplings. After plucking off the last leftover bites, they passed the finished plates to the waiter.

Sakaguchi stared at the wall. "We must have missed something."

Sugamo and Osaki grunted.

Takamatsu lit a cigarette. "We'll go through it all again tomorrow."

Ishii sipped her beer. It was still half full.

A waitress started clearing away the plates, all of them empty save for a little sauce at the bottom.

The waitress came back with small bowls and Chinese-style *renge* spoons and then brought in two party-size plates heaped with fried rice for everyone to share.

Chapter 20

Hiroshi took a taxi home. It was just a ten-minute ride and he got out a few blocks from the apartment to let the cool autumn air clear out the sake and frustration. He didn't want to think, which is what he'd done all day. He just wanted to walk. As always in Tokyo, he wasn't the only one out walking around. He headed home.

In the apartment, all the lights were on. Ayana was usually the one trying to conserve resources. Hiroshi clicked off the switches as he headed to the bedroom.

Ayana had taken over the bed with an iPad, two laptops, and papers strewn every which way.

Hiroshi dropped on the bed and bounced.

"You're messing up everything." Ayana screamed, snatching at the papers.

He breathed out on her before closing in for a kiss. "See? Not drunk."

Ayana pecked his lips and pushed him away. "Be careful of my notes."

"Notes for what?"

"The wedding speech." Ayana stayed focused on her screen.

"Let me hear what you have so far."

"Take a shower first."

Hiroshi got undressed.

Ayana kept her eyes on the screen. "You're coming with me, aren't you?"

"To the wedding ceremony?"

"I told you about it." She hummed as if it was decided. "But what am I going to wear? I have to stand at the front with everyone staring at me."

"So, do some shopping."

"What do you think I'm doing?" Ayana held her laptop out. One-piece dresses filled the screen.

"I thought you were working on your speech?"

Ayana looked at him and sighed. "Help, or don't help, but don't interrupt."

Hiroshi tickled Ayana's foot poking out under the covers as he headed in for a shower.

He turned the water on high. When he felt warm, he remembered Ayana told him one of her younger colleagues at the National Archives was getting married and she was asked to give the best friend speech. It was the first time she'd ever mentioned marriage at all. He didn't know what to say.

At dinner the week before at one of their favorite neighborhood trattorias, she started searching for wedding speeches and wedding dresses. Hiroshi finished his meal and the bottle of wine, but she didn't talk about anything on the way home. Was that just a set-up? He was happy with how things were, but didn't mind talking about it. He loved living with her. It was that simple.

Ayana's apartment wasn't ostentatious like the 4LDK in Azabu. It was the right size and within walking distance of three stations with eight train lines, cozy restaurants, takeaway delis, a decent liquor shop, and a cool neighborhood vibe that was modern by day, traditional by night.

It was all so easy living there. He'd never thought of himself as comfortably middle class, as settled in any sense, but he was getting used to it. He could get married, sure. Why not?

He couldn't do worse than his parents, whose home had been a warzone of unspoken acrimony right up to his mother's death from cancer. The silence became complete when his father's heart gave out soon after. Maybe they'd been in love, but from the outside, that was hard to see.

After they died, Hiroshi's uncle offered him a place, but Hiroshi wanted to live on his own near his university. His uncle pushed him toward something more practical than history. Not knowing how to argue against it, he went to Boston to study accounting and English. He ended up liking America, and all the places he lived in, dorms and funky apartments, a string of girlfriends' places. He liked them knowing they wouldn't last.

When he came back to Tokyo after years in Boston, his longest-term girlfriend, Linda, came with him. That was exciting at first, but she was basically on a long vacation and Hiroshi didn't want to move back to Boston. So she left and he stayed in Tokyo. Without any big argument scenes. It wasn't even a breakup, more like a move, for her, and a stay, for him.

For a couple of years after Linda left, he kept the cheap apartment with its view of a too-close hillside overrun with bamboo grass. Once he got the detective job, he often slept in his office where the heating had two settings—arctic or equator. With the time difference, he made phone calls to overseas police departments and Interpol mostly at night, so it didn't much matter where he woke up sleep-deprived.

That was when he re-met Ayana on a case. The spark from their brief college affair reignited, more strongly than he'd been ready for, and in a short time, he moved into her apartment. Though it was part of her divorce settlement, it was the first place that ever felt like home.

He turned off the water and the pipes gave out their familiar clunk. The towels smelled fresh and clean. He dried off and stepped into the bedroom.

Ayana was still working away.

He dug in the drawer for something to wear. "How's your new boss?"

"Well, he's certainly the most unpleasant librarian I've ever met."

"He's taking over while, um, what's her name again?"

"Whose name?"

"The colleague getting married."

Ayana sighed. "Rina. I told you a hundred times."

"So, the boss is unpleasant?"

"A total asshole." Ayana used English.

"It's temporary, while Rina's gone, right?"

"That was supposed to be a month, but now it might be nine months."

"Nine?" Hiroshi pulled on his shorts, realizing what she meant. "Oh, that kind of wedding."

"That's the fashion now." Ayana smiled.

He pulled on a T-shirt and snuggled into bed. He rolled on his back and tugged her arm. She set the computer, iPad, and notes on the other side and rolled close.

"Do we have enough money?" he asked. Between the apartments and the wealth management, he'd been doing estimates of cash flow all day.

"We have this place, jobs, us, who needs money?"

"Yeah, but, a little more would give us more, what, security?" Hiroshi wasn't sure what he was saying but he wanted to say something.

Ayana patted his chest. "In my experience, money dissolves trust."

"You mean your husband."

"He made a lot of money, but it only fueled his pride, his affairs, his ambitions. He thought money bought anything. Me included."

"Is there something you want or need?"

"Is this about your job again? If you want to quit, quit. But I think you'll go crazy with a boring job, even if the salary's better."

Hiroshi thought about that. "All these other people fill up their lives with things. They buy cases of wine, new cars, bigger apartments—"

Ayana kissed him to shut him up. "I had all of that. Business-class flights, the apartment in Paris, charge accounts. I spent all day at museums, movies, cafes, and shopping. But it was all at my husband's expense and he kept track. I was never more lonely."

"I want to pay for half of this apartment."

Ayana laughed. "It's already paid for. You're here. End of story."

"I don't want to live for free."

"You're not living for free."

"My former girlfriend always wanted to split everything fifty-fifty."

"And that didn't last, did it?" Ayana thumped his chest with each syllable.

Hiroshi coughed and held her wrist. "This apartment I saw today—"

"On a case?"

"A 4LDK in Azabu."

Ayana whistled. "Not cheap. And...?"

"And... well... nothing."

"I want you here, not us somewhere bigger."

Hiroshi pulled her tighter.

"If you want to help with something, why not help with the wedding speech?"

He started kissing her. "Want me to check your speech right now?"

"No, you're doing something more important." Ayana climbed on him.

Afterward, Hiroshi stared at the ceiling with Ayana's hair spread over his chest. "What do you think about marriage? Kids?"

"What is all this?" Ayana sat up.

"I don't know. I'm just asking."

"Our work-life balance is just right as it is, except you work too much."

"Well, what do you think about all this?"

Ayana pulled on her T-shirt.

Hiroshi shrugged. "OK, you don't want to talk about it."

"What's this all about?" She lifted her hips and wiggled her shorts on.

"Do you want children?"

"Can we have this discussion another time? I have to give this wedding speech at Rina's wedding. It's a lot harder than you think." She opened her laptop and settled it in her lap.

"Well, do you want to get married?"

Ayana put her laptop down. "Can we talk about this when we're both ready? Let's plan a trip to an *onsen* hot springs and talk about it then? In a private *rotenburo*, looking out at the mountains and a forest stream."

"Naked, you mean?"

"Unhurried, I mean. Without having to get up in the morning and go to work. Without having to write a wedding speech and find a wedding dress."

"Don't talk to me like I'm a traditional Japanese—"

"What? You're not even making sense. Plus, you *are* more foreign than me, sleeping with all those American—"

"You speak English *and* French and lived abroad longer than I did."

"You're the one who knows pillow-talk in English."

"And you don't?"

"No, I don't."

Hiroshi pulled her to him, but she pushed away. "I have to finish this wedding speech and find a dress."

"Can I help?"

"You can help by not bringing up serious topics at the wrong time."

Hiroshi scooted toward her, threw his leg close, and pressed himself against her. "Speaking of serious topics coming up."

She shifted away and picked her computer up. "Do you need a new suit or wedding tie or anything? I found a template for a 'speech from an older colleague at work.' I'll copy that, add some anecdotes..."

He gave up and rolled on his back and looked at the ceiling. "Put something funny in, something archive related."

"Funny? Archive related?" She bit her lip, irritated, and stared at the screen.

When he turned over, in submission, she leaned over and kissed the back of his neck.

He let her work, wondering why she wouldn't let him pay half.

Maybe because he didn't really have the money. A detective's salary wasn't much.

Chapter 21

Hiroshi heard the tink and ping of bowls and plates, the sucking sound of the refrigerator door, and the shush of the faucet. He smelled coffee, or a dream of coffee, and rolled over to smell Ayana on the empty pillow next to him.

Maybe Takamatsu was right about the need for food, drink, conversation, and sleep. He felt restored. And sex. Especially sex.

His phone was ringing. It was Watanabe at the Tax Agency. "Can you stop by here on your way to work? I found some things you might like."

Hiroshi told Watanabe he'd be there in less than an hour and hopped in to the shower.

After he got dressed and picked up the client list and his cellphone, he found a message from Takamatsu that they were already at work, reminding him he missed the morning meeting, again, and asking where he was.

Hiroshi sent him a message to meet at the Ministry of Finance building.

Takamatsu wrote back to say he and Ishii would be waiting outside.

Hiroshi found Ayana standing at the kitchen counter typing on her laptop, a cup of coffee and a bagel beside her.

"I don't know how to give a speech, or write one, or anything." Ayana stuffed the bagel into her mouth and shut her laptop.

"Improvise. Like a jazz musician."

Ayana chewed slowly. "You're always full of suggestions after you get some sleep."

Hiroshi poured a cup of coffee. He took the other half of the bagel from the toaster and slathered it in cream cheese. "I wish I had suggestions for this case."

"Maybe I'll call in sick today. A personal day. I can get this finished and shop for a dress."

"The archives can run themselves for a day."

"But not detective work, I guess. Forensic accounting is so necessary for the functioning of the world."

"You want me to take a day off too?" Hiroshi's phone rang.

Ayana pointed at it. "Nice try. I'll see you tonight. Or not, if the forensic accounting runs late."

Hiroshi watched her getting ready to leave as he listened to Sakaguchi tell him he missed the morning meeting, a brief one due to lack of progress. He listened politely. He'd slept longer and deeper than he thought. No one had found anything from the hotels. There were no sightings of the two girls.

Ayana waved from the front hall, blew him a kiss, and was gone.

Hiroshi stuffed the rest of the bagel in his mouth and finished the coffee. He washed the dishes and hurried outside to catch a taxi.

Ishii and Takamatsu were waiting in front of the Ministry of Finance building that housed the Tax Agency and Watanabe's office. Takamatsu was talking to the security guard and Ishii waved.

Hiroshi called Watanabe to let him know they were downstairs. They went through security and Hiroshi wondered if the list Mehta had given him was going to help. It was just as likely to get a hit as calling hotels, but he had to try something.

Takamatsu held the elevator door open and they got in.

Hiroshi pressed the button. "Who has wealth in this country? Wealth they want to hide?"

Takamatsu turned to Ishii. "See, happens every time. Hiroshi starts expanding the investigation. We were supposed to find two abducted girls but Hiroshi wants to look at tax compliance for the moneyed elite."

Ishii said, "If it's connected..."

"Everything's connected, according to Hiroshi."

Hiroshi patted the file of investor names. "If some of the investors Patrick Walsh helped had been *sokaiya*, would that catch your interest, Takamatsu?"

Takamatsu's eyes widened. "It might, yes, but that was a long time ago. They're all somewhere else, working some other line." Takamatsu frowned.

"You were the one who brought it up yesterday."

"I was drunk."

"You mentioned it before you got drunk. Call it nouveau *sokaiya*."

Takamatsu scoffed, mumbling "nouveau" in Japanese pronunciation.

Ishii interrupted. "*Sokaiya* are old history, aren't they?"

"That makes me old history too." Takamatsu laughed.

"I read about their extortion and blackmail. Did you work on those cases?" Ishii looked at him.

The elevator door opened, and Takamatsu walked out first. "Everyone did in those days."

Watanabe welcomed them into his office. He had on the usual suspenders and pinstripe shirt with a white collar. It gave his elegant bow even more charm.

"This is Takamatsu and Ishii," Hiroshi said.

Watanabe opened his arms wide. "I'm glad homicide is taking an interest in these kinds of tax issues. They're killing the country." He waited for them to laugh at his joke, but only Ishii smiled.

They sat down and Hiroshi handed him the list of clients from Mehta.

Watanabe put on a pair of glasses, leaned back, and read slowly and carefully. His face lit up at some of the entries. He hummed with interest.

Ishii waited with her hands folded calmly in her lap, attentive and patient. She was going to be an asset to the homicide department.

Takamatsu squirmed in his chair. Hiroshi wondered if he had attention deficit disorder.

At the end of the final page, Watanabe folded the list shut. "Quite a collection."

"Do you know any of them?"

"A few. One of them was caught up in a scandal with some of London's EMIs."

"What are EMIs?" Ishii asked.

Watanabe smiled. "Electronic money institutions, the love child of cryptocurrency and crooked banks. Used by all sorts of high fliers. Started as a way to move cash for investing in start-ups, but it was quickly taken over by high-risk customers."

"High risk?" Ishii asked.

Takamatsu smiled at her being first on the questions.

Watanabe nodded. "High risk could be anything. A lot of the clients on this Nine Dragons list would fall into that category. Someone who's received too many SARs would want to slip their remaining transfers through the EMIs instead of regular banks."

"EMIs hide everything?" Ishii leaned back in her chair, thinking.

"Not everything, but they're below the radar. Way below." Watanabe smiled. "E-money companies have fewer regulations than banks, especially in the EU. Transactions aren't protected by deposit insurance, but that's one of the risks they're willing to take."

Hiroshi heard about this on a case he worked with Interpol, but he was told there was no international agency tracking EMI transactions. The money moved too fast. "Can you tell us which of these clients was involved in EMIs?"

"I can do better than that." Watanabe handed Hiroshi a printout. "I found this. From my side."

Hiroshi took the list and recognized a few of the names.

Watanabe took a fountain pen from its holder and put a checkmark by a dozen names on the client list Hiroshi had given him and handed it back.

"So, these check marks mean…?" Hiroshi held up the printouts.

"Who you want."

"Can we take your list?"

Watanabe closed his eyes. "Hide it in your pocket while I'm not looking." He laughed. "What I'm concerned with is who's moving money without paying taxes. Like this guy on your list, name of Kosugi. He's been in my crosshairs for years, but he's just too good. He knows the value of paying professionals like Nine Dragons."

Takamatsu quit fidgeting. "Kosugi, that sounds familiar."

"It should. He was one of the first yakuza to start transferring illegally obtained profits to legal activities after the nineties bubble burst."

Takamatsu took out his lighter and flicked it open and shut.

"He seems to have a knack for balancing unreported income with reported, so some taxes are paid and everything looks good enough for lazy auditors, and he's free from taxes on the rest. Before the financial system internationalized, the lack of transparency was the cover. But now that it's internationalized, it's just too much money moving too fast."

Takamatsu laughed. "I remember Kosugi from twenty-some years ago. There were articles in the paper about how he was one of the good guys trying to reform the yakuza."

Watanabe laughed. "I wonder how much that article cost him."

"It pays to advertise. Even for people like him." Takamatsu played with his lighter.

"So, why would people need a firm like Nine Dragons?" Ishii asked.

Watanabe nodded. "Some of their money has been 'liberated,' as they say. But not all. They have ties here, and who knows how many old accounts are sitting around, earning no interest but drawing no scrutiny, either. They probably want Nine Dragons to launder what's left, or at least give it a rinse and spin dry."

Hiroshi had seen how much was parked in savings accounts working a case on scammers who targeted the elderly. Because older Japanese often put everything into Japanese postal savings accounts, Japanese banks had some of the largest reserves of low-interest accounts in the world. If that money were put to use, it would boost Japan's economy. And if it was taken out of the country, it would avoid a lot of taxes. "So, Nine Dragons helps drain the country."

Watanabe shrugged. "There's a lot of money in Japan, a lot of illegal money, and a lot of savings that might or might not be illegal. Even if it's legal, moving savings to high-interest accounts hidden in an overseas trust sounds pretty good to most people."

Hiroshi looked through the list in his hands.

Watanabe popped his suspenders. "And Nine Dragons knows all the new-style tax avoidance tricks. If one of the Nine Dragons employees was in Wyoming, I don't think it's because he knows how to wear a cowboy hat and sits a horse well."

"It's because he knows his way around the trust fund shell company heaven." Hiroshi folded up the list and put it in his pocket. "Are you going to freeze these accounts?"

Watanabe smiled. "I put in a request for that, but they're negotiating. Nine Dragons has connections to Chinese banks, so they don't want to upset any international investment schemes. International cooperation and all that."

"But they will soon?"

Watanabe shrugged. "Maybe a day or two. If we can't freeze them, you and me both won't be able to find anything."

Ishii leaned forward. "If the wife is working at Japan's largest bank, she must know the small banks and how to use the SWIFT messaging system."

Watanabe shrugged some more. "Any account manager could move funds from their legit accounts to someplace outside Japan."

"And from there to less legit money institutions before

dropping it into a shell account." Ishii whistled at the ease of it all. Takamatsu pointed at Ishii. "Now she's thinking like a criminal!"

Hiroshi's cellphone buzzed. He took the call and listened as Takamatsu and Watanabe chatted about the importance of thinking like criminals.

Hiroshi hung up. "We've got to go. Seems like financial crimes have bumped against human realities again."

Chapter 22

Through the haze and pain, Kyle heard Miki's howls and whimpers. He felt her fingers brushing his face as he struggled from some black underwater space to the surface of light and air. Nausea swept through him. He turned to the side and threw up. He coughed and choked, throat burning from the stomach acid. The pain made him shiver and start to black out.

"Miki?" Kyle's voice echoed inside his own head.

"Kyle, Kyle, honey, you're awake, you're OK, people are coming, I called them."

"Fucking Christ." His hand shook as he touched his head. His hair was sticky and wet.

Miki wiped his head with the moist cloth. "They're coming now. Baby, what happened?"

Kyle felt Miki's hands on his head and arm. He could hear her, but could only pry open one eye a sliver.

Miki kneeled on the tatami beside him with a cloth and a bowl. He couldn't inhale through his nose and swallowed a wad of snot and blood down the back of his throat.

Miki howled. "Just hang on, baby, the police are coming, the ambulance is coming. Don't move."

Kyle shivered, his body alternating waves of numbness and spikes of pain, like his body was no longer his. Miki was cooing in a high-pitched voice from very far away.

Kyle could see the blood in the bowl, his blood.

Miki wiped up the vomit and took the bowl and cloth back to the kitchen. It hurt to breathe. He heard the water running. She was back with a new bowl and fresh cloth.

"What happened, Kyle, baby?"

Miki was beside him with her hand on his. His wrist ached. Kyle tried to clear his throat. "What time is it?"

"It's morning. Have you been here all night?"

The cool water on his face and head made him shiver, even with a blanket over him. His jaw ached and there was a loud ringing in his left ear. Snot and blood flowed from his nose down the back of his throat. "Someone came in. Two guys."

"Two guys?"

"Three guys." He clutched her hand. "Where are Patrick and the girls?"

"They're not here," Miki said. "Their stuff is gone."

Kyle thought back. The first gut punch doubled him over. They hit him outside the door, took his key, shoved him inside, hitting him until he dropped on the tatami in the same room where Patrick and his daughters slept. After that, it was a question and a slap, another question and a fist to his stomach. They slammed his head into the tatami again and again. It hurt at first, but then he didn't feel anything.

Miki didn't come until morning, he realized, or they'd have gotten her too. Good that he told her he was out drinking so she stayed in her own apartment.

"Who did this?" Miki started to cry. "Oh, where's the ambulance?"

Kyle tried to sit up, but the pain and nausea knocked him back.

Miki put cushions behind him and adjusted the blanket. "They'll be here in a minute."

He looked at Miki and her tears started to fall heavier. She wiped her face, kneeling beside him in her work outfit, which was splattered with his blood.

Kyle touched his face. Each breath hurt. "Where's my cellphone?"

"What?"

"Find my cellphone." He heard himself twice, once inside his head and once from far away.

Miki got up to search for his cellphone. Kyle could see her through one eye, mumbling to herself and stooping to look under

164

the furniture.

"Here it is!" she shouted. It had slid under the kitchen counter. She hurried back to Kyle and handed him the phone.

His hand was shaking too badly to press the screen, so he handed the phone over and told her the password.

"Find the call from yesterday without any name on it. He called from a new phone. Afternoon. I missed the call, but it must have been him."

Miki found it and held the phone to his ear. He waited for Patrick to answer. "Booster? It's me. We gotta talk."

Patrick had been sleeping. "Horndog. Sorry we just left, but I...hey, you don't sound so good. Hangover?"

"That and then some." Kyle coughed. "Someone jumped me."

"Where? When?"

"Last night, at the door to my apartment. I didn't even get a punch in."

"Are you OK?"

"Not really."

"Who were they?"

"Three guys. Dressed in black suits. They wanted you."

"I'll come."

"Don't do that. Miki's here. The ambulance and police are coming."

"Jesus, man, quit talking and go to the hospital."

"Tell me what trouble you're in."

"How did they find you?"

"I didn't have time to ask them while they were smashing my face into the tatami. Is this because of Nine Dragons?" Kyle coughed and moaned.

Patrick didn't answer.

"If they found me, they'll find Miyuki. You better tell her. And you better keep moving. Get out of Japan. Get Jenna and Kiri out. And Miyuki."

"I'm working on it."

Miki took the phone from Kyle. "Patrick? Do you know who did this?"

"Take Kyle to the hospital and call me back when he's stable. I'm so sorry."

They heard a loud knock on the front door and Patrick hung up.

"Don't open it." Kyle tried to get up but couldn't.

The knock came again. "This is the police. Open up."

Miki checked the camera screen feed from the hall. "It's the police."

They knocked again and held up their badges. "Police. Open up."

Miki opened the door.

Two uniformed police rushed in. One of them went to Kyle and checked his vitals, pulled another blanket over him to keep shock from setting in. The other called for backup and checked on the ambulance.

Miki wiped her eyes. Her work suit was soaked in tears and blood.

Hiroshi and Takamatsu came in without knocking. Hiroshi kicked off his shoes and hurried to Kyle. After Hiroshi got the call, Ishii had put the siren on to halve the fifteen-minute drive. They almost got there faster than the local police.

Hiroshi turned away when he saw Kyle's battered face. He turned to Miki. "I'm Hiroshi Shimizu and this is Detective Takamatsu and Detective Ishii. And who are you?"

"I'm Miki Shitani. Kyle's girlfriend."

"You found him like this?"

"I sometimes spend the night here, but I stopped by this morning on my way to work. About an hour ago."

"Any idea who did this?"

Miki started to cry.

Ishii led her away from the room to the kitchen, comforting and questioning her at the same time.

166

Hiroshi kneeled down on the tatami beside Kyle. He closed his eyes for a minute and then focused on what he had to do. Kyle's face was bruised, swollen, and bloody. There were no open wounds and no bones sticking out. He could talk.

From the kitchen, Miki spoke to Hiroshi in Japanese. "He doesn't speak much Japanese. But I can interpret."

"I speak English." Hiroshi leaned over Kyle. "Tell me what happened. This is related to your friend Patrick, isn't it? He was here, wasn't he?"

Kyle rasped as he took a big breath. "He came here yesterday. I hadn't heard from him for months."

"And he just showed up?"

Kyle nodded.

"And he had his daughters with him?"

Kyle nodded.

"And where did he go?"

"I don't know."

"When did you see him last?"

"Late morning. I went to work around noon and he was still here."

"You didn't hear from him after that?"

"I was working."

"And when did you come home?"

"I was drinking in Roppongi with clients."

"And you left them when?"

"Around two. I took a taxi home. They jumped me at the door."

"What did they ask you exactly?"

"They asked about Patrick."

"What about him?"

"Where he was. Where he was going. The same thing over and over. They hit or kicked me after every question. Or smashed my head into the tatami."

"How did they find you?"

Kyle shook his head

167

"What did they look like?"

"They hit me too quickly. And too often. I couldn't see well, but they all wore black. Like a uniform or some shit."

"How many were there?"

"Three. And they called someone in the middle of it."

"What did you hear of that call?"

"My Japanese is not so good and I was out of it. That's the last I remember."

"You're lucky."

Kyle smirked. "Yeah, I feel really lucky."

"So, where is Patrick?"

"I don't know."

"Give us your best guess."

"He's still in Tokyo. But he didn't say where."

"Come on. You know him better than anyone. He had other friends?"

"Just his wife." Kyle shook his head. "He has money. I gave him some."

Miki came back into the room, knelt beside Kyle, and tried to shield him from more questions. "Please."

Hiroshi ignored her. "Why did he take the girls?"

Kyle winced and Miki put her hand on his shoulder.

"He was your best friend in Japan, right? And you don't know anything?"

Kyle squeezed his face and shook his head. "I wish I did."

"We need to find him before they do."

Kyle coughed and it took a couple of breaths to recover. "If I knew where he was, I'd tell you, to keep the girls safe. And Miyuki. His wife. Can you check on her?"

"We already did." Hiroshi stood up to get out of the way of the ambulance crew who just arrived. Ishii led them in.

"After you're fixed up, we'll talk more. At the hospital." Hiroshi stood back to let the paramedics check for bleeding, breaks, and injuries, and make sure he was stable. They were surprised he wasn't in shock.

They got him onto the gurney with Hiroshi and Ishii's help. Miki kept hold of his hand.

"Take him to the police hospital in Nakano," Hiroshi told the ambulance crew. "Someone will meet you there to watch him."

Takamatsu called Sakaguchi to arrange for one of the younger detectives to guard him.

When he was gone, Takamatsu started surveying the room. "They left him alive for a reason. Not sure what the message is. We're coming for you, I guess."

The apartment was a mess. They'd tossed the place. "We better have the crew go over all this and we'll go talk with Kyle's boss at Pacific Investments."

Takamatsu took out his lighter and started flipping it open and shut.

Chapter 23

Patrick stared out the window at Tokyo wondering who had gotten to Kyle and how. Maybe the city wasn't as large and anonymous as he thought. Kyle was right. They had better move—and move soon.

Kyle was right about Miyuki. She was in danger too. He hoped for the sake of the girls, she would help. If she took the girls out of the country, he could take a separate flight to Honolulu, open the accounts on his laptop, and be done with it all. It seemed like years ago he was driving to Haneda Airport with the girls for a clean getaway.

They could shelter in Wyoming after he set things right with Nine Dragons. The house in Jackson Hole was under a trust that didn't have his name on it, onshore/offshore, as they called it there. But if they found Kyle, they could find that house.

He called Tim. "Anything yet? We're ready to go." He didn't want to mention Kyle.

Tim sounded like he'd been sleeping. "I'm on it. We'll find something before the end of today. So just hang tight."

"I think we need to move."

"I'll call you back in a couple of hours. You can wait that long, can't you?"

Patrick growled yes and hung up.

He felt hungry for the first time since coming back to Tokyo. Breakfast in the hotel restaurant would be an hour, packing another hour. Maybe Tim would have something by then.

Ordering room service might be safer, since the guy from the pool could be lurking around, but he had to go down to get more cash if they were going to stay another half day. There would be an ATM in the lobby for Kyle's account. He owed Kyle a lot more than money now.

He wondered if the police would monitor Miyuki's calls. If it felt wrong, he'd hang up. He had to let her know.

Miyuki picked up right away, waiting for him to say something first. Patrick pulled the window curtain around him to dampen his voice. "It's me."

"Are the girls safe?" Miyuki asked.

"They're fine," Patrick answered.

"They're with you?"

"Right here, still sleeping."

"What are you doing?" Her voice was even, angry, steady.

"We've got to get the girls out of Japan."

Miyuki didn't answer for a few moments. Patrick hoped it wasn't going to be one of those conversations where she used silence like a weapon. That was worse than getting hysterical, which she was also really good at.

Miyuki cleared her throat. "I want to talk with them."

"They're sleeping."

"I have my mother's *funeral*."

"Your mother's *what*?"

"Tied up in her futon, she couldn't breathe."

"She was sleeping when I saw her, drunk on *shochu*, as usual."

"Her body's at the crematorium. I want the girls to be there."

"Things are more serious than you think."

"*More* serious? Taiga's in the hospital. In a coma. My mother is dead. You took my daughters. There's *more*?"

"We need to leave Japan."

"I can't understand what you're doing. Are the girls in danger? Why would you take them? Because of the divorce?"

"It's more than that. I need to know they are safe. This is the only way."

"Why wouldn't they be safe anywhere?"

"I'll explain later, but first I have to get to my laptop in Honolulu."

Miyuki injected a long, heavy silence. "What are you not telling

172

me?"

"A lot. It's worse if you know."

"Nothing is worse than coming home to my girls gone. Nothing."

"You filed for divorce."

Patrick wondered if the police were with her. When she spoke, her voice choked. "I got a package of photos. Of you."

Of him? Now he understood. He'd been set up. By Leung or someone. Were they trying to blackmail him? He could guess what the photos were. He'd had some of the wildest sex of his life with one of the paralegals he met in Wyoming. It was all physical and all too easy.

But he'd received photos, too. Of Miyuki, with a man, and of Kiri and Jenna on the way home from school. That's why he came back.

"Joseph Leung screwed everything up. I'm trying to fix it. He's been using me. For a long time. And he didn't answer at Nine Dragons."

"That's because he's dead."

"He's *what*?" He should have insisted on talking to Leung when he called Nine Dragons. He should have followed up, should have called Mehta. He should have done a lot of things.

Miyuki lowered her voice. "They interviewed me about you."

"Who? What did they ask?"

"Detectives. They asked about our relationship."

"Did they ask about Wyoming?"

"The divorce. I was with my lawyer."

"You know, if you hadn't sent those divorce papers—"

"You were fucking some blonde. What was I supposed to think?"

"I got a photo of you, also. You think I wasn't angry?"

Miyuki went silent.

Patrick let her have a few moments of silence. "So, are you coming with us? We can discuss the photos later."

"What photo? I have no idea what you're talking about."

Why couldn't she kick into practical mode and they'd fight it out when they were safe? If they could get out of Japan, he'd be able to sit down with her and tell her everything. Or almost everything.

"I will never forgive you for taking the girls without telling me. Why should I believe anything you say?"

"I had to do it this way. I had to make it seem it was nothing to do with work."

"Even though it is. What was Nine Dragons doing?"

Patrick started to explain more, but stopped himself. "Listen to me. Are you in our apartment?"

"I can't go anywhere without detectives or private investigators following me."

"That's good. They'll keep you safe." He hoped.

"Go into your mother's room, pull the tatami up, and get the USB I hid there. It's at the far end closest to the kitchen."

"Under the tatami? What are you talking about?"

"You have to pry one of the mats up. And inside the closet in Jenna's room, there's a ceiling panel. Get a chair. There's a blue bag inside."

"What's in it?"

"A lot of money. Don't open it. It's wrapped to carry."

"More secrets."

"It wasn't a secret. Just not shared."

"That's what a secret is."

"For now, you have to trust me. For the girls' sake. I can fix this, but I need to be in Honolulu and be sure the girls, and you, are safe."

"Now you're scaring me."

"You should be scared."

Jenna turned over, arched her back, and snuggled into the pillow. Kiri made a rapid little sniffle, about to talk in her sleep, then sniffled again and drifted back.

"Just bring the USB and the money. Don't let anyone follow you. If I can get to my computer in Honolulu, this will all be over."

Miyuki went silent again. "Why is your computer in Honolulu? And why are you here? Where are you?"

"I went to Wyoming to make double the money. It was the retire early plan like we talked about."

"We didn't talk about this."

Patrick watched the girls sleep, letting the silence hang between them. The girls were stirring. "Jenna, are you awake enough to talk with your mom?"

Jenna sat up, wiggled off the bed, and reached for the phone.

Patrick handed it to her and helped Kiri wake up and be ready to talk. He heard their answers to Miyuki's questions.

Jenna was smiling when they finished. "Mom wants to talk with you."

Patrick took the phone back and watched them skip off to the bathroom.

"I want to be with the girls," Miyuki said with the decisive final tone he knew too well.

"I'll call you in two or three hours." He hung up before saying anything more.

He would have to figure out who moved the money inside Nine Dragons, and why before they could really be safe. They'd better move, but where?

After their shower, they started packing and getting ready. When they had things together, he decided to leave their bags in the room while they went downstairs to eat. He kept the girls inside the door while he leaned outside to check the hallway. It was empty.

In the elevator, Patrick asked them what their mom talked about, but Jenna laughed. "She said we should be on our best behavior."

Kiri giggled. "We always are, poppa."

"I know you are, sweetie." He kissed them on the top of their heads.

In the lobby, Patrick used Kyle's card to withdraw cash. He hoped the police wouldn't track it, but that was a risk he'd have to take. Maybe he could manage one more withdrawal without being caught. He took the cash quickly and headed toward reception to pay for a half day if that was possible, and if not, for whatever was.

The receptionist smiled at Kiri and Jenna and turned back to the screen and tapped the keyboard. She cocked her head to the side. "It says here that your stay is paid for."

Patrick leaned on the counter, thinking the receptionist's English was not good. "I got permission to pay in cash yesterday. I put down a small amount, but didn't—"

Kiri tugged on his pants and Jenna leaned against him. "We're hungry."

The receptionist read one page and then another. "Someone put a card number on file for you. Maybe a grandparent, friend, or your workplace? That sometimes happens."

"I don't think so..." Patrick started running through the possibilities. None of them were good. "Is there a name there someplace? Please, I need to know."

Smiling in a practiced way, she adjusted her uniform and clicked the keyboard. "Well, it seems the name is Kosugi." She pasted a smile across her face and lifted her eyebrows.

"Kosugi?" Patrick answered her fake smile with one of his own. "Of course. Thank you."

"Enjoy your breakfast. All expenses are covered."

Patrick pretended to know who it was, keeping the smile on his face as he leaned down to Kiri and Jenna. "OK. I'm hungry. What about you two?"

"We want pancakes."

"Pancakes it is." He took the girls' hands and they headed to the cafe.

Halfway across the lobby, a man in a maroon turtleneck with a gray camel hair jacket circled in front of him, speaking in rapid-fire Japanese. Patrick shook his head and pulled the girls close.

The man smoothed back his longish hair. "You don't speak Japanese?" He said in English.

"Not very well." Patrick clutched the girls' hands.

The man spoke in halting English. "We have a situation. And we need your help."

"We?"

"Kosugi."

"Kosugi?"

"As I understand it, you handle his accounts at Nine Dragons."

Patrick saw two men by the door, loose, limber, and vigilant. They were younger than the man in front of him, with buffed biceps and workout shoulders tight-packed in turtlenecks. Even their masks seemed muscular.

Kosugi. Before he left for Wyoming, Leung had told him to put a little extra effort into Kosugi's account. And he had. He'd reset Kosugi's trust details and added a layer to his shell company in Wyoming. Kosugi wasn't one of their richest clients, but Patrick suspected Nine Dragons wasn't his only wealth management company, either.

"We need to go. Kosugi is waiting. He would like you to come without a fuss."

"The girls…?"

"They come with us. This won't take long."

Patrick stood holding the girls' hands, deciding. He looked around the lobby and then stooped down and looked the girls in the face. "We need to go with these guys for a little bit and then we'll be back here right away, OK?"

"Is this a work thing?" Jenna asked.

"Where did you hear that phrase?"

"Mom says it all the time." Jenna nodded.

"I'd like to see you work, poppa," Kiri said.

"Now's your chance." Patrick squeezed their hands, hoping this wouldn't be their last chance.

Chapter 24

The men from the lobby led Patrick and the girls to the elevator and rode down with them from the fortieth floor. When they arrived at the ground floor, a dark blue six-seater SUV idled in the drop-off circle. The man in camel hair opened the door for them.

Patrick picked Jenna up and set her inside, and then picked Kiri up, tickling her as he put her into the seat. He buckled them in carefully. Patrick had a good idea what they wanted. He just hoped it was all they wanted.

The man held his hand out until Patrick realized he wanted his cellphone. He gave it to him. The other two men climbed in the back seat. The camel hair coat got in front telling the driver to lock the doors and drive. "Please keep your masks on until we arrive," he advised.

Patrick leaned forward. "My girls haven't had breakfast yet."

The man turned around, frowning. "What do they like?"

Patrick turned to the girls. "What do you want to eat? These guys are going to buy us breakfast."

"They don't have pancakes?" Kiri asked.

"I don't think so." Patrick looked at Jenna.

"What about donuts?" Jenna smiled, pleased with her suggestion.

The man in front made a call.

"Poppa, why are the windows so dark in this car?" Kiri asked.

"It keeps out the sun." Patrick tapped on the window. "You don't want to get sunburned, do you?" That seemed to satisfy her and they rode the rest of the way in silence.

Patrick tried to keep an eye on passing landmarks, but the car veered into tangled streets with a blur of ramen places, print shops, pachinko parlors, Chinese and Indian joints, and clothing stores that could be in any part of the city. The dark windows removed all detail so each street was tinted the same. The SUV slowed to navigate narrow blocks of one-way streets before pulling into the entryway of a shabby building that just fit the vehicle's width.

A guard came out from a small glass-fronted cubicle. One of the men in back got out and held the door open for Patrick and the girls. They stepped onto an oily circle of metal set into the concrete floor.

The driver pressed buttons on a control panel on the wall and a grinding of gears erupted behind the inner door. The door opened and a Ferris wheel mechanism rotated down. The driver eased the car onto the lift, got out, and sidled back to the panel to press a large red button that rolled the doors shut and the SUV rotated up and away.

The man in the camel hair coat waved them into a cramped concrete area with metal stairs and an elevator. Kiri and Jenna held hands. The elevator creaked down. Not everyone could fit in so Patrick and the girls got on with two of the men.

"What is this place?" Jenna whispered.

"Today's workplace," Patrick whispered like he was reading them a bedtime story.

The girls giggled. "It's not like your office with the dragons and all the windows."

The elevator let them out in front of a door. Inside was a neat room with long, flat tables resting on horizontal cabinets but no windows. A row of open white shelves ran along the wall, strangely empty. Wide flat drawers lined the space below a wide countertop. Overhead, air ducts and support beams were painted white.

Three women in white blouses and black skirts stood and bowed. One of the women hurried over, holding out her hand toward two sliding doors. She pulled the doors open to a Japanese-style room with tatami and a low table that could seat ten or twelve people.

In the center of the table was a box decorated with bright red donuts, some drawn with smiley faces and sunshine rays. Bottles of juice in different sizes, shapes, and colors were set together like a cheery set of dollhouse skyscrapers.

Kiri and Jenna looked at Patrick for permission. He waived them on. What else could he do? They sat on the edge of the tatami and pulled off their shoes, then hopped up, polite but excited.

"Save me one, will you?" Patrick said.

"We're going to eat them all," Kiri said, giggling.

The woman kneeled down and opened the donut box. Inside were two dozen donuts of every glazed, sprinkle-covered, and food-colored description.

Kiri and Jenna lost themselves in their sugary decisions.

The woman turned to Patrick. "Your girls are so cute."

"Yes, they are." Patrick nodded. "But they need to wash their hands."

The woman led the girls to a small sink at the other end of the room.

The other two women finished what they were doing and came over. One of the women asked Patrick in English if he'd like some coffee.

He had enough adrenaline, he didn't need caffeine. After the girls washed their hands, Patrick made sure they sat down.

"We'll watch them," the woman said in English, pulling the sliding doors shut.

The man in the camel hair coat waved Patrick to the other side of the office. He knocked on a Western-style door and pulled it open without waiting to a room with a high ceiling, clean design, and ergonomic chairs. Behind the desk sat a man in his sixties.

Patrick recognized Kosugi instantly. His face was as tanned, rugged, and focused as a boat captain's, but his clothes were a pro golfer's. He wore a tight-fitting lime green polo shirt over his taut, stocky frame. He was on the phone and motioned for Patrick to sit.

The shelves were filled with golf trophies, a golden golf ball, framed certificates, and square boards signed by famous athletes.

Patrick started running through what he imagined Kosugi wanted done. He tried to think of Kosugi as just another client, but he was clearly a guy who could order anything done without a second thought.

Kosugi glanced at Patrick and kept nodding and humming into the phone without saying anything. He twisted in his chair, listening, until he wrote on a pad of paper and hung up.

Patrick sat up.

"I'm Kosugi. You're the guy who did everything for Leung, who knows how to seal the money airtight. In Wyoming, wasn't it? Any golfing there?"

"I don't know. I was too busy."

"I had my girls out there trying to break in, but they couldn't. And they break into all kinds of things. That's why I hired them. And that's why I'm hiring you."

"Hiring me?"

"Unfortunately, the compensation is not the monetary kind, but rather the going-free kind. Your girls are comfortable?"

"They're eating donuts. Where are we right now?"

"Near Kanda. I picked up this place from an architect who went, well, bankrupt. He gave me a deal on his computers. He used them for design, 3-D modeling, that kind of thing. They're high speed, they tell me. My staff set them up for you."

Patrick tried to hold Kosugi's gaze, but he couldn't. He had to look away. "I want you to promise my daughters will be safe. I won't do anything until I'm sure they're going to be safe."

Kosugi chuckled. "Ah, you Americans. Always imagining the world is infinitely negotiable." His voice was as deep-throaty and dry as a smoker's, but Patrick didn't see any ashtrays. "You've got it backwards, I'm afraid. It's your daughters who are keeping *you* safe."

Patrick took a breath.

Kosugi continued. "I trusted Leung with important investments. But that's over. For obvious reasons. So I need you to move them for me." Kosugi spoke slow, steady, accented English, as if translating every word in his head into commands that wouldn't be misinterpreted.

Patrick sat forward. "Do you know what happened to Leung? Do you know who...killed him?"

Kosugi shrugged. "I know he handled money for a lot of people who, like me, don't like their accounts played with. So, let me give you some hard-won advice. When business colleagues disappear, you're on your own. You should learn from them, find out what makes them tick, when they're alive. You apparently didn't do that with Leung, did you?"

Kosugi was right. He should have paid attention.

"You just took your pay and did your work, right? You missed the chance to learn how *not* to do things. Leung toyed with things he shouldn't have."

"Toyed with?" Patrick had the feeling of being measured, inside. "I had nothing to do with that."

Kosugi leaned back, nodding. "But you're still the guy who set things up. And more importantly, you're the guy who can fix things. Like my money. Right?"

"If I can get in, I can do that." Patrick was far from sure he could do that, but he'd worry about alternatives later. Leung might have put Kosugi's money out of reach. He doubted he could ask Kosugi to go with them to Honolulu.

"Then what I need you to do for me is straightforward. I never caught up with the computer age. Why I have to hire those women out there. They're smart as whips, but even they couldn't get into Nine Dragons. That's how I know you're good."

Patrick tried to remember the last time he checked on Kosugi's accounts. He'd reset them carefully in Wyoming, layering them into a trust fund packed inside shell companies run through various countries. Leung had urged special care with Kosugi, but he'd never told Patrick why. And he hadn't asked. Now, he knew why.

"My staff will, what's the word? Ah, *babysit* your daughters while you transfer the money from my Nine Dragons account into this new one." He pulled the top sheet from the notepad and slid it across the desk.

The paper had a golf ball with "Great golf quotes" and a quote from Sam Snead: "Of all the hazards, fear is the worst." Below were the numbers of Kosugi's accounts.

Patrick fingered the sheet. "And if I do this for you?"

"There's no 'if.'"

"*When* I do it."

"We'll give you a ride back. I'll cover your hotel bill for the inconvenience. I've found that positive motivation works better. Maybe I'm getting old."

"That's it?"

"That's it."

Patrick looked at Kosugi and back at the account numbers. Patrick took a breath. "What happened to Leung?"

"You know, I sent a lot of clients his way. Some were long-time associates."

"To Nine Dragons?"

"That's what really hurts—the damage to my reputation." Kosugi shook his head.

"You're threatening my daughters."

"Right now, they're eating donuts. I'm sure they'll save you one."

"And if I don't help you?"

"Like I just said, there's no 'if' here. And I don't do circular conversations. We've talked enough." Kosugi nodded at the numbers in Patrick's hand. "Is that all you need to get this done?"

Patrick stood up with the account numbers in hand. "That and a high-speed internet connection."

Chapter 25

After an hour of examining bloodstains and broken furniture, Takamatsu told Hiroshi to let the local police and crime scene crew finish Kyle's apartment. If the three guys beat up people for a living, they were unlikely to leave clues.

In the car, Takamatsu lit a cigarette. "How can they understand each other if they don't speak the same language?"

"Who are we talking about?" Ishii pulled out into traffic.

"That couple. Do you speak another language, Ishii?"

Ishii nodded. "I studied criminal law in America."

"Why did you come back?"

"A long-time relationship ended, and my degree wasn't much use there. Maybe no use here, either."

"Your boyfriend was American?"

"Not that it's any of your business, but yes." Ishii looked at Takamatsu until he rolled down the window and concentrated on smoking.

"Isn't that lighter heavy?" Ishii asked.

Takamatsu held it up. "It is heavy, but it reminds me to smoke."

"You need reminding?"

"Sometimes."

Ishii kept the car weaving through traffic. It was only a twenty-minute drive to West Shinjuku, the skyscraper side of the station opposite the host club side.

Hiroshi called Akiko, listened closely, and hung up. "Akiko called ahead for us. The chief now wants her to call every airport and boat entry port in Japan. There are about a hundred of each."

Takamatsu tossed his cigarette out. "The smaller the entry points are, the less they follow procedures. You can come and go as you like if you're rich enough."

Ishii pulled into the ramp for the underground parking lot of the triangular skyscraper housing Pacific Investments. On the lobby floor, they checked in at reception and took security passes. A guard pointed them to the right elevator.

In the elevator, Takamatsu started flipping his lighter. "It's harder to get in and out of this building than Japanese ports or small airports."

The elevator opened to wide windows that framed Tokyo. Ishii and Takamatsu lingered a moment at the spectacular view, but Hiroshi walked quickly to the reception counter of Pacific Investments. He'd had enough of heights on another business-related murder case just six months before. He'd nearly fallen stopping a girl from jumping. The memory, and the anxiety, had yet to subside.

A neatly dressed woman bowed deeply and led them along a corridor with offices on both sides. Unlike Nine Dragons, the company had offices with walls and doors. The door to the CEO of Pacific Investments was open.

From inside, the view was again stunning, as if the entire city had been positioned for just that view. Hiroshi kept his attention on Kamiya's face. He was sixty-something, in good shape, with lively eyes and a calm manner.

He stood for introductions. "I'm Kamiya. Thank you for taking the time to come here and update me on Kyle Shawcross. I'm very concerned. Shocked, actually. Is he all right?"

Hiroshi nodded. "He's in a protected hospital and we stationed extra guards there. They are used to injuries of that sort."

"Of what sort?"

"He was beaten pretty badly."

"I was told he wasn't found for several hours." Kamiya eyed each of the detectives. "So, who did this? I want him found."

"We're working on it. We think it wasn't about him, but about his friend, Patrick Walsh."

The receptionist brought in tea, and Kamiya found his manners and asked them to sit down. Hiroshi moved his chair to face the wall instead of the window.

Kamiya's eyes closed tight, as he sat down, thinking. "Kyle has never been any trouble. I worried he'd be lured away too. Patrick always overshadowed him, but when he left, Kyle came on stronger."

Hiroshi nodded. "Patrick stopped by Kyle's and stayed the night."

Kamiya frowned, thinking about that with his hands together. "They were the first two foreigners I ever hired. I had to brush up my English to work with them. The other employees learned, too. Japan was opening to the world economy, kicking its Galapagos syndrome, trying to be like other countries. All this old wealth was stagnating, so we wanted to put it to work for investors. Those two were pivotal in making that happen. But they were naive too, never quite understanding what kind of wealth was here."

"The kind that gravitates to Nine Dragons."

Kamiya nodded. "It was like trying to untangle a century or two of tightly knotted connections. There were a lot of unexpected opportunities."

"There's profit in that."

Kamiya smiled. "We still get high-risk clients every week. They're good at covering their trail, but after getting burned a few times, we started to screen them more carefully."

"Nine Dragons welcomed those types of clients."

Kamiya shrugged. "Some of the clients we rejected went there."

"Can you give us their names?"

"I can pull a list together." He called one of the staff, told her what he wanted, and asked her to hurry, explaining why.

"So, your clients are always—"

"High-net-worth individuals, yes, but Leung aimed for the *ultra*-high-net-worth clients. Patrick bought into it."

"What's ultra start at?"

"Thirty million US or so. At Pacific, we tend to work with the next tier down. They're more grateful, more mature, and safer. At whatever level, clients require a lot of personal attention."

"Patrick was good at what he did?"

"He had the knack of evaluating portfolios, enhancing tax efficiency, planning financials, establishing goals. He communicated well to clients. That's invaluable. But I warned him against going to Nine Dragons."

"Because?"

"I wanted him to stay, first of all. He made a big difference. When Patrick was headhunted by Leung, it must have flattered him. He was no doubt lured by Leung's promise of larger portfolios, the selective marketing, and surely a bigger salary and bonuses. More freedom. Nine Dragons and Pacific have different philosophies. Here, we're more conservative. Plenty of money to be made within the clear confines of the law."

A well-dressed woman brought in the printout Kamiya asked for. He thanked her and asked her to stay, but she said she was busy with another client and Kamiya let her go.

Kamiya handed over a copy of the list. "So, this list is of appointments we didn't follow up on."

Hiroshi found the name on the list and showed it to Takamatsu and Ishii.

"Some were straight up about what they wanted—offshore investments far from the prying eyes of Japanese tax regulators. There aren't many regulations in the first place, to be honest. Still, some of them want to avoid them just to prove they can. Others are used to working in the gray zones. In the bubble years, that was easy. Less so now."

"How gray are the gray zones?" Hiroshi asked.

Kamiya shrugged. "For some clients looking for legitimacy and long-term strategy, we might overlook the sources of their wealth. I mean, we have almost every pachinko parlor company in Japan. Where does that fall? Legal, yes, but it's still gambling.

Others have money sitting around in obscure accounts going back to the war. Some are honest and easy to work with. Others lie and demand the impossible. The latter are just not worth it."

"So, what happens to the demanding clients?"

"They go elsewhere."

"To Nine Dragons?"

"It would be the next logical stop." Kamiya nodded. "Some old-school *sokaiya*, for example, well, we just don't want that kind of money. I left the firm where I started for just that reason."

Looking out the window, Takamatsu chimed in at last. "The *sokaiya* were great at breaking up company meetings, hiring *sokaiya* to get rid of *sokaiya*, luring executives into compromising situations."

Kamiya smirked and shook his head. "They'd follow you, learn your secrets, take photos of you, contact your wife. Cheap blackmail, most of it. It was how they did business then."

Takamatsu sat up. "That was business as usual in the bubble years. But even now, wherever there's money, there's blackmail and extortion. "

"I'm glad we've steered clear." Kamiya hummed. "The shame of public exposure used to kill more executives than smoking. They were horrified of whatever the *sokaiya* found on them, which usually wasn't that much. I'm glad those days are over."

Hiroshi tried to get a read on Kamiya. "And those guys still have money to invest?"

"Sure. One guy, Nozaki, came with a group of them. He was leading them like an investors group. I checked up on him before agreeing to anything. Glad I did. Another investor, an old friend, told me they tried to pull that threatening stuff with him. I made sure Nozaki and his group never came back."

"How did you manage that?"

"I called the police. They cooperated. Unlike in the old days. And I hired a security company, too. Not cheap but worth it."

Takamatsu held up his hand. "Hey, in the bubble years, we

were hobbled by regulations, codes of conduct, lack of budget. We're trying to catch up. That's why we've hired people like Hiroshi here."

Hiroshi fidgeted. It was Takamatsu who was calm and patient at this interview. "What kind of investors group would someone like Nozaki put together?"

Kamiya put his hands together under his chin. "Back when I started, things ran on trust. One person would front a group of investors who wanted to remain unknown. An old-style firewall. As long as that person never divulged where the money came from, the others were protected. People like Nozaki worked that way, shielding others' investments. The original shell company."

Takamatsu nodded. "And they were people whose trust you couldn't break and stay alive too long."

Kamiya cocked his head to the side. "That's how it used to work. Things have changed so much."

Hiroshi shook his head, still not clear. "So, Nine Dragons welcomed clients of that ilk?"

"That's what I heard." Kamiya shrugged and smiled.

"You heard that from Patrick?"

"I haven't seen him since he left for Nine Dragons."

"From Kyle?"

"We don't talk about other firms here in the office, and I'm too old to go drinking anymore, where the real info is exchanged. But you hear things about competitors and their methods. I'm sure that old-style investing still exists, but not with us. I focus on my company and let the rest go. We have enough to work on here."

"Security must be a major concern."

"Hacked passwords, intercepted emails, opened accounts...our security budget balloons every quarter. I'm sure you're doing your best to catch up, but the criminals are always a few steps ahead of regulators and the tax office. They're always quite a few steps ahead of us. That's why we're so cautious."

Hiroshi thought of Watanabe. He wasn't behind, the

bureaucracy was. "I still don't understand why Nine Dragons set up an office in Tokyo."

Kamiya nodded. "When regulations started to be enforced, there was a rush to get money out of Japan and shelter it as soon as possible. Government regulators were scrambling, so there was a rush to tap into it while they still could. Japan changes slowly, so probably it was last on the list. Leung has offices in Hong Kong, Shanghai, and the rest of Southeast Asia, so he must know what he's doing."

Hiroshi sighed. "He's not doing anything anymore. Someone killed him yesterday morning."

Kamiya didn't look surprised.

Chapter 26

One of Kosugi's female assistants stood beside Patrick and the other sat behind two monitors opposite his. That was fine. He didn't mind being monitored. He was going to move Kosugi's money and get out of there as soon as possible.

He heard Kiri and Jenna in the other tatami room through the sliding doors.

Patrick opened Nine Dragons system. After all the legal fluff, a shell company was basically a series of passwords inside passwords, gradually obscuring ownership through a series of access points. Leung had once told Patrick that the secret was neat record-keeping. If you lost the path, you lost the money.

Patrick remembered most of the paths, but the others were on his computer in Honolulu. He wanted to check his own account, but the women were watching him too closely.

Even with the fast connection, the transfers took time, so he asked one of the women for another computer. She brought over a laptop and set up a second monitor, so now Patrick had two computers and four monitors.

She bowed and smiled as brightly as any other service industry professional. By the door, one of the buffed men who'd picked them up at the hotel stared as dully into space as any bodyguard or bouncer.

Patrick plugged in the second set of numbers. He had a system for passwords, changing them regularly according to the date, but opposite one hundred and eighty degrees so the passwords were different every day and easily calculable. He logged in and set the transfer going. If his own passwords still worked and if the transfer went smoothly, the whole nightmare would soon be over.

The numbers clicked into place and Kosugi's accounts were

where they were supposed to be. Kosugi had three separate accounts. Patrick wondered if anything were missing from them, prayed there wasn't, and wondered how Kosugi made all that money. He had a pretty good idea it wasn't from golf bets.

In the other room, Kiri was singing the theme song to "Doraemon," or was it "Anpanman"? He remembered the melody, the girls played it so many times watching the show with their grandmother.

He started transferring Kosugi's money to the new accounts. One of the two women went in with Kiri and Jenna and he was left alone with the woman at the monitors across from him and the bouncer on a stool by the door.

Nine Dragons' head office or the police would get into the accounts and freeze them soon. Maybe they were tracking them already. He'd logged on at the hotel, but maybe Kosugi had better security.

The first account of Kosugi's finished. He waited for follow-up messages, but none came, so he turned his attention to the other two. The second started smoothly so he let it roll and turned to get the third account started. It was set up in Wyoming with a backup connection to Panama, routed through Latvia and Luxembourg.

Leung had a thing about bouncing the transfers through several countries. That added layers of security but could draw attention. Just one SAR could pause transfers or put them under scrutiny. He'd do things differently when he and Kyle set up their firm.

He checked the second transfer and an error message popped up. It was taking too much time and stopped. He kicked the third account back up on the screen and glanced at the woman and the bouncer. He started the procedure again, and decided to check Leung's past month.

He heard Kiri and Jenna's voices behind the sliding door in the tatami room.

He opened the other accounts, hoping the woman wouldn't notice where he was or what he was looking at. He could always say he needed to check other accounts of Kosugi's to be thorough. The accounts clicked open and he slid back in his chair. Nothing more than the same out and in strategy he'd seen when he logged in at the hotel.

He switched to his own master account, the one he used for temporary transfers, and scrolled back a few months.

And there it was!

Money was moving in and out of an account in Patrick's name. He had never seen that account before. Leung must have set it up to make it seem that Patrick—not Leung—was executing all the transfers. He'd been so busy getting the new accounts set up in Wyoming, he'd barely even checked his own transfer account.

Leung had a master password for all accounts. He used it mostly for oversight, but for the past few months, he used it to shuffle funds in a way that made it seem Patrick was the one doing it. Without a more granular check of settlement delays, routing codes, and endpoints, he couldn't be sure where the money went.

What he could see was that Leung made it appear that it was Patrick, not Leung, misusing floats, churning accounts, and kiting other people's money. All this on-the-run shit was because Leung dipped into the wrong accounts, imagining no one would notice. There must be a lot left unreturned when Leung was killed. If Kosugi had noticed, others would also, if not now, soon enough. This could drag on for a long time.

He'd like to kill Leung himself.

Patrick made sure the women were drinking coffee before he started to download the information to his cloud storage folder, but he was startled by a hand on his shoulder.

"Everything going OK?" Kosugi asked. He had a grandfatherly manner to him, a grandfather who could do whatever was needed.

"All good so far." Patrick smiled at him as cheerily as he could muster.

Kosugi looked over his shoulder. "You're really a genius with these things. My girls here," he gestured at the women in the office, "really liked how you set up everything over there in Wyoming. It's just too bad Leung had to mess with it."

Patrick noticed that the screens of account numbers didn't mean anything to Kosugi. His assistants would know exactly what they meant, though. That's why he had them there. And Kosugi would call the bank eventually for confirmation.

Kosugi talked as he balanced himself for a practice golf swing. "You should learn to enjoy your money before you're too old. I misspent my youth, encouraging executives to pay, extracting insurance from wealthy companies. Profitable but boring. I should have done the fun stuff when I was young. You can't put 'good at golf' on your tombstone, can you?"

Patrick sighed. "I'm sorry about Leung. I don't know what he was thinking."

Kosugi patted Patrick's shoulder again. "I know it wasn't you. My assistants checked. They figured out that much already. We still needed you to get in and move our money out."

Patrick looked at the two women standing in front of the two monitors opposite him.

"I've never been the kind to quibble about a percent here or there. But to take our money, use it for a quick profit, and not tell us? And to do that to friends I recommended?" Kosugi swung his imaginary club and stayed in place for a long follow-through.

"I wasn't involved in that."

"I know you weren't. Like I said, we check on things like that. We know you set up the shell companies and those trust fund things. You should go into business for yourself. Let me know if you ever do."

Patrick nodded, hoping the third transfer would hurry up.

Kosugi settled his stance for another practice swing. "I still have a lot of good friends from the old days. A lot didn't make it, of course. It's a hard life. After the bubble years fizzled out, I decided to take my share and invest it. I barely knew what interest and dividends were."

He spun into his swing hard and steady. The women looked where he hit as if following the ball down a green.

Kosugi loosened his shoulders and turned to Patrick. "I pay a couple of golf pros to keep me from embarrassing myself at Tara Iti, Dornoch, or Cape Wickham. The women like the resorts in the south of Portugal, and the new ones in China. You should learn to enjoy yourself along the way. I wish I had."

"I might refocus. But for now, I need a flight out of Japan," Patrick said.

Kosugi dropped his hand on Patrick's shoulder again. "I always use private jets. You arrive rested. No immigration headaches. Some services skip logging flight details. From Tokyo, head to Guam. You're in America there. Get another private jet from there to wherever you're going. Google it. You're a smart kid."

"Was it you who's been following us?"

Kosugi cocked his head. "It wasn't me, but I found you easily enough. Who was following you?"

Patrick looked confused. "You sent me, and her, photos, right?"

"Photos?" Kosugi gave him a hard look. "It wasn't one of my people. Mine are all here and I never hire out anymore. Too many things go wrong."

Patrick looked back at the screen. Then who was it? The transfer finished. Patrick wanted to shout hallelujah, but he stood up calmly and backed away from the screen. "All done."

Kosugi leaned down, but he didn't really read it. "Wait here, all right?" Kosugi went back to his office.

The women smiled at Patrick and stood in place. Waiting patiently was probably a lot of what they did. They were too polite to ask questions and Patrick hoped the silence would speed things along.

Kosugi came out tossing a golf ball into the air. He was lithe and worked out a lot, not just golf, more like personal trainer workouts. "All good."

"And my girls?"

"Just be glad you were with your daughters or this might have taken a different turn." Kosugi called and the door to the tatami room slid open. Kiri and Jenna were sitting at a low desk covered with bright-colored squares of paper and origami figures.

Kiri walked on her knees to the edge of the tatami. "Look what I made."

"What is it?"

"A turtle, can't you tell?"

Jenna finished her creation. "Look at mine."

"That's a crane." Patrick turned it over in his hands, impressed at the neat folds and deft tucks that formed the complex angles of the paper crane.

He gave the girls a big hug, but it was really he who needed the hug.

Chapter 27

In the elevator down from Pacific Investments, Akiko sent a message that the tech guys had got a hit on a car outside the Azabu apartment. She sent the name and address of a foreigner living in Mejiro to whom the license plate was registered. Hiroshi read out the address, and Ishii inputted it to the car's navigation.

Hiroshi settled into the back seat. "An American. A different one than the father who took the girls."

"We don't know that yet, do we?" Ishii sped north to Mejiro Station.

Takamatsu rolled down his window and lit a cigarette. He seemed lost in thought and unusually quiet.

A few minutes west of the station, Ishii turned down on a narrow lane lined by two-story homes and unit apartments built right to the curb. Ishii slowed to avoid utility poles, community bulletin boards, and trash pick-up spots along the curb. At every corner, mirrors set on orange poles allowed a view of the cross street.

Hiroshi pointed at an apartment building with an overgrown hedge and Ishii pulled into a jigsaw puzzle of a parking lot across the street. Hiroshi looked for the car they found on the surveillance footage, a matte black Toyota Harrier, but the lot only held off-duty taxis, subcontracting delivery vans, late-model sedans, and gravel.

Hiroshi got out and surveyed the nine-unit, tile-covered building for exit routes, a practice Takamatsu drilled into him. The apartments had balconies wide enough to hang laundry and squeeze in a patio stool, but not much more. No back exits.

Takamatsu put his hands on the car and pushed back to loosen his hamstrings. He pulled his arms behind him and stretched his back.

"You running the Tokyo Marathon?" Hiroshi asked.

"Without Sugamo and Osaki here, I want to be ready." Takamatsu rotated his neck. "My doctor recommended stretching a bit."

"You go to a doctor?"

"Wife dragged me."

"Doctor didn't say anything about the smoking, I guess."

"No, he said a lot. I just didn't listen."

Hiroshi walked to the side of the apartment building looking for the entrance. Ishii and Takamatsu followed.

The entry was down a half-flight of stairs. A superintendent in a stiff uniform jacket greeted Hiroshi with a pleasant smile. It was a little strange to have a superintendent for such a small apartment. The building must have been ultramodern in the 1960s, and it was still well maintained.

"I'm looking for a foreigner, Tim Branson. Is he here?" Hiroshi asked.

"Ah, Tim-san? He's out now, but he said he had a package coming today." The guard looked at the stack of deliveries.

"Which floor is his apartment on?"

"Third floor. Can I help you with something?"

"Hiroshi?" Ishii called from the top of the stairs.

Hiroshi turned to see a heavy-set foreign guy ambling down, loose-limbed like all Americans, in a sweatshirt, wool overshirt, and baseball cap. He stopped next to Takamatsu.

Tim was as big as a linebacker. Sugamo and Osaki would have been welcome.

Hiroshi spoke in English. "Are you Tim Branson?"

Takamatsu made the mistake of reaching for Tim's arm.

In a flash, Tim grabbed Takamatsu's hand, bent it sharply at the wrist and shoved him against the wall. Takamatsu groaned and clutched his wrist.

Ishii pulled out her friction-lock baton, whipped it to full extension, and held it out in both hands to block him.

Tim shoved the baton with his forearm and ducked to the side.

Ishii swung and landed a sharp blow to his ankle.

Tim stumbled and yelped but kept going.

Hiroshi took the stairs two at a time.

Tim got to the top and sprinted down the street.

Hiroshi kept after him with Ishii behind.

Up ahead, Tim turned down a side street blocked by a row of tall hedges. Hiroshi raced to the turn, but Tim was gone. He could see straight to the end of the empty lane, so he hurried to the next turn. Still, nothing. The streets zigzagged through a maze of odd-angled lots.

Ishii caught up and they picked different directions. Soon they were lost in the dogleg tangle of neighborhood lanes. The houses and apartment buildings were close to the street, so it was impossible to see more than a short dash ahead.

Hiroshi lost sight of Ishii, and couldn't hear her running, either. He pulled out his phone and saw calls from Takamatsu.

Out of breath, Hiroshi called back, looking down each of the lanes as he jogged forward.

"Where are you?" Takamatsu asked.

"Can you see Shiinamachi Station? Higashi Nagasaki?"

"Is he heading that way?"

"I lost sight of him. And Ishii too. Maybe he turned south. Can you angle south?"

"Yes."

Hiroshi could hear Takamatsu breathing hard through the phone. "He must be staying on small streets."

"Smart guy. Where are you now exactly? On my app, the whole area is called Higashi Nagasaki?"

"You see the station? Turn south and keep going until it turns into Senkawa Dori. Maybe he's heading for the train."

"You were right, we needed Sugamo and Osaki. Where are those tracking apps we used to have?"

"Chief didn't want to pay for them." Hiroshi hung up before

Takamatsu could curse the chief and headed to a large street with taller, commercial buildings. A short way down, Ishii was crossing a pedestrian bridge.

By the time he got to the other side, Ishii was gone down the streets on the other side. He headed after her, checking every side street, hoping that Ishii had a visual and they weren't just wasting their time.

The first street ended in a park, and on the far side Ishii stood turning in all directions.

The park was larger than most with benches, a playground, and a public toilet. Beyond a chain link fence at the end, an urban farm spread out with fine black dirt from which poked the white tops of daikon. A greenhouse of plastic sheets and steel frames stretched along the daikon patch.

A group of elderly women in jogging outfits was fast-walking the circumference, and a trio of housewives watched their kids playing in a round sandbox.

Catching his breath, Hiroshi walked over to the housewives. Two of them stood and moved to the sandbox where the kids were shoveling and dumping sand.

Hiroshi pulled out his badge. "We're looking for a foreign man, big, baseball cap?"

"We almost called the police," one said. The mothers hovered over their kids and pointed at the public toilet.

Ishii jogged from the far end of the park and pulled her friction-lock baton out again. She reached under her jacket to her waistband. "Here's my backup."

"You carry two?"

"If you were a woman, you would too."

Hiroshi took the baton from her, flicked it out, and weighed it in his hand like a kendo sword.

They advanced on the public toilet, which was, like most public toilets in Tokyo, doorless with windows of open, concrete lattice. You could see inside if you stood in the right place at the right angle, though no one would.

Hiroshi moved toward the men's entrance, and Ishii circled toward the women's.

When they got close enough, Hiroshi shouted in English. "Tim? Come on out. We just want to talk."

Ishii started around the back. Hiroshi went into the men's side. Above the sink, Tim was stuck halfway out a shoulder-high window above the sinks. He heard a whack and Tim's legs kicked out.

Hiroshi heard another crack from the other side.

Tim screamed. "Goddamnit, that hurt!"

"Don't fucking move," Ishii shouted in English from the other side of the back wall.

Tim twisted in place. The upper window wasn't big enough for him to get through, and he was wedged in, trapped. Hiroshi grabbed his legs and tugged. They really needed Sugamo and Osaki for this one.

Pulling on his legs, Hiroshi yanked Tim free, and got up upright. Ishii came around, set herself, and braced to hit him again, but Hiroshi held Tim's arm tightly.

Hiroshi started to think how far away the car was and wondered where Takamatsu was. When he looked at the exit, Tim threw a punch, putting all his weight into it, but he was too slow.

Hiroshi ducked, and Tim's fist glanced off the side of his head.

Ishii struck Tim's hand as he raised it again and gave him another whack on his forearm.

Tim clutched his arm.

Ishii jammed the baton between his arm and back, grabbed the end, and twisted. Tim tumbled over and she dropped a knee into his back and snatched his wrist, twisting hard. She struck him on the shoulder blade with the butt of the baton. "Stop wiggling." She hit him two more quick blows until he stopped trying to squirm free.

Hiroshi was surprised by her deft movements and by how small she looked on top of the mountainous American. He dropped down to hold Tim's legs, while she pulled cuffs out and got both wrists secured.

Feeling better with Tim facedown and cuffed, Hiroshi realized they should have sent someone to check Tim's room. Was this guy really trying to escape or was he just leading them astray? They might have just missed Patrick and the girls hidden in his room.

It was too far back to run there now. He called Osaki and Sugamo to tell them to hurry to the apartment and search it. He regretted racing after Tim. Why didn't Takamatsu think of checking Tim's place?

Takamatsu arrived, directed by the mothers. He leaned over to catch his breath, coughing. When he could speak, he patted Ishii on the back. "Not bad."

A local police car pulled up, and two local cops pedaled over on their bicycles.

Feeling exhausted from the chase, Hiroshi took Tim's wallet out of his back pocket. The name read "Tim Branson," the same as the one Akiko sent. Ishii was talking with the local cops, arranging for transport.

Hiroshi pulled Tim up to a sitting position and if the local cops hadn't been there, he would have smacked him. He was sick of this case and sick of tracking down suspects. Maybe this wouldn't be a dead-end, though. He leaned down to Tim. "Do you want to talk here or back at the station?"

Tim spit. His face was scraped and his sweatshirt torn. "The story's the same either place."

Chapter 28

Back at headquarters, Hiroshi stopped by his office and bolstered himself with two double espressos before heading down to the interrogation rooms. He felt the run in his legs, and Tim's punch had caught more of his head than he realized at the time. He thought about putting some ice on it. The headache was already starting.

Takamatsu and Ishii were waiting outside the rooms. Instead of flipping his lighter, as usual, Takamatsu was shaking the wrist Tim Branson bent. Ishii stood to the side as if they had done nothing more than sit in office chairs all morning.

"Go put some ice on it," Hiroshi told Takamatsu, though he didn't do that for his own head.

Takamatsu shook off his suggestion. "Ishii and I will watch his body language. Give us a summary of what he says after you're done."

"Ishii doesn't need a summary. Only you," Hiroshi reminded him.

"Oh, yeah, I forgot, we're internationalizing." Takamatsu headed to the observation room with Ishii, bending his wrist up and down.

Hiroshi entered the interrogation room and sat down across from Tim. He was getting really tired of this case, tracking two girls and their father with nothing to show, waiting for access to the Nine Dragons' files, getting punched in the head, and missing meals. He was starving. The room was overheated. Tim was sweating in his hooded sweatshirt and wool overshirt. Hiroshi took off his jacket.

"Was all that necessary?" Hiroshi stared at him.

Tim sighed. "I thought you were someone else."

Hiroshi waved for the camera to be turned on.

Michael Pronko

Tim ran the handcuffs back and forth through the eye bolt anchor in the table. "Are these necessary?"

"If you want me to bring in my colleague whose wrist you bent, he'll show you why they're necessary. You caught my head too."

Tim nodded apologetically. "My wife sent people to rough me up. Twice. They did a very good job. I thought you were the third round."

"It seems like you know how to fight."

"I do aikido."

"For self-defense?"

"That and it helped me quit the booze."

"Hitting a police officer—actually three officers—is a serious offense."

"You didn't identify yourself."

"There wasn't time."

Tim was sweating heavily. "Could you open a window or unzip this sweatshirt or something?"

The room was stifling. Hiroshi waved for the policewoman at the door to undo the cuffs so he could pull off his sweatshirt. She undid them, remaining poised in case Tim tried something.

He pulled off his wool overshirt and sweatshirt, wiped his face, and crumpled them on the table in front of him. The policewoman slid his cuffs back through the eyebolt in the table. His T-shirt was soaked with sweat.

Hiroshi asked for a bottle of tea. He pulled out his cellphone and scrolled through the information Akiko sent him. "Stalking, abduction, assault, disrupting a school zone, and mail fraud. Was that all in one day?"

"The mail fraud was a letter to my daughters. Assault was self-defense. It was my wife who abducted the kids. She dragged them back here from America and denied me custody."

"When was that?"

"Five years ago. There's a warrant out for her in Maryland, but it's not recognized in Japan."

206

"What's her name. I'll check on it."

"Saori Kano. Please check on her, and my daughters. Now, I'm just waiting for them to grow up. Once they turn eighteen, I can contact them without being arrested. I post a lot on social media, hoping they'll see it. They can find me if they want to."

"And while you wait, what are you doing for work?"

"They give me temporary visas, but that doesn't allow me to work. A lot of help that is."

"You're independently wealthy?"

"I work at a bookstore, teach English, do some modeling, which is why I came over here in the first place."

Tim had a rugged face with a strong jaw and a two-day beard. The kind of foreign man in countless ads. With just a T-shirt on, Hiroshi could tell he worked out. Probably had nothing much else to do.

"A car registered to you was at the scene of a crime. It was connected to the abduction of two girls. You want to tell me about that?"

Tim sighed. "I also register cars in my name. They're rented out short-term to foreigners in Japan."

"You own the cars?"

"They're just registered in my name."

"Looks like one of your cars is going to land you in jail. And this won't be any short-term thing."

"The car's used by whoever makes the reservation. Usually from abroad. Saves time with Japanese paperwork. You can see it on the website, Friendly Japan."

"My assistant found that. But we couldn't find a name and address for the owner."

"His name is John Smith."

Hiroshi stared at him. "John Smith? You expect me to believe that?"

"It really is his name. I don't know his address."

"So, you know nothing about the car or its whereabouts?"

"Like I said, all the rentals go through the site. I maintain the cars, do airport pick-ups, hand them the keys, that's it."

Takamatsu had taught him to back off when one direction wasn't working and return to it later. "Why did your wife send someone to work you over?"

Tim sighed and shook his head. "I wanted custody of the kids, or at least visitation rights. I got a lawyer, she got several lawyers, and they went at it. But in Japan, it doesn't matter what the wife did, they award custody to the mother. The husband, especially if he's a foreigner, is always wrong. *Gaijin* is a word I know well."

"Where is your wife from?"

A young guard brought in a bottle of tea for Tim. She set it down in front of him and stepped back to the door. Tim bowed thanks, cranked open the top, and leaned over to drink clumsily, the cuffs rattling. Tea spilled. Hiroshi didn't try to help.

"My wife's family is from all over. At least they have houses all over, Karuizawa, Hakone, and two apartments in Tokyo. I didn't know she was rich until we got married."

"With that kind of money, they usually don't resort to violence."

"They don't need to. My wife's family sent people twice, though. I can't imagine what whoppers she told them bout me. I was in the hospital for two weeks after the second attack, and they put it on *my* record. That's not against the law? That's not admissible in court?"

"How do you know it was her family?"

"They told me." Tim shook his head. "And she's the one who cheated on me. Right after my daughter was born. And not just once. I thought we'd work it out. I wanted to. She was such a beauty. In the end, she did what her family told her to do—lie to the judge."

"All of that was presented in evidence?"

"Of course. I refiled with a new lawyer and got help from a group of other parents in the same situation. Then I started

208

helping others."

"Do you know Patrick Walsh?" Hiroshi held up a photo of him on his cellphone.

Tim looked away.

"He's driving your car... or wait a minute, maybe it was you who abducted the girls?" Hiroshi let that sit. "Look, we need to find the girls. You need to help us. Now."

Tim leaned back in his chair. "I'm working shit jobs, waiting for my daughters to reach the age of majority so I can contact them without violating Japanese law. Why not wait in jail?"

"You want me to tell you why? You'll be fighting every day in there. There's no special American section with comforts from home. You'll be a sparring partner for everyone in there."

Someone knocked on the door and Hiroshi realized he was leaning halfway over the table. Sugamo was waving Hiroshi out to the hall. Hiroshi let the camera roll and walked out of the room.

"What did you find in Tim's apartment?" Hiroshi asked.

Sugamo shook his head. "There was nothing there. Photos of his daughters, his CV, a computer, some aikido stuff, luggage, clothes like he has on. Two tatami rooms and a small kitchen. Didn't take us long to find nothing."

"Is someone working on his cellphone?"

"They're trying."

Hiroshi went back into the interrogation room. His head was aching. He should have put ice on it. He sat down and stared at Tim. This was going nowhere and it was starting to piss him off even worse.

Tim shook his head. He was still sweating.

"So tell me where you met Patrick Walsh. Did you help him get a car, or something more?"

Tim took another sip of tea, looked at the wall, and resigned himself. "Through the support group. Some of them had some crazy ass shit with their wives and wives' families. We pool our knowledge, help each other out."

"Did you see the two girls? They could be in danger."

Tim looked up at the mirrored glass of the observation room and down at his cuffs. "They're not in danger. They're with their father."

"You saw them?"

"Briefly."

"So, you know where they are?"

"I told you, no."

"Where are the safe houses for this network?"

"There's nothing like that."

"You gave him the car and he drove off with the girls. That's it?"

"Yeah, that's it." Tim looked at Hiroshi. "Japanese think their country is so special that it doesn't have to follow the laws all other developed countries follow. So, it's really Japan that's breaking international law, not me."

"Unfortunately, aiding and abetting an abduction, fighting with police, and lying during an investigation are all crimes in every country."

Tim yanked on the cuffs. "Japanese always want to say they're unique, but that's not an explanation, it's an excuse for all kinds of bullshit."

Hiroshi smacked the table. "You think Americans don't spout off about how unique they are? You think Americans are open-minded about foreigners?" Hiroshi leaned forward and looked into Tim's eyes. "Why did Patrick come back?"

"He wanted to see his daughters. That shouldn't be a crime."

"How much did he pay you?"

"Nothing. He donated to the group's legal fund."

"Didn't you ask him about his money?"

"To me, he's just another father trying to take care of his kids."

"His trouble is working with the wrong people."

"So, you want him for his kids or for his work?"

"Both." Hiroshi tapped the table with his fist. "So, help us on the kids."

"He'd be treated unfairly in the courts here."

"You're not getting it. The girls are in more danger with him."

Tim looked away. "I want to see a lawyer. There's one in the father's support group who handles this."

Hiroshi pulled out his cellphone. "Tell me where he took the girls and I'll call the lawyer right now."

The door opened and Ishii ducked her head in. "We need to go," she said.

Hiroshi waved for the recording to be turned off and leaned his face close to Tim's. "You're in some seriously deep shit, so you better start helping us, or you're going to get in a lot deeper. Keep up that fucking attitude with me and you'll never see your daughters ever again. I'll make sure of that. You got it? Anything happens to those girls, it's on you."

Tim set his jaw and stared at the one-way glass to the observation room reflecting a blurred image of him and his situation.

Chapter 29

After Kosugi's men dropped them off at the West Shinjuku hotel, they hurried upstairs where they'd left their packed bags. Patrick got the girls to brush their teeth while he called Tim to see if he'd arranged something out of the country yet or not. Tim's phone rang, and flipped to message.

He redialed and heard it pick up. He waited patiently. Tim would have spoken right away. He'd always answered, overflowing with advice, comments, opinions.

Patrick hung up. Someone else had Tim's phone.

Tim had given him a backup number in case of emergencies. He looked at it for a minute, and let it go. It would be better to move on his own. But maybe Tim was right about one thing—the more conspicuous they were, the less they'd be noticed.

All right, they'd do conspicuous. There was only one place an American with two daughters would draw zero attention, and it would distract the girls until he could get the private jet arranged and try to figure out the best way to reunite with Miyuki.

The city gleamed outside the picture window. The sun threw sharp-angled shadows from the buildings, a skewed checkerboard of light and dark to the horizon. The landowners, development companies, and city planners planted cash and up grew buildings, each one a corporation of its own. From twenty-some floors up, it all looked easy.

Not so easy was figuring out who'd followed him and sent him the photos of the girls. If it wasn't Kosugi, then who was it? Who was the man in the pool the day before if not Kosugi's man? And where did he go? Was he one of the men who harassed Arisa at work?

He thought over what he'd seen when he logged into the accounts. Leung was moving money into short-term, high-risk investments, and then returning it, but why? There was enough cash to do that anyway, or enough to borrow on. Fiddling with investors' accounts in that way was asking for trouble, ensuring it.

Now that Leung was dead, he'd never know for certain. All he could do was damage control, and he'd better do it quickly. He was furious with himself for not bringing his computer with him. That was probably the stupidest thing he'd ever done in his life. He wouldn't let it be one of his last.

His phone rang. It was a number he didn't know. He didn't answer the call. Instead, he sent a text message to Miyuki telling her where they were going.

Miyuki wrote back, "Finalizing funeral stuff for my mother. Meet you after. I can't leave without doing that."

He hoped that's all it was. Was she being agreeable or just leading him on to get to the girls? Maybe she had the police sitting right beside her as she wrote. Or maybe she understood they had to get out of Japan, that this was serious.

The girls came skipping out of the bathroom in their bathrobes. He'd wanted them to shower again after Kosugi's place, which he knew was not really needed and mostly symbolic, but they didn't mind.

"Can we have pancakes for lunch?" Jenna stood behind Kiri and tickled her.

"You just had donuts. How much sugar can you hold?"

"More." They both giggled.

"We're going to get something healthy to eat at the new hotel. Let's get dressed."

"New hotel? What's wrong with this one?" Kiri put her hands on her hips.

"Can't we go back to the pool?" Jenna swam her arms around for dramatic effect.

"I think you'll like where we're going."

"Where?" Kiri had squirmed away from her sister.

"Where's your favorite place in the world?"

"Home?" Kiri wondered if that was the answer he wanted.

"I think we're supposed to say 'school.'" Jenna corrected her little sister.

"I mean, favorite *fun* place."

Kiri's eyes got big. "Disneyland?"

Patrick patted her little shoulder. "Wouldn't you rather have pancakes with Mickey's face on them?"

The girls pounced on him, hugged his legs, Kiri reaching up like she had when she could barely walk, begging him to pick her up. He pulled her up into his arms and Jenna jumped up and down. "Disney!"

Jenna tugged on him. "But what about school?"

"Listen, in America kids miss school for important things all the time. We're moving into our big house in Wyoming. We have a huge field with horses. And Mom's going to be so surprised. It's going to be fun."

Patrick's phone rang again. He ignored it and kneeled down and pulled them close. "So, can you help me until we get there? Mom's going to join us at the hotel. She doesn't know anything yet, so you'll have to promise to keep it a secret from her. Can you do that?" He gave them his serious face until they both nodded yes. "We better get packed."

The girls leapt for their clothes, picking out what new clothes to wear. "You didn't fold them right." Jenna frowned at her dad.

"Well, refold them correctly and let's get a move on. You think they're going to wait for us at Magic Mountain?"

"OK!" They started chatting about their day, which rides, which food, which shows, which photo spots.

Patrick took their passports and tucked them in his jacket pocket, arranged his own clothes, and hopped in for a quick shower. He bit the tags off with his teeth and pulled on his new clothes while the girls asked a million questions, trying to be good so the plan would not get changed.

After he checked under the bed, under the covers, in the bathroom, everywhere, he hoisted their two bags on his shoulders and Jenna took the laundry bag and her small carry-on. Kiri carried her own backpack and tucked her hand under Jenna's bag, trying to help.

Patrick stepped out of the room and scanned the hallway in both directions. He started toward the elevator staying ahead of the girls and looking behind. Down the hall was nothing but a flower arrangement in a blue vase and an abstract painting.

In the elevator, Jenna looked up at him. "Is Mom really going to meet us there?"

"You don't believe me?" He was trying to reassure himself as much as them.

"And it's OK to miss school?"

"You'll catch up."

They both nodded seriously, their loyalties divided, unsure if it was OK, but ready to go.

When they got to the lobby, he scanned every chair, pillar and visible space, but he couldn't see anyone. He rescanned it all. They got halfway across the lobby before the concierge came running over.

Patrick ignored her. His phone rang and he ignored it too. He told the girls not to move while he made sure the bill had been paid and they were all checked out.

The concierge brought over two bags with pink, silver, and purple characters on the outside for Kiri and Jenna. They set their bags down, bowed, and thanked her in polite Japanese. The new gift bags wouldn't fit inside their other bags.

The concierge smiled. "Can I arrange transport for you? Where are you off to today?"

"Disneyland!" the girls chorused.

"We couldn't get a flight on such short notice, but we have one for late tomorrow. That gives us today and tomorrow morning in Disney. We can take a taxi."

"Our service is very reliable and not much more expensive." The concierge pulled out her phone and called to arrange it.

"We're fine." Patrick leaned down to the girls. "Can you put those nice presents in your bags?"

"They won't fit," Jenna said.

He carefully zipped open the top of his laundry bag and jammed them in, harder than he'd intended.

"Don't break them," Kiri said.

He left them to go over and be sure they were checked out and they could get away without being noticed. The clerk waved the paper in the air and tucked it into a file below the counter, assuring him it had all been taken care of.

Patrick got the girls to pick things up and move toward the elevators.

The concierge came after them. "The car is expecting you downstairs. Let me get a bellhop for your bags."

"We're fine." The elevator came right away and they got on, waving politely to the concierge as the doors shut. The girls were excited and he put a hand on them to calm them as they rode down.

At the entryway, he hurried toward the drop-off circle. A bellhop came to help with the bags and Patrick waved him off. He set the bags down and looked for a taxi, hoping to get away as quickly as possible. Shinjuku Station was not far through an underground walkway with entrances all through West Shinjuku.

A black sedan, similar to the one Patrick borrowed from Tim, pulled up to the curb. Patrick searched along the circle for a regular taxi, the quickest way out. Taxis were parked at the far end of the circle, but didn't come when he waved to them.

Out of the black sedan, a tall Asian man in a white T-shirt and blue blazer turned and smiled with both hands on top of the car. "Are you Patrick Walsh?" he asked in English, smiling.

Patrick looked at him. Who was this? The guy from the pool? Another of Kosugi's men? Was this who the concierge called? The bellhop stood by the bags, looking back and forth at the car, Patrick, and the bags.

The tall Asian man frowned when Patrick didn't budge, and waved them inside with a smile. "Tim sent me."

Another car pulled up behind the black sedan and an older driver wearing white gloves got out and hustled over to the bellhop. The bellhop was confused and tried to explain to the driver who had called him. The bellhop pointed at them, but Patrick ignored him. He didn't want to get in any of those cars. He didn't trust any of them.

He stooped down to whisper to Kiri and Jenna. "We're going to walk to the station, OK? There's a tunnel that goes there. It's fun, but you've got to stay close to me and move fast."

"Why aren't we taking the car?" Kiri asked in a whisper.

"Yeah, why not?" Jenna pulled on her bag.

"The train is better." Patrick took the bags and hoisted them on his shoulders. He headed the girls toward the underground pedestrian walkway to Shinjuku Station, ignoring the bellhop and the tall Asian man. He wanted to get out of there, and the train would work. Public spaces felt safer.

At the end of the drop-off area, the door of a black van with tinted windows slid open. A man stepped out wearing a shiny orange tie that gleamed against his black outfit. He had a pale, concave face that arced down like a bony shovel.

When he pulled off his sunglasses, Patrick saw the man from the pool the day before.

Chapter 30

The shovel-faced man in black took a step toward him, but Patrick kept going toward the stairs to the underground walkway. He heard him give the car three loud raps with his palm, but he didn't look back.

The stairs led to a walkway lined by coffee, lunch, and drinking places for the workers in the skyscrapers towering above. The girls were following along like little angels on their journey to a Disney ending. He hoped.

"I want to go on the pirates one and the world one," Kiri said.

"We're going on all of them," Patrick assured her.

"Splash Mountain for me," Jenna said.

"Can you swim?" Patrick teased her.

"You just saw us in the pool," Jenna protested.

Kiri looked up at him. "It's in a boat, Dad."

The underground passageway was busy with people heading from Shinjuku Station to West Shinjuku. When they arrived inside the station's busy open area, Patrick herded them to the ticket machines. A huge train map of Tokyo with each line in a different color spread across the wall above.

He didn't know the *kanji* for Maihama, the Disney station, but knew roughly where it was. They had to transfer at Tokyo Station. He got three tickets and hurried them to the gate. He would redo the fare when they got off.

He looked behind for the first time, worried what he would find. All he saw was the fast flow of people through the station, some headed to the department stores above, some to other train lines, others just passing through the tunnels crisscrossing the station.

There was no man in black with an orange tie and no tall Asian guy in T-shirt and blazer.

Patrick went through the ticket gate first, followed by Jenna. He saw the sign for their platform, but Kiri gave a little shout. Patrick whipped around. The wicket had shut with Kiri outside and the ticket on the inside of the machine. How did she manage that?

He hurried back to the gate and waved Kiri toward the office at the side. He spoke to the guard in rapid-fire English. The guard nodded listlessly, frowned at Kiri, and waved her through.

"I'm sorry, poppa. I didn't go through quick enough, and it shut."

"It's OK, baby, let's go."

They walked awkwardly through the dense crowd. Kiri and Jenna weren't quite used to commuting, especially with heavy bags, and he stepped back to help them. They didn't commute on their own yet. That's why they needed Taiga.

When they got to the top of the escalator to their platform, the express train arrived, and Patrick fast-stepped the girls on and found a place by the door. He watched the doors close and ducked down to survey the platform through the window. The doors opened to let someone off or on in another car, then shut again, and the train took off.

Patrick pulled Jenna and Kiri close, positioned the bags at their feet, and then told the girls to enjoy the ride. "First ride of the day," he whispered.

"Slowest ride of the day," Jenna said. Kiri kicked her feet.

In the Disneyland hotel, they could stay hidden amid the families and he would have time to get the private jet arranged.

The tall Asian guy speaking perfect English maybe was from the support group. Did the group send him in Tim's place? Why didn't they let him know? Was that who had called him? They must have his number. Maybe he was going to contact him after he arrived at the hotel.

And where was Tim? Who was the guy from the swimming pool if he wasn't one of Kosugi's men? Someone else after their money from Nine Dragons? The other clients would not be so accommodating as Kosugi.

The train made its first stop. The doors opened, letting in a cool stream of air to the sun-warmed interior. The passenger sitting next to Kiri got up suddenly and hurried off. Kiri plopped down and patted the seat for Jenna, both of them so thin they could fit into one person's space. He adjusted their masks and arranged the bags into a tight stack at their feet.

At the next stop, more passengers got off than on. He searched both directions and was startled to see the tall Asian guy in a T-shirt and blazer and white mask. Patrick averted his eyes but noticed him sending a message on his phone.

Immediately, Patrick got a message. "The network sent me."

"What network?" Patrick wrote back.

"Support network."

Patrick frowned.

"To help. Told to stay with you. Easier in the car."

"Where's Tim?" Patrick looked over at him. He was Asian, but maybe not Japanese, or he lived outside Japan for a long time. His blazer and T-shirt were designer brands and his cellphone a new, large model.

The text said: "Something happened."

"What happened?"

"We're not sure yet, but I'm here to be sure you're all right."

"Tim didn't answer my calls."

"I'm taking his place. We have a plan."

"Poppa, are you OK?" Jenna tugged on his pant leg.

He smiled. "I'm fine. Just thinking."

Kiri kicked her feet and whispered, "I have to pee."

"One more stop and we switch trains. Can you wait?"

Kiri wiggled on the bench and nodded. Jenna patted her and advised her to think of something else. Patrick put his phone away.

The train pulled into Tokyo Station and Patrick gathered their bags, letting the other passengers jackrabbit off wherever they were going. The Asian guy at the other end of the train car got off slowly, checking his phone.

And that's when Patrick saw the man in the orange tie, the one outside the hotel, from the pool. He couldn't see his shovel-shaped face below his black mask, but it was him.

Of course it would have been easy for them to catch up on the way to the station and to stay hidden in the throngs of commuters and the crush of people on the train.

"Can we hurry a little?" Kiri said. "I really have to pee."

"It's just downstairs. Let's be careful on the escalator."

The two-story escalator down to the central walkway of the station moved at a slow pace. Patrick steadied the bags with one hand and held Kiri's arm with the other. Jenna was behind her. Several people behind Jenna stood the shovel-faced guy and several steps above him was the guy replacing Tim. Had they seen each other? If he was going to lose them anywhere, it would be in the crowds of Tokyo Station.

Patrick patted Kiri's shoulder. "We'll be there in a minute, sweetie." She put her hand on his and he felt the familiar circuit connect.

When they got to the ground floor, Kiri started dancing. Patrick didn't bother to look back at the two men. He scanned the overhead signs, dozens of them, for a female figure in red and a male figure in blue. An arrow mercifully pointed the way.

The crowd flowed around them as they hurried past bento shops, souvenir stands, and chain restaurants to the side hall where the toilets were. Patrick wanted to drag all three of them into the diaper changing and handicapped toilet, but it was occupied. Kiri was close to losing it.

Patrick leaned down. "Jenna, can you take your sister inside?"

"Sure. I need to go too."

"Yes. But hurry, OK? And don't talk to anyone. Come right back out."

They scampered to the entrance and Patrick watched them dart around the wall to the interior where he couldn't see.

Patrick rebalanced the bags by a row of lockers and scanned the fast-moving crowd for the support group guy and the shovel-faced man in black. Not seeing them made him more nervous.

He peered into the toilet and drew a concerned stare from a woman coming out. Patrick stepped to the side, trying to appear innocent. He needed a piss himself but he'd have to put it off. What he really needed was Miyuki.

If he could dodge the two guys and get to the hotel at Disneyland, they'd have time to talk after the girls were worn out from the rides. He could arrange the private jet, and together they'd decide what to do and how to do it. Even a temporary fix would be better than nothing.

Plus he had his backup plan for Nine Dragons.

All of that depended on shaking the two guys trailing him.

He stood by the women's toilet again, drawing glances from women coming out, and resigned himself to waiting a little longer. He searched the crowd but saw nothing unusual. After Wyoming, Tokyo was exhausting. So many people in constant motion, too many to consider. He wondered if this would be the last day he'd ever see the place.

A tiled wall blocked the view inside. He moved to the side, wondering whether he should call in to them. The handicapped toilet was still in use, or broken. Patrick left the bags and walked closer to the entrance of the women's toilet to peer in.

A businesswoman with a briefcase and a navy blue trench coat over her arm came out and stopped in front of him. "Can I help you?" she said in curt English.

"Oh, you speak English. Yes, actually. My two daughters are in there. They've been in there for a long time. My wife's not here and..."

She scrutinized the toilet, Patrick, and the bags. "What are their names?"

"Jenna and Kiri."

"Do they speak Japanese?"

"Yes."

She frowned at him, reset her bag on her shoulder, and marched inside. In a few minutes, she returned, frowning more deeply and shaking her head. "They went in when?"

"Ten minutes ago."

"Kiri and Jenna?"

"Yes." Didn't she trust him to know his own daughters' names? The woman went back in again.

Patrick walked over and kicked the bags, then went close to the entrance again.

Two young women, with shopping bags crooked over their elbows, came out, surprised at him trying to peek inside. They started whispering.

Patrick pointed inside. "*Musume*," he said, knowing the word for "daughter" better than any other in Japanese.

Patrick felt a tap on his shoulder from behind. He turned to see the woman in the trench coat.

"There's another exit." She pointed around the corner.

Patrick walked to the side and stared down the busy passageway at the other exit to the women's toilet.

Chapter 31

Patrick walked back and forth between the toilet entrances. How could the girls have gone out the wrong door? Surely they were old enough to figure it out and come back. They just got turned around. He looked around wildly, but the constant flow of people blocked any clear view of someone Kiri and Jenna's height.

The businesswoman in the trench coat gave the two young fashionistas an explanation about the girls. They covered their mouths in horror. The women discussed the situation, and a few more women gathered listening intently.

If he'd spent more time learning Japanese and less time moving money overseas, he'd be better off at the moment. The women finished talking and everyone but the businesswoman scurried off.

In English, she said, "They'll look for your daughters and you come with me over to the *koban* police box."

"No," Patrick said.

This was not the answer she was expecting. "The police will help," the woman said. "You need to tell them quickly so they can hurry. Those women will go that way, and the young women will go the other way. Come with me."

Patrick felt like a stupid child unable to manage even the basics of life. What kind of father was he? The businesswoman took Patrick by the arm and pulled him along.

Patrick didn't see any way to avoid the *koban*. He picked up their bags, trying to think of how to keep the police from seeing his face. The police would surely have a photo of him and Kiri and Jenna, but he'd let himself be arrested if he could just get them back.

At the door of the *koban*, housed in a small glass-walled room at the end of a row of souvenir stands, two uniformed policemen dragged in a red-faced drunk shouting belligerently. The officers hustled him to the back room and dropped him onto a chair.

A portly officer with a round, red face came to the counter and listened to the businesswoman explain what happened. He nodded placidly and picked up the phone. He made several phone calls in brisk tones. When he hung up, he called the two officers who'd brought the drunk in and explained. They looked at Patrick and hurried off into the crowd.

The drunk man tried to stumble out of the room, but the portly cop grabbed his wrist, twisted gently, and moved him back inside the room as easily as opening a door. He scolded the drunk until he flopped down and dropped his head in his hands. Patrick wondered why they didn't handcuff him or punch him or something.

The portly officer came back and spoke to the businesswoman.

She translated. "Do you have photos of your daughters?"

Patrick kept his face away from the officer and held out the wallpaper photo of them on his cellphone. Kiri and Jenna beamed out, and Patrick choked back another surge of panic.

The police officer examined the photos and called to the back room. A female officer came out, took a photo of the photo and hurried off.

The businesswoman translated. "She'll check the other women's toilets."

"Where were you going today?" the officer asked.

Patrick understood that much Japanese. "Disneyland."

The officer nodded and turned his attention to someone asking for directions.

The businesswoman patted Patrick on the arm. "They won't get out of the station, don't worry."

Patrick stood outside the door and kept looking through the crowd for Kiri and Jenna, hoping the officer wouldn't figure out who he was. He was sure he'd be on every list in every *koban* in the country, but Tokyo Station was a city unto itself. A million people a day passed through. Or maybe the officer was waiting to find the girls before arresting him.

The girls could be waiting for him by the Keiyo Line entrance. They knew the name of the train line that went to Disneyland. He wanted to run off in that direction, but that would seem suspicious. He'd just have to wait.

The officer stepped out beside Patrick with his hands in his pistol belt. In the unceasing flow, it was hard to pick out individual people, much less two little girls, even his own.

The police phone rang, and Patrick turned to it expectantly. The phone seemed to be some inter-station system, not the regular phone. The officer hung up and picked up one of the cellphones on the counter. He set it down again, still calm, as if two girls were lost in the station every day, and maybe there were.

The drunk in the backroom started yelling again, and the plump officer went back, and told him to be quiet. He and Kyle had been stopped by Japanese police several times in their first couple of years in Roppongi or wherever they happened to be partying. Kyle thought it was because they were foreigners, but Patrick thought it was because they were drunk.

The guy in the backroom yelled again. Patrick wondered, again, why they didn't do anything about him. He turned back to the stream of commuters and thought of his own father.

He'd gotten his father out of the drunk tank in the South Boston Police Department when he was young. Many times. He'd learned it was best to say nothing to the cops, pay the fine, and take his father home. His father once claimed he was beaten by the police, but Patrick knew it was a bar fight or a money lender.

His mother had stuck with his father even when he gambled away the mortgage and they'd been evicted. Patrick came home from university one day to find out they moved into his aunt's place, or his mother did. His father was off on a bender.

His father spiraled down from there. The last time he'd seen his father was when he left his Econ final to get him out of jail. His father asked him what he was going to do with his life and Patrick told him, "Get the hell out of here." "Good," his father replied. Those were the last words they exchanged.

He wasn't sure why he thought about that. It wasn't the police. It was the promise he made that day not to have kids unless he provided for them. His father was a gambler, always waiting on the big win, always losing. Patrick realized he was a gambler too, only at a different level with different bets, a different sort of waiting on the win. He wasn't going to lose, though. He wasn't going to end up like his father.

And then there they were.

Jenna was talking with the young policewoman, and Kiri was between the two fashionable shoppers, all of them giggling like they were out shopping, like it was nothing.

When the girls saw him, they ran to him, and Patrick stooped down and wrapped them in his arms. "Where did you go?"

They hugged him and wiggled, too excited to explain.

Jenna bowed to the policewoman and got Kiri to bow too.

He held them close. "What happened? You gave me a scare."

Jenna switched to English. "We washed our hands and went out the door. I got turned around."

Patrick squatted down. "Did someone lead you out the wrong way?"

Jenna looked down, ashamed. "No. I had to wait for Kiri and she said it was the right way, but I was looking in the mirror and thought it was the other way and you weren't outside. There were a lot of people."

The businesswoman smiled, and Patrick thanked her. She spoke to the girls, giving them advice about toilets in train stations. They nodded obediently and thanked her in polite Japanese.

Patrick surveyed the surrounding people for the two guys he

suspected were still following them, but he couldn't see either one. They must have stayed at a distance to avoid the police. Or maybe he'd lost them and they were gone.

This was their chance. Patrick thanked the two shoppers in the few polite Japanese phrases Miyuki made him memorize. The young fashion-loving women cooed at his daughters. "Your daughters so cute!" one managed in English.

Patrick told Jenna to tell the police they were fine and that they were late to meet their mother at Disneyland.

"Mom's coming?" Jenna smiled. She straightened up as if she was five years older and explained to the police.

Patrick bowed his thanks, keeping his face averted. "All right, all right. We're late for Disneyland. Let's go."

The drunk in the other room started to push his way out. He was agitated but could barely walk. The two young policemen blocked the doorway, and the older officer turned his attention to a phone call. If it were South Boston, he'd have been clubbed silent long since.

Patrick pulled the bags onto his shoulders and hurried them off toward the Keiyo Line. He could feel his cellphone buzzing, but he ignored it as they headed down a long passageway with moving sidewalks that would deliver them to the Disney-bound train.

He realized he wasn't going to manage much more of this without Miyuki's help. He leaned against the moving handrail and checked his messages.

"You're always checking your cellphone," Jenna said. "You should learn to be in the moment."

Patrick laughed. "Where did you hear that?"

"Taiga says that. He studied Buddhism."

"He what?" Patrick hoped he was OK, that it had been just a bump and a bruise and nothing more.

Kiri tugged on Patrick's pants. He still felt like scolding them for getting lost, but it was fantastic to have her tugging on him again. "Taiga went to a temple in the mountains. I want to go too."

Jenna laughed. "Will you take us, Poppa?"

"We can do that instead of going to Disneyland if you want?"

Jenna and Kiri looked at each other. "Can't we go to Disney now and to the temple later?"

"We're going to America tomorrow. Do you think temples have horses? Do you know how to ride a horse?"

Jenna and Kiri laughed and shook their heads.

"Well, you're going to have to learn. What color horse would you like?"

"What are the choices?" Jenna asked. Kiri shrugged and giggled.

"Let's go or we'll miss the train." Patrick looked behind him and hurried the girls down the escalator, across the platform, and onto the express train. The station nearest Disney wasn't far.

Patrick sent a message to Miyuki, telling her they were fine and not to worry. He realized he was trying to tell himself that. He suggested she come the next morning. They'd be fine at the hotel until then. He hoped that was true. It seemed like she trusted him, but what did that mean anymore?

She wrote back, "OK." What did that mean anymore?

Chapter 32

Ota had been following Miyuki Walsh all day on simple errands. It was confusing trying to connect the law office in Akasaka with the small lane in Kokubunji, but following anyone through Tokyo when you didn't know what they were doing was confusing.

Ota was Shibutani's best private investigator. Shibutani, who had worked with Takamatsu in homicide for years, coordinated from the office while Ota put shoes on the street and eyes on the suspect.

Ota's deafness occasionally presented a hurdle, but he and Shibutani worked fine with it. A plain leather jacket, which held everything he needed, good walking shoes, and neat but longish hair allowed Ota to blend in anywhere. Being deaf, he saw more and was seen less. For most work, he didn't need to hear. He needed to watch.

Miyuki walked out of the building. He'd waited outside her apartment all night, dozing on a bench and reading all afternoon with nothing happening. He took a couple chances going to a convenience store to pee and restock *onigiri* rice balls and bottled tea. At last, he could move.

Ota slipped a telephoto lens on his cellphone and tested the resolution, taking a few shots and deleting them. Miyuki was dressed in black funeral clothes with low heels. She was very beautiful, like a model for funeral outfits.

When she headed to the subway, Ota had to move quickly to stay with her. He guessed she was heading to make funeral arrangements for her mother, but it was getting late, and he wondered if the funeral parlor would still be open. He'd been briefed on the story from Shibutani.

He was about to follow her down the steps to the subway when a tall man cut in front of him. He'd seen him somewhere.

Ota hung back and let the guy get ahead so he could move parallel and squeeze off photos of the man's face.

As the man turned down the stairs after Miyuki, Ota took a few more shots and had to hurry to get on the same train. Once he got on, he stored the telephoto attachment in a pocket—he had a pocket for everything—and sent the photos to Shibutani in his Akabane office.

Shibutani wrote back telling Ota to get a better shot.

He couldn't do it on the train, so he waited until she and the man got out at the stop nearest Zoshigaya Cemetery. He wore all black, too, as if in mourning himself.

Upstairs, the exit led to a busy road between the Gokokuji Temple and the cemetery. The surrounding lanes were lined by wooden buildings selling flowers, incense, and brooms for cleaning graves. One or two stone-carver workshops remained, but most were converted to showrooms, the actual carving done elsewhere. To Ota, the cars whizzing by, their rush-rush, high-speed vibrations, felt like a violation of the sacred area.

Miyuki entered a brownish-beige, two-story box of windowless concrete. Ota assumed it was the cemetery office. He took a photo to make sure. "Sato" was the name of the funeral service.

The man in black walked to the corner. He wore a shiny maroon tie against a black shirt, covered by a black jacket and black overcoat. He probably had black underwear.

Ota walked halfway up the stairs of the overpass to get a better angle. He slipped the finger-sized telephoto back on and pretended to be looking at the cemetery grounds while pointing the camera at the man. He caught the man's face—pale and concave—from different angles.

Ota stopped to look at the photos. He was one of the men harassing the woman in Kokubunji when he'd followed Miyuki there. How did he get so close to Miyuki? Ota thought back to whether he'd been followed. In Kokubunji, they'd driven off in their car.

Ota sent these better shots to Shibutani. He still couldn't figure anything out and neither could Shibutani, but they made a record of it all, as Takamatsu asked.

Miyuki came out of the building and strode up the overpass, walking right past the man in black without noticing him.

Ota sent a quick message to Shibutani, asking about limits, something he always did before going over them. Shibutani told him to go ahead. Takamatsu would sort it out later.

The pale-faced man followed Miyuki from a few paces behind, much closer than Ota would have. Ota waited patiently until they got across and then hurried across the overpass after them.

Shibutani texted Ota. "Nothing in the database from that photo. Try another angle."

Ota texted as he walked. "If they split up, do you want me to follow the guy or Miyuki?"

Shibutani texted back. "Stick with Miyuki. Don't let her out of your sight until she's safely back in her apartment."

Ota sent back an OK emoji and hustled to keep them in view.

Miyuki went down to the subway and Ota hurried to catch up. He hustled down the escalator and got to the platform as the Yurakucho Line train pulled in. They got on three separate cars, Miyuki in the middle and Ota and the pale-faced guy on either side.

Miyuki switched to the Hibiya Line and got off at Hiroo Station. On the street, she turned in the opposite direction of her apartment, the guy still following her. Ota followed them down a narrow, winding street with a railing dividing the pedestrian and car lanes.

Miyuki stopped in front of a new-looking building so narrow the stairs were on the outside. She climbed up to the top floor and entered without knocking.

Ota ducked behind a concrete planter for a large tree set below a curved wall. The guy in black stopped on the opposite side in front of an apartment building fronted by maple trees and thick ivy.

They both waited, on opposite sides, for Miyuki to emerge.

After a half hour, Miyuki came down the steps talking with a handsome man in loose-fitting pants and a retro paisley shirt. He had collar-length hair and kept his glasses on top of his head. He stopped at the bottom of the stairs with a hand on her arm, nodding at everything she said.

Ota squeezed off several nice, clean shots.

They gave each other a hug and kiss on the cheek, just a bit closer than with a client, and closer than most relatives. Miyuki headed downhill, and the man stood there watching her walk away.

Ota hurried over to snap a photo of the company names on the building. "Sato" again, but there were millions of Sato's in Tokyo. He turned back, but the pale-faced guy in black had disappeared. That was not a good sign.

He waited until Miyuki turned at the big street ahead and then hurried after her with one eye out for the guy and one on Miyuki. He texted Shibutani the company names.

Shibutani texted back that it was probably a client of hers from the bank. Ota wrote back that it was something more, but he'd missed a photo of their embrace.

Miyuki headed back to her apartment, thankfully, where it was easier to keep an eye on her. He needed a break and didn't want to sleep on the bench another night. He texted Shibuta to ask if the police were still in the apartment.

Shibutani texted he didn't know. "Just follow her to the door."

Ota waited until she put the code into the small password panel. The automatic glass doors slid shut behind her. The guy in black didn't seem to be anywhere around. Ota searched in all directions, waiting for him to emerge.

Ota turned toward the convenience store down the street, but a sudden blur of motion from the apartment lobby caught his eye.

He hurried to the automatic doors and pressed his face to the glass. Two men, one on each side, were pulling Miyuki into the elevator.

He looked at the password panel in frustration and texted Shibutani.

Shibutani texted to wait while he called Takamatsu.

A couple arrived, arm in arm. The man put in the security code, and Ota slipped in after them, holding his phone to his ear like half the people in Tokyo did, acting like a resident.

Ota rode the elevator to Miyuki's floor and ran down the hall to her door. With one hand, he banged on the door, and with the other unzipped the pocket in his leather jacket for what he needed. If the police were still there, they'd answer right away.

They didn't, so he pounded again, in short, hard bursts, ready. He couldn't hear if they said anything, so he pounded again.

The door opened a crack. It wasn't police. Ota jammed his shoe in and reached his arm toward whoever was on the other side.

His handheld stun gun connected and the door loosened. He shoved his shoulder into the door and stepped past a young guy clutching his chest and trying to breathe.

Ota kneed him on the side of his knee and he spun backward.

Miyuki was on her knees on the floor with the other guy standing over her.

Ota charged forward and jammed the stun gun into his back before he could turn around. The guy bucked, spun, and dropped to the floor.

As he turned to help Miyuki, Ota felt hands on his shoulders. He jammed his elbow back, hard and square, spun around, and rammed the stun gun into the guy's gut. He fell over and flailed like a harpooned fish.

Before he recovered, Ota kneeled down and slipped zip ties around the guy's ankles. He rolled him over, the guy still shaking from the zap, and zip-tied his wrist.

The first guy started crawling. Ota put his boot on his back and flattened him to the floor. He dropped both knees onto his back and held the stun gun so he could see it to get him to stop wiggling. When he stopped, he zip-tied him.

Ota stood up slowly.

Miyuki looked at him, confused.

Ota tried reading her lips, but she ignored him and swung her purse down on the head of the guy at her feet, landing it again and again until he curled up. She started on the other guy worming his way toward the wall, but she was crying too hard to land a solid blow.

When she slowed down, wobbling, Ota caught her arm and held his hand up for her to stop and calm down.

Miyuki spoke to Ota.

He couldn't read her lips because she was breathing so hard and her lips were trembling.

"I'm deaf," Ota said in slurred speech.

Miyuki blinked at him.

Ota pointed at his ears. "I'm deaf." He'd been through this a thousand times. He pulled out his cellphone and gestured for her to read what he was going to write on his cellphone.

"My name's Ota. I'm deaf." He showed her the message, and she nodded at him. "I was sent to watch you."

"By who? Patrick?"

"No, not him. But I'm sure he'd approve."

Miyuki nodded, trying to compose herself, wiping her face. She took his cellphone from him and typed, "Thank you."

Ota typed. "Do you know these guys?"

"They're hosts from Taiga's former club," she typed. She pulled back her foot to kick the guy in the ribs but Ota held his hand up to stop her.

He handed her the stun gun. There was plenty of charge left.

Chapter 33

Hiroshi had gone back and forth from his office to interrogating Tim most of the afternoon. Tim didn't give up much, but each time, something flaked off, like chipping a block of ice. Takamatsu had given up and went to fill in paperwork.

Ishii called Hiroshi and Takamatsu and told them to wait at the back door of the station. Taiga was out of his coma. Ishii was the only one with energy left, and that was a help in itself. He wondered if interrogating anyone else would help. Tokyo was too big to search for two girls.

Waiting for Ishii to pull the car around, Takamatsu lit a cigarette. "At least we've got everyone we need to interview in the same place now—the hospital."

Traffic was heavy but it wasn't a long drive. In the car, Takamatsu opened the window and blew his smoke outside. "I don't buy this parent snatching his kids thing."

Hiroshi checked his cellphone. "Parents get jealous, angry, vengeful."

"Over their kids? That's why I don't like these marriage cases, especially international ones."

"You sound like that judge."

Takamatsu took a drag of his cigarette. "The judge doesn't like international marriages because it offends his sense of purity. I don't like them because they're messy and dangerous. Families are inherently screwed up. Man and wife were not meant to live together peaceably."

"You'll win this year's all-Japan award for marital fidelity."

Takamatsu smiled. "Some people have affairs to keep their marriage together. Others to wreck it."

"What's your wife do while you're working?" Ishii asked.

Takamatsu laughed. "Lunch, shopping, yoga. Her chatterbox

sister moved close to us. They talk half the day."

"I didn't know you were so traditional?" Ishii smiled.

"I'm not. It just worked out that way. I've been married for forty years. Never a fight." Takamatsu lapsed back into quietude.

At the Nakano Police Hospital, they parked close and the three of them stopped by reception to get the room number and a map of the hospital. Taiga was put in a new ward none of them had been to before.

"Should we talk to Kyle again? He might have thought of something," Ishii suggested.

Takamatsu sighed. "Let's not and say we did. He's probably too sedated."

Hiroshi held up the map to see how to navigate to the room. The hallways were confusingly connected. Hiroshi wondered how the different buildings had been joined. None of the corridors seemed to line up. After a wrong turn and a backtrack, they found the right ward.

At the nurses' station, Ishii showed her badge to the head nurse writing on a chart. Ishii smiled and leaned across the counter. "Did Taiga Smith Sato say anything before he woke up?"

The nurse put down the tablet with the charts. "We kept him sedated, but he was disturbed and restless. When we let him wake up, he said many things that made no sense. That often happens. We got the name of his brother out of him and he's on his way. He mentioned two girls' names so many times all the nurses remember them—Jenna and Kiri."

"Any other visitors?"

"One. A man in a black suit and shiny tie."

"What did he look like?"

"Tall, thin face, longish hair. He asked if Taiga was awake, but then left. We called security in case he returns."

"No one else?"

She shook her head, busy filling in blanks on the chart.

"And how is Taiga now?"

She flipped through the tablet computer holding his charts. "Extensive bruising, cracked rib, broken nose. Internal bleeding, but we got that under control." The nurse closed the chart. "Also, he had signs of anorexia and traces of amphetamines in his system."

"Those were recent, the amphetamines?"

"It stays in urine for five days or so." The nurse gave them an "I'm really busy" look.

They let her go and walked to Taiga's room. The local policeman stationed there overnight bowed to the detectives.

Taiga's face was covered in bruises, his nose wrapped in a small pyramid of bandages, his body barely visible beneath the sheet.

Taiga's eyes opened when he heard the detectives. He nodded like he knew what was coming. He propped himself up, shifting the IV drips snaking into his arm.

Hiroshi and Ishii stood close to the bed. Takamatsu stood back and watched.

Hiroshi rolled the drip stand to the side. "I'm Detective Hiroshi Shimizu. We're investigating what happened to you and to Jenna and Kiri. What do you remember?"

Taiga's face was too swollen to show any emotion. His eyes dropped deep inside the bruised, puffy flesh. "Jenna and Kiri's father was in the living room when I came back." He spoke in a crow-like voice, distant and raspy.

"You're sure it was the girls' father?"

"I'd seen him in photos."

"You're sure it was him?"

"I only saw him for a minute before he swung a heavy bag."

"He hit you?"

"I can't remember exactly." He closed his eyes and took a huge breath, which made him wince. "Next thing I know, I woke up with someone smashing my face into the tatami."

"Patrick?"

Taiga frowned and shook his head.

"Could you see him?"

"Them."

"It wasn't Patrick?"

"They dressed in black."

"So, the father had help?" Hiroshi looked at Ishii, who was listening with her arms folded.

"He wasn't there. He was gone."

"He wasn't watching from a distance?"

"I couldn't see. Two guys held me down and kept hitting me. One gave the orders."

"In English?"

"Japanese. It was strange-sounding, like from an old movie." Taiga resettled his bandaged head on the pillow.

"How do you know it wasn't the girls' father?"

"The girls told me he only spoke English. These three guys swore fluently in Japanese."

"And then?"

"And then I blacked out. They kicked me. Many times." Taiga pulled up the hospital gown to show his blue and purple ribs. He shivered. "The nurses told me to keep breathing deeply, but it hurts too much."

"And then what?"

"Miyuki came back. I felt her hand and passed out again."

Hiroshi stepped back from the bed and looked at Ishii. Takamatsu shrugged and walked into the hall.

Hiroshi tried to make sense of Taiga's story. If there were three people in the apartment after Patrick left, how did they get in? And what did they want?

"Are the girls OK?" Taiga asked.

"We're trying to find them. Their father took them, it seems."

"I'm glad it wasn't those three guys."

"Did they ask about Kiri and Jenna?"

Taiga nodded. "They shouted 'Where are the girls?' I wanted

to get up and kill them, but I couldn't move. They held me down." Tears poured down both sides of his face. "You'll find them, won't you? I'll watch them better next time." He started to cry harder. "And their grandmother?"

"She died."

"I thought so. I heard them attack her too." Taiga's face wrinkled up. "Kiri and Jenna's father hit me. But it wasn't him who beat me up."

"Your wallet, keys, and cellphone were missing."

Taiga shook his head and shrugged. "Are you going to find the girls?"

"How did those guys get into the apartment?"

Taiga wiped the tears, touching his nose, shuddering in pain. Ishii handed him a tissue from the bedside table.

A tall, well-dressed salaryman rushed into the room. Ignoring the detectives, he went straight to Taiga and hugged him. "What happened?" he asked in English.

After they talked for a minute, the salaryman turned to the detectives and bowed. "I'm Leon. Taiga's brother. I'm sorry for this trouble. I've been away on business."

"I'm Detective Hiroshi and this is Detective Ishii. That's Detective Takamatsu by the door."

Leon patted his brother's shoulder. "Tell them what they need to know. Whatever it is."

Taiga's face clouded over. It took him several tries to start explaining. "I thought she changed the locks after she filed for divorce. She gave me a new key. I thought the old one wouldn't work. I thought it would be OK."

"You thought what would be OK?" Ishii asked.

"The other hosts at my old club said they helped people get into places to steal a few things. Some of the hosts stole keys, and sold them. I never did that before. I thought I'd trick them and sell them the old one. But she didn't change the lock. She just made new keys."

"How much did they pay you?" Hiroshi asked.

Leon tightened his grip on Taiga's shoulder. "Taiga. Tell them everything."

"I'm so sorry." Taiga took his older brother's hand. "I was doing so well, Leon. I took care of the girls and I was studying. All I did was sell them the key."

Hiroshi leaned toward Taiga. "Who did you sell the key to exactly?"

"I'm glad it was me they beat up instead of the girls."

"Who did you sell it to?"

"I handed it to the hosts at the club. They were going to sell it to some guy named Nozaki. The owner of the club knew him. They were just going to take things, and that's it."

"That's what they told you?" Ishii asked.

Taiga nodded. "I was so stupid."

"You didn't see who they sold it to? This Nozaki?"

Taiga shook his head.

Leon handed his brother some tissues. "I told you to not borrow any more money from anyone."

"I didn't want to bother you again." Taiga squeezed his brother's hand. "I was doing so well. I had to have some help to stay awake to study."

"You took that again?" Leon shook his head. "You know that's not good for you. That's what pushed you over the brink before."

"I just wanted to stay awake." Taiga turned back to Hiroshi. "I had debts. From the host club."

Hiroshi looked confused. "They told me you were the most popular host, with champagne calls every night."

"They charged me for things. A new suit, taxi fare, dinner, whatever. They kept saying the women hadn't paid for it, so I had to." Taiga turned to his brother. "They were only going to rip the place off. Nothing more. They promised."

"Looks like their promises weren't worth much." Ishii let go of the bed rail and stepped back, shaking her head.

Taiga started to cry again. "They are so wonderful, Kiri and Jenna. You have to save them. I wouldn't do anything to hurt the girls. I was taking care of them." He turned his face to the other side, his body heaving with sobs.

Takamatsu stepped back into the room with his coat on and motioned for them to go.

Hiroshi turned to Leon. "Take care of your brother."

Leon sighed. "I've been trying."

Takamatsu held his cellphone up and waved for Hiroshi and Ishii to hurry up.

Chapter 34

Hiroshi, Takamatsu, and Ishii hurried out of the hospital to the parking lot. Takamatsu got in the front and Hiroshi got in the back.

Ishii slipped a bill into the payment machine and smacked the side when it didn't give her a receipt. She pulled into the street with a quick turn. She still had the energy to act on her impatience. Hiroshi wasn't sure he did.

Takamatsu said, "Back to the rich part of town. Ota followed Miyuki and has something for us. Saved us a lot of time."

Hiroshi hummed. "What did he find?"

"The hosts"

"What hosts?"

"From Kabukicho. Prod them into action and catch them at it. Worked perfectly."

Ishii drove more quickly than usual. "Even if we have the hosts, we still haven't found the girls."

They rode the rest of the way to the apartment in Azabu in silence, each of them looking out a different window at the city.

They parked and hurried to the front door, and Miyuki buzzed them in. The elevator ran slow, and Ishii pressed the button to speed it up, in vain. When they got to the floor, Ota had the door open waiting for them.

Takamatsu went in, and Hiroshi and Ishii followed, all of them taking off their shoes at the *genkan*.

Takamatsu, who knew a little sign language from a cousin, signed to Ota, nodding at what Ota signed back. When Takamatsu hit the limit of his sign language ability, he took out his cellphone and typed questions.

The hosts from the Shinjuku club sat on the floor against the sofa with their wrists and ankles cuffed. The younger one, the sassiest, rested his head back on the sofa with his eyes closed, his face blotchy red. The other host, disheveled and sweaty, eyed them warily. They looked nothing like their glamour photos on the display board outside the club.

Miyuki handed the stun gun to Ishii. She pressed the button, but it was empty. She tried it again, but the charge had all been used.

Takamatsu pulled a chair over in front of the two hosts.

Hiroshi suggested Ishii take Miyuki to the other room. She led Miyuki off, asking her soft questions.

Takamatsu leaned toward the hosts.

They squirmed and pushed back against the sofa, but there was nowhere to go.

Takamatsu checked to be sure Miyuki and Ishii were out of sight. He backhanded the kid on the left so hard he dropped over on his side.

Takamatsu grabbed his collar and yanked him up.

The host eyed Takamatsu defiantly and Takamatsu slapped him on the other side. This time, he waited until the kid sat back up on his own. "What's your name?"

"Sono."

"Sono what?"

"Sono Daisuke."

"Daisuke, I think you remember us, don't you?"

Daisuke nodded.

"Good. So, yesterday when we talked, I said you better share your deep knowledge base. So you can keep your job as manager. Do you remember that?"

The other host looked away, exhausted.

"But it's fine to talk here since we've bumped into each other so fortuitously."

The hosts resettled themselves, both of them watching Takamatsu. Hiroshi stood a few steps back, and Ota observed from the other side.

Takamatsu turned to the second host. "Maybe it's you who abducted the girls and killed an old woman?"

The hosts' eyes widened. The words "abduction" and "kill" got their attention.

Takamatsu took his time. "What are you doing here in this apartment?"

Daisuke started to answer, but before he could, Takamatsu cracked his face with the flat of his hand.

He dropped onto the floor in the other direction. His body had no strength left. The stun gun and the slaps had taken their toll.

Takamatsu pulled him back to a sitting position.

Daisuke braced himself.

"This is your second time here, isn't it?"

The two hosts looked confused.

"The first was to murder a grandmother and abduct two girls. So where are they?"

They looked indignant. "We don't know anything—"

"Oh, but you do know something I need to know. That's why we stopped by the club. Remember?"

"How much did you cheat Taiga out of?"

Daisuke sighed. "We took a fee. That's business."

Takamatsu slapped him but not hard enough to knock him over. "What was the name of the guy you sold the key to?"

"Nozaki."

"Who is he?"

"Some old-school guy. The owner of our club knew him from before."

Takamatsu smacked him again. "From before what?"

The host screamed and sat up, trying to act tough, but the slaps were getting to him. Takamatsu grabbed his chains and yanked him forward. "What's he look like?"

"I never saw him."

Takamatsu pulled the chains tighter. "Taiga had his nose smashed in. His ribs were kicked and broken. What do you think

Nozaki will do to you?"

Daisuke's eyes held a glimmer of understanding.

Takamatsu laughed. "You're starting to understand. That's good."

Daisuke took a breath and wiggled upright.

Takamatsu pulled the chains back and forth. "Let's try again. Nozaki, right? Got a first name?"

"Just Nozaki."

"And what's he look like?"

"Like anyone."

With one hand, Takamatsu grabbed his hair and yanked. "What's he look like?"

Daisuke tried to pull away. "He was tall. Dressed in black."

"Black what."

"Black everything. He had a colored tie, bright purple, or orange, or whatever."

"So you did see him. Who did he come with?"

"Same two guys every time. They dressed like him. Three of a kind. They had longish hair, all of them."

Ota tapped Takamatsu on the shoulder and signed to him. Takamatsu gestured for Ota to show what was on his cellphone to Daisuke.

"Is this the guy?" Takamatsu pushed Ota's phone closer.

"Yeah, maybe." Daisuke looked up at Takamatsu, hopeful that was all he needed to say to get out of this.

"Take another look."

Daisuke nodded. "That's him."

Ota took his phone and typed a long message to Takamatsu.

Takamatsu read it carefully and turned to Daisuke. "Now, you're really in trouble. This guy is worse than you think. How do you contact Nozaki?"

"I don't. He just stopped by a few times recently."

Takamatsu put his foot in between Daisuke's legs.

Daisuke tried to squirm away, and the other host reset himself.

"I will break your balls, his balls, and the balls of your boss. You'll be on the run for the rest of your life. With crushed balls. So, how do I find him?"

Daisuke moved his legs to avoid Takamatsu's foot. "I don't have my phone."

Ota had it on the kitchen table and brought it to Hiroshi.

"What's the passcode?" Takamatsu pulled his foot back to kick him.

"Six, two, three, five."

Hiroshi inputted the numbers.

"And what's the owner's name?"

"It's under 'Acquire' in the directory"

"You leave a message for him and tell him to call you right back."

Hiroshi pressed the number and held it to the side of Daisuke's head. "*Shacho*. I have a situation. Call me back."

"You call him *shacho*?" Takamatsu laughed. "CEO of a host club. Nice."

They waited for the phone to ring, but nothing came.

Takamatsu stared at Daisuke. "I hope you're not lying to me."

Hiroshi sighed. "He might not call back all night. Let's call Sugamo and Osaki to clean up here."

Takamatsu pulled his foot back and stood up, resigned to the dead end. Takamatsu signed to Ota. Ota showed him the photo.

Takamatsu froze in place. He signed Ota and Ota signed back. Takamatsu examined all the shots that Ota had taken, scrolling up and down, his face tightening.

Hiroshi wasn't quite sure what it was, but Takamatsu's face was rigid. Hiroshi looked at Takamatsu. "Who is it in Ota's photo?"

Takamatsu closed his eyes. "Someone I haven't seen in many years. I'll explain later, over a drink."

Daisuke pushed himself up. "Can you let us out of these cuffs? They're too tight."

Takamatsu ignored him.

"She nearly zapped us to death." Daisuke put on his tough face again.

"I didn't see anyone using a self-protective device, did you, Hiroshi?"

Hiroshi shook his head.

Takamatsu signed Ota. Ota shook his head.

Takamatsu leaned close to Daisuke. "Just be glad to get out of this with your balls intact."

Hiroshi called Osaki and Sugamo to come and pick up the hosts. They were checking a hotel nearby and said they'd be there in a few minutes.

Takamatsu straightened his cuffs. "We just called your ride. They'll be here shortly. We'll talk again tomorrow. Get a good night's sleep." Takamatsu leaned down again. "Unless Nozaki has someone inside. Then you won't sleep at all."

Takamatsu asked Ota to write down all that happened that day, but Ota told him Shibutani already had it in order, so Takamatsu called him, walking to the corner of the spacious LDK room to talk more privately with Shibutani in a low voice.

Ishii returned from the back bedroom with Miyuki.

Miyuki jumped when her cellphone buzzed in her bag on the kitchen island.

Ishii encouraged her to take the call, but Miyuki ignored it. Ishii whispered it was OK, but she refused. She picked up her phone, turned it off, and dropped it back into her bag. "Just work."

Her phone buzzed again. She picked it up and looked at the call. "Just an old college friend." She dropped the phone back in her bag again and leaned against her oversized refrigerator, looking stricken, but who wouldn't be after fighting with the hosts, handing over photos of her husband's infidelity, arranging her mother's funeral, losing her daughters, and her dream apartment turned nightmare.

Hiroshi wondered if it was Nozaki who had sent her the

photos? Was this old-school blackmail? Break up the home and then pick the person apart until they complied. Takamatsu had described it to him several times. It seemed so old-fashioned.

And how were they going to find Nozaki? Wait until he found Miyuki? Or wait until he found Patrick and the daughters? That would be too late.

Osaki and Sugamo arrived and took charge of mopping up and getting the two hosts to the station. They declined Takamatsu's invite for drinks after they were done, reciting the tasks remaining in their workday.

Takamatsu, for once, didn't insist. They'd been running all day. They'd have to wait until tomorrow to figure out something more. Hiroshi didn't argue against something to eat and drink. He wanted to find out what Takamatsu knew about Ota's photos.

Chapter 35

Ota smiled at their invitation to *yakitori*, but he decided to keep watching Miyuki, even though other detectives would stay. Miyuki insisted they all watch from outside the apartment.

After parking in Ikebukuro, Takamatsu led them across a wide street into a warren of pedestrian lanes that led away from the station. "I hope you like sake and *yakitori*." He spoke to Ishii more than Hiroshi.

"My two favorite food groups," Ishii replied.

"And I hope you don't mind standing?"

Ishii smiled. "That way you won't fall asleep if you drink too much."

Takamatsu turned to Hiroshi. "See, she went to America, but remained a real Japanese."

The buildings sloped to four or five stories punctuated by rickety one-story shops. At the end of one lane, Takamatsu headed up the stairs of a brand-new building of exposed concrete and hanging *kokedama* moss balls spilling ivy. Takamatsu pulled back an artsy steel door into the sleek interior of a modern *yakitori* place.

Savory aromas gushed from the glassed-in grill. Jazz played from wall-mount speakers. A long row of refrigerated cases held sake bottles in careful rows. Wooden plaques with hand-painted *yakitori* choices hung along the wall, a few turned over, sold out for the day. It was the kind of place that didn't advertise because it didn't need to.

A young man in a thick blue apron with moussed hair led them to one of the concrete tables jutting from the wall. Takamatsu ordered beer and a set plate of *yakitori*.

"I haven't eaten all day." Ishii hung her jacket up and handed a hanger to Hiroshi.

Takamatsu hung his camel hair coat on two hangers and brushed it neat and straight. He lit a cigarette before he even sat down.

The beer came and they hoisted their glasses and mumbled, "*O-tsukare-sama desu*," for a toast before downing the cooling, foamy relief. Small dishes arrived, a slice of tofu topped with teensy mushrooms, a plate of grilled *iwashi* sardines, and a little blue bowl of potato salad.

A waiter brought over three fist-sized white cups with blue circles in the bottom, and two bottles of sake, a *daiginjo* from a traditional *kura* brewery and a *shinshu* labeled with a single Western number instead of the usual poetic phrase. The waiter poured the cups right to the brim.

"*Kanpai!*" They let the sake settle in and their humanity return.

Assorted chicken skewers on a brown, glazed plate arrived, and they eyed the *yakitori* for a moment, deciding what they wanted before plucking one of their favorites.

Takamatsu slid his empty stick into the bamboo container. "You think the wife was screwing the babysitter?"

Ishii dropped her skewer in the container. "I had an odd impression when I asked her about him. She knows more than she lets on."

"So who sent her the photos and why?" Hiroshi pointed with his empty skewer.

"She said she didn't know." Ishii cocked her head. "I believe her."

"Was that why she filed for divorce?"

Ishii finished chewing. "Can't be the only reason. Even with a big settlement."

"More *yakitori*?" Takamatsu asked.

"I'd like more hearts and gizzards," Ishii said. "And some liver."

The waiter wrote down the order and hurried off.

"You're not like this spoiled kid," Takamatsu pointed at Hiroshi. "He only likes breast meat or *tsukune*."

Hiroshi pulled the soft, white *sasami* skewers onto his plate and let the sake dissolve the fatigue and frustration of the day.

The door of the restaurant opened and Sakaguchi ducked inside. He sprayed disinfectant on his hands from the bottle by the door and ambled across the room, limping on his injured knee.

Takamatsu waved the waiter over and ordered for Sakaguchi. Ishii took Sakaguchi's overcoat, weighing the heavy black wool in her hands as she hung it up for him.

Sakaguchi pulled over a stool and set it next to the wall so he could lean back. His beer arrived, and he hoisted the large mug in one hand.

"*Kanpai!*"

"Not your usual kind of place, is it?" Sakaguchi asked Takamatsu.

Takamatsu lit a cigarette. "The chef's father ran a place in Shinbashi. It's a nice change, this place."

"Women can feel comfortable here." Ishii looked around. There were quite a few groups of women.

"Another reason to like it." Takamatsu laughed.

"So, tell me you found something." Sakaguchi drained this mug and held it up for another.

Another set plate of *yakitori* arrived. In front of Sakaguchi, the skewers seemed as small as tooth picks.

Hiroshi slid another *tsukune* onto his own small plate and shook his head. "The abducted girls, the parents, the CEO of Nine Dragons, the babysitter, the husband's friend, the hosts, Nozaki, none of it connects."

"Don't forget the dead grandmother." Takamatsu raised his glass. "To the elderly."

"At least they didn't smash her nose," Ishii said. "After the conversation with Miyuki, I felt she's protecting her husband."

Hiroshi sighed. "You think she's in on this with him?"

"Not in on it but on his side. She said she had always trusted him, and always would."

Takamatsu sighed. "Interrogating men is a hundred times easier."

Ishii was about to argue with him, but a waiter reached up to turn over two of the wooden boards on the wall, the *yakitori* choices sold out.

Hiroshi sipped his sake, wishing he could spread the case across the two monitors in his office and have it all come together with the press of a button. "You think Nozaki was fronting other investors?"

"He was always fronting something." Takamatsu finished his cup but, unusually, didn't order another.

When the plates were emptied, Takamatsu flipped his lighter. "So, *nijikai?*"

Sakaguchi drained the last of his sake. "I have something to announce. So let's all go."

They paid and reassembled in the lane downstairs. A short walk away, Takamatsu stopped at the frosted glass door of a dilapidated wood-frame, tin-walled shop. He slid open the door and Sakaguchi stooped sideways to get in. Hiroshi and Ishii followed.

The small square room was lined with narrow plywood shelves holding tin cans and small packets of snacks next to handwritten prices. Rows of one-cup sake, more brands than Hiroshi thought possible, were arranged by prefecture. A refrigerated cabinet with bottles of beer was jammed to the side. A large bottle of *shochu* rested on top.

In the back, a wood counter blocked off a living room area where a TV cast its pale glow through *shoji* dividers. An old man looked over from where he sat under a *kotatsu*. He pulled his hand out from under the heated, blanket-covered table and gave a calm wave.

It was too cold inside to take off their coats. There was no place to hang them, anyway.

From the shelves, Takamatsu pulled down tinned sardines and Sakaguchi took down *umeboshi* pickled plums.

Hiroshi went for beer and got a bottle to share with Ishii. The opener was tied to a grimy piece of string taped to the cold cabinet door. Takamatsu and Sakaguchi poured their own plastic cups of *shochu*.

Sakaguchi held up his plastic cup of *shochu* and cleared his throat.

Hiroshi, Ishii, and Takamatsu stopped to listen.

Sakaguchi's hand wasn't trembling exactly, but there was a shake, of uncertainty, or fatigue, Hiroshi couldn't tell. "I'm being promoted to chief and I need your—"

"So, it's true?" Takamatsu's face broke into the widest grin Hiroshi had ever seen him make.

"You'll have our full support." Hiroshi tapped his beer cup against Sakaguchi's *shochu* glass.

"Congratulations!" Ishii held her cup of beer overhead with two hands.

Takamatsu kept smiling. "We'll get you a Borsalino hat."

"They don't sell them in my size." Sakaguchi patted his head.

They drank without another word and that was all the congratulations Sakaguchi needed.

Hiroshi broke the awkward silence. "So, the daughter-abducting father was really talented at setting up shell companies and individual trusts."

Sakaguchi stretched his knee. "With dirty money?"

Takamatsu drained his *shochu*. "If it's Nozaki's money, it isn't just dirty, it's bloody."

"Nozaki?" Sakaguchi ate sardines from a small tin.

Ishii finished her beer. "Nozaki is probably the one who broke into the apartment—"

"I thought that was the father?"

Ishii nodded. "After the father."

"There were two break-ins?"

Ishii nodded. "The second was Nozaki. He's the one who beat up Taiga. And then Ota followed—"

"Who called in Ota?"

"I did, chief." Takamatsu shrugged.

Sakaguchi sighed. The chief was adamant about not using outside help. Probably why Takamatsu did it.

Hiroshi interrupted. "Nozaki was also on a list of clients for a wealth management company."

Ishii continued. "And Ota found one of Nozaki's men following Miyuki this afternoon."

Sakaguchi dug into his pocket for his cellphone and scrolled up and down. "Here's the video from outside Nine Dragons."

Takamatsu pulled up the photos that Ota had forwarded through Shibutani. The body sizes matched, as did the black outfits, but with a mask on, it wasn't certain.

Takamatsu put his phone away. "Nozaki was a cop. A couple years younger than me. You could tell who he brought in because their noses were always broken. There were a lot fewer restrictions in those days, but still he got fired. He started working for *yakuza* roughing up cheating girlfriends, making collections, or just showing up when needed. He was smart and smooth-talking, and gradually moved from muscle work to *sokaiya* corporate extortion."

Ishii interrupted. "I don't get that. Why didn't the companies just throw out anyone who disrupted their meetings?"

Takamatsu smiled. "Nozaki owned shares in the companies, so he had the right to attend meetings. Of course, he'd pay someone to disrupt the meetings, and pretend to stop them. Then collect money from the company for stopping them. Companies would do anything to avoid the shame of disruption. A very lucrative form of theater. In the bubble years, corporate accounting was whatever you made of it, so they could always cover payoffs."

Sakaguchi reached down to massage his knee and stretch his leg. "In my neighborhood growing up, it was easier to pay suppliers who overcharged. *Especially* those who overcharged. You paid for things *not* to happen."

Takamatsu flipped his lighter. "Nozaki took that to another level. He started to show up to collect at the main offices. He published trade magazines and forced the companies to buy them at inflated prices. He'd threaten journalists to get puff pieces in respectable magazines, and charge for that. He was a master."

"And don't tell me, he'd follow the executives, find them in compromising situations, and photograph them for blackmail," Hiroshi added.

"Another type of shame that worked well." Takamatsu lit a cigarette and flipped his thick gold lighter.

Sakaguchi interrupted. "So you knew this guy, Nozaki?"

The old bar owner behind the counter started snoring in front of the TV.

"One year, there was a directive to stop all corporate extortion. The *sokaiya* were going to be stopped, at last. We were given a free hand to arrest anyone for any reason. So, when the annual meetings started, we were ready. Shibutani, his cousin, and I were assigned to the same place."

"As expected, the *sokaiya* started shouting and things quickly turned into the usual tussle. But that day, the theatrics turned violent. Shareholders and company employees were slugging it out with Nozaki's men. The police were bashing heads. In the middle of the fight, I saw Nozaki smiling at me. In his hand, he held a knife. Before I could get to him, he turned and tossed it out the window."

"Tossed it where?" Ishii asked.

"Below the window was a canal." Takamatsu closed his eyes. "When the fighting was brought under control, three detectives lay bleeding. One was the son of a Diet member who wanted to be a detective. He had to have part of his intestines removed. The other was Shibutani, who as you know is still kicking. The third was Shibutani's cousin. He bled out before the ambulance arrived. Shibutani never got over it."

"Shibutani and I looked for Nozaki for years. We'd get reports now and again from Interpol and overseas departments. Nozaki must have siphoned off enough during those years to stay hidden forever."

Takamatsu ground out his cigarette in the leftover oil of his empty sardine can.

"But now, he's back in Japan, out of hiding, and he won't be hard to find."

260

Chapter 36

From Ikebukuro, Hiroshi took the Yurakucho Line toward Edogawabashi Station. He wondered if Takamatsu knew how to find Nozaki. He probably did and would go find him. And not answer his phone until he did. He should have insisted on going with him.

The dull yellow lights of the passing stations cast a balance of light and dark into the train car, making him drowsy and roused, a bad combination. Usually, a train ride, even a short one, cleared his head. But with this case, his head was full of nothing. He needed two monitors for his brain.

Where would a father go if he were taking his kids out of Japan? He'd slip out wherever he could. Private transports were rarely searched, rarely recorded. Several scam artists he'd tracked had escaped that way after ripping off elderly pensioners, leaving Hiroshi with plenty of evidence and nowhere to pin it.

Even public transportation like the ferry from Shimonoseki to Busan, Okinawa to Taiwan, or Osaka to Shanghai, was easy to sneak through. The Maritime offices might not contact Tokyo with the passport information until Patrick and his daughters were long gone.

Still, that was better than Nozaki finding them.

The train stopped at Edogawabashi and Hiroshi got out to walk the rest of the way to Kagurazaka in the cold, quiet, empty streets.

Wandering toward Ayana's apartment—*their* apartment—the lanes meandered up and down slopes steep enough to require circular indentations in the concrete for traction. Even with strong gripping shoes, it was sometimes too slippery to walk in the rain.

He walked past the more expensive grocery with better produce, past Ayana's favorite bread shop where light at the back signaled the baker already at work on the morning's breads and pastries. The liquor store with the best selection of wine had its display cases and signs pulled tight against the front wall.

He headed past the ultramodern shrine Ayana didn't like. Every time he and Ayana walked by, they had the same pointless argument about the design, an argument whose real meaning he had yet to untangle. He didn't really want to, though. He hoped he'd have the same argument with her forever.

When he got to Kagurazaka Dori, he stopped to watch two cats skitter down a narrow lane of cobblestone steps. Old wooden walls lined each side, but the cats scurried into a break he could barely see. The yowling of the neighborhood cats sometimes woke him in the night, but they owned the night streets. The shadowed passages and dark hideaways were theirs alone.

He trudged down the street and up the stairs to their apartment building and took the elevator. Inside, he toed off his shoes and called, "*Tadaima!*" in a soft voice in case Ayana was asleep.

"*O-kaeri nasai!*"

His only complaint about Ayana was she didn't use the traditional "I'm home" and "Welcome home" greetings. For that matter, she didn't say "*Ittekimasu*" or "*Itterashai*" when one of them left. To Hiroshi, it felt like living alone, like living in the silence of his parents' home.

When Hiroshi complained, Ayana laughed, surprised at his seriousness about something so trivial and traditional. But she promised to do that if it made him happy, and she had. Hiroshi sometimes said it twice just to hear her answer again.

Ayana was on the sofa in sweatpants and a wraparound shawl. Crumpled printouts spread around her, two laptops angled open on either side, and an empty glass of wine rested on the coffee table, or wine table, as Ayana called it.

Hiroshi tossed his coat over the chair by the kitchen island and headed to the refrigerator. He took out the jug of filtered water and got a glass.

Ayana held out her cheek toward him. "I said '*Tadaima*,' but what do I get? No kiss?"

"You'll just criticize me for drinking."

"Have you been drinking?"

"Just water." Hiroshi held the water up as evidence and leaned down for a kiss.

"Working on my wedding speech." She tried to smile but grimaced, frustrated.

Hiroshi sipped the water. "How was work?"

"This new boss is a complete asshole."

"You said that."

"He wants to redo our entire system. Some of the librarians said they were thinking of quitting."

"That bad?" Hiroshi looked at her.

Ayana bit her lip. "Yes, it is that bad. He's clueless."

"Why was he put in charge of things? Why not you?"

"He's a man, I guess. And the rumor is he only worked at prefectural libraries. He was pushed out of each one after a couple of years. I don't know what connections he had to get transferred to the National Archives. He must have been kicked out of every other place."

"Demoted upwards? Why not demote him to some solitary project?"

Ayana picked up her glass of wine, swirled the last drop, and bent back to finish it off. "Eww, sour."

Hiroshi wanted to leap on her lovely neck and tickle her until she screamed. Instead, he said, "I'm sorry you have to suffer."

"Not as sorry as I am. As all of us are. We promised not to talk about it at the wedding."

"When's the wedding again?"

She stared at him. "I told you. Tomorrow. Today, I guess. It's after midnight."

Hiroshi nodded like he remembered. He had already told Sakaguchi he needed time off, but he couldn't remember the time or place. Maybe she'd sent it to him. He'd search his messages.

"I bought you a new white tie." Ayana didn't look up from the pages she was working on. Or re-re-working.

"What was wrong with the old one?"

"The dry cleaner couldn't get the stain out."

"What stain?"

Ayana scoffed. "My point exactly."

"I don't think I even used that tie. I can't remember the last time I went to a wedding." Hiroshi took the jug of filtered water back to the fridge.

"Can you listen to my speech?"

Hiroshi sighed. "Can I take a shower first? I've been running, and I mean, literally running, all day."

"Like through streets and up stairs and things?" Ayana looked amused.

"Yes, as a matter of fact. Lots of streets. All of them dead ends." He was too tired to be indignant at her lack of sympathy.

"But can you listen to my speech after you shower? I can't tell if it's any good or not."

"What do you have so far?"

"About how she was a great student, a reliable worker, always on time, knows the archives inside and out…"

"You're supposed to entertain people, liven up the proceedings, not recite her CV. Did you put in any jokes?"

Ayana wrinkled up her face, leaned back on the sofa, recrossed her legs, and growled.

"Put in something funny."

"Like what?"

"Like something funny at the archives."

"Nothing funny ever happens there."

"Well, put in something funny she said."

"She's an archive librarian. She's the most serious person I know." Ayana bit her pencil, typed something into her laptop. "She called twice tonight. I had to talk her out of canceling the whole thing."

"It's already paid for. It'd be a headache to reschedule—"

"That's what I told her. She used the virus as an excuse the first time, and the second time claimed her husband wanted to cancel, but wouldn't admit it."

"That's just nerves. They're already legally married at the city office, aren't they?"

"Yes, but they've only half moved in together. Everyone's nervous about next steps like that."

"Were you?"

"Now we're back to the marriage discussion?"

"Were you?"

Ayana stared at him. "You mean when I got married, or when you moved in?"

Hiroshi regretted starting this conversation again. He was too tired to get into it. Maybe if he stayed silent like Ayana did sometimes, it would pass.

"I wasn't nervous at my wedding. Or when I divorced the creep. But I was nervous when you moved in. Very."

"And now?"

"Now... what?"

"Are you still nervous?"

"Not about us, but when you're at work. Or you don't answer. Or you come home drunk. I get worried. I mean, the things you tell me I'm sure are not the whole of it."

"Mostly, I work in my office."

"But not today."

"Not today. Why are you using two laptops?"

"You said you had two in your office. You were right. It works wonders." She set them both down and stretched her back and neck. "I shouldn't have done kendo tonight. I needed a workout, but someone whacked my shoulder."

"You need new pads."

"I need new shoulders."

"My shoulders need a shower." Hiroshi pointed toward the shower, and Ayana made a girlish face and turned back to her wedding speech.

After the shower, Hiroshi pulled on shorts and a T-shirt and flopped backwards on the bed for a minute before he went to help Ayana with her speech.

When his cellphone rang, Hiroshi looked around for it, confused, and for Ayana, even more confused. She wasn't there, only his cellphone was. Sometime in the night, Ayana must have thrown a blanket over him and went to sleep on the sofa.

Moving the phone from ear to ear as he sat on the edge of the bed, he tried to get his brain focused on what Sakaguchi was explaining to him from the morning meeting, which he'd missed again, and what they had found on the case, and how Ishii had to go on ahead without him. Sakaguchi never got angry, but it sounded similar.

Dressing while he listened, he was half-ready by the time he hung up. He couldn't believe he'd slept in again. At least he'd slept. There was a lot to do, to catch up on. He texted Takamatsu, but there was no reply.

He went out to the living-kitchen-dining room. It was small, but perfect. Why was he even asking Ayana about money and about marriage? Everything was fine as it was.

There was no sign of Ayana other than fresh coffee and a Danish wrapped in a napkin.

After burning his tongue drinking too fast, he ate the Danish in big quick bites as he sent Ayana a text message apologizing for not helping with the speech.

He slipped on his jacket and shoes at the *genkan* and checked he had everything.

He had to hurry.

Chapter 37

When Hiroshi got to his office, Akiko was in her seat at work on her computer. He was so pleased she was back, he shut his eyes and stood by the coat rack for a moment.

"You missed the morning meeting. The chief called. Ishii is waiting for you. And check the notes on the back of your computer..." Akiko rattled off a list, a delight just to hear her.

Hiroshi tried not to look immensely relieved as he hung his coat on the rack and disinfected his hands. "How did you manage to escape?"

"Sakaguchi said I'd contribute better from here. He's making more decisions. It's great he's going to be chief, isn't it?"

"I hope he doesn't get chewed up by the bureaucracy."

"I think it'll go the other way. Would you want to go up against him?"

"Wouldn't ever think about it." Hiroshi headed for the espresso machine—a double for him and a double for her—to celebrate her return.

Akiko clicked away on the keyboard. "Look at all these unanswered emails. Did you read any of these while I was gone? And I still need to finish calling a couple more hotels and ports. Ueno wants me to translate for him."

"Translate?"

"Sakaguchi wants to have another go at that American guy, Tim. He's the one who saw Patrick last."

Hiroshi finished his espresso. "Where's Ishii?"

"She's at Nine Dragons."

"Oh, that's right." Hiroshi remembered Sakaguchi told him that on the phone.

"The chief arranged with the Chinese Embassy officials to let us sit in on interviews with clients. Special privilege, he said. You

267

weren't here so she went on her own."

"I better catch up with her." Hiroshi headed to the coat rack.

"I think she can handle it." Akiko scowled.

"That's not what I meant." Hiroshi put his coat back and called Ishii. It took a few rings.

Ishii whispered when she answered. It sounded like her hand was cupped over the phone. "The chief insisted I go ahead without you."

"Isn't Sugamo or Osaki with you?"

"They were busy. Takamatsu didn't answer this morning. There was something strange in how Sugamo and Osaki put me off. They must be covering for him."

"Takamatsu is trying to find Nozaki. I should have stopped him." He checked for a reply from Takamatsu, but there was nothing. He texted him again.

"These interviews are a waste of time. It's just apologizing to clients for screwing their accounts up."

"We better find Takamatsu. I'll meet you."

"Text me when you're near and I'll leave. I've had enough of listening to rich investors whining." Ishii hung up.

Hiroshi put his coat on.

Akiko looked up. "Where are you going?"

"To find Takamatsu." Hiroshi hurried downstairs and out the front door to grab a taxi.

In the taxi, Hiroshi called Sakaguchi.

"I didn't send Ishii there," Sakaguchi explained. "It was the chief. It's his last case, but he's acting like it's his first. Coroner narrowed the time of death down. Not sure that helps any. The grandmother was choked. No sighting of the girls or the father."

"They could be anywhere. Nozaki could be anywhere."

"I'm stuck in a meeting for another hour. It's starting now."

"You don't know where Takamatsu went?"

"He said he'd be with you," Sakaguchi whispered and hung up.

Hiroshi called Takamatsu but got no answer. Takamatsu

screwed up following his hunches a few times before, putting himself and the case in danger. Settling an old score with Nozaki wasn't likely to improve his judgment this time, either. When Tim bent his wrist, it was the first time he'd seen Takamatsu get hurt in a fight.

Hiroshi put his phone away and watched the flow of traffic. The road south was wide enough that taxi drivers could park along the curb to take a nap, a rare chance on Tokyo's cramped roads. New apartment buildings loomed on either side, forming a corridor of affluence down the center of moneyed Minato Ward. The elite names of the areas alone jacked up real estate prices. The buildings, tall and solidly built, stored wealth in their floorspace, upper-floor views, elegant construction, and prestige.

When Hiroshi got out of the taxi, he called Ishii. She sounded relieved and said she'd be right down. He called Takamatsu again. No answer. When he hung up, his phone rang. Akiko. "Give me some good news," he begged her.

"I think we might have found something." Akiko hummed pleasantly. "We talked to that American guy, Tim."

"Already? You went alone?"

"Already. Ueno was right beside me and two guards stayed inside the room. All I did was translate."

"And...?"

"We didn't ask him anything. Ueno just stared at him. Even I was getting uncomfortable. Finally, Ueno had me tell Tim, in English, that if he didn't give us something, we'd make sure he was deported by the end of the day."

"He believed that?"

"He did. And then he whined and asked a lot of questions."

"Americans love questions."

"Ueno didn't reply. He just sat there while Tim tried to bargain, debate, demand a lawyer. Finally, our silence drove him insane."

"Americans can't stand that." Maybe he should bring Akiko with him on interrogations. She could be sweet and she could be vicious. Hiroshi pitied her boyfriends, past, present, and future. "So…?"

"So…Tim told us he dropped Patrick and the girls at an expensive hotel in Shinjuku. He couldn't remember the name, but he described it well enough we narrowed it down. And sure enough, they had a father with two daughters there the night before."

"Why didn't they say something when you called the first time?"

"They said the mother was going to join them, so technically it wasn't a father and two daughters. It was a family. Only the mother never arrived. The hotel apologized. Innocent enough mistake."

"Innocent if nothing happens to the girls. We'll head there."

Ishii pulled out of the parking garage and stopped by the curb. Hiroshi got into Takamatsu's usual front seat and they headed back to West Shinjuku.

Sakaguchi called.

"I thought you were in meetings all morning."

Sakaguchi grunted. "I used this excuse to get out. We finally heard from the local *koban*."

"Whoever is in charge of police box reports needs to speed things up."

"Not their fault. Several local *koban* did report seeing foreign fathers with two daughters, but the chief wanted to announce it at the meeting."

"So he'd get credit for it? Didn't he understand this is urgent? Who let him keep it quiet?"

"Police commissioner I guess. I'm not cut out to be chief if that's what I have to deal with every day."

"You wouldn't do that. Where were the sightings?"

"Most credible one was at Tokyo Station."

"All right. We'll head to Tokyo Station instead of the Shinjuku hotel."

Without a word, Ishii changed lanes and took the next right.

Sakaguchi continued. "I told the *koban* inside the station to give this top priority. Ask at the outside gate. They'll be waiting. I told the hotel to send their security footage. So take a look. We might not be too far behind. Any word from Takamatsu?"

"Not yet. I hope he didn't... but I know he did." Hiroshi hung up. Nothing to do about Takamatsu but wait for him to emerge. He'd call Osaki and Sugamo and work on them.

Ishii pulled in front of the old brick edifice of Tokyo Station that sat like a fancy brick dollhouse over the vast nexus of train lines, Shinkansen platforms, subways, and shopping arcades that stretched in all directions below.

Hiroshi hopped out and ran to the small door of the *koban*, his badge held out to the officer on duty. "I'm Hiroshi Shimizu, detective, homicide. My chief, Sakaguchi, said you had a sighting of a father and two daughters."

The officer in charge picked up the phone and spoke for a few seconds. "The officer who helped will be here in a minute. We pulled all the footage for that time period. Is there anything else we can do?"

"Any idea which way they were heading?"

The officer spoke into his walkie-talkie. He turned to Hiroshi. "They told one of the officers Disneyland."

Hiroshi wondered vaguely why they were heading there as if on vacation. But there must be some other reason than the rides.

A young officer ran up, stood rigidly, and waited.

Hiroshi pulled out the photos. "Were these the three you saw yesterday?"

The officer examined the photos carefully. "*Hai.*"

"Why didn't you call us yesterday? We had this out everywhere." Hiroshi closed his eyes.

The first officer picked up a stack of papers, printouts, faxes, and notes. "All these are requests to keep a lookout for someone. Every *koban*, city office, and worried mother in Japan sends them to us, as if everyone who comes to Tokyo goes through Tokyo Station." He bowed deeply in apology.

There was nothing to do but let it go. "And where's the video footage?"

The young officer waved them inside the small police box. He pulled out a laptop and set it on a file cabinet. He opened the video files, found the footage, and scrolled ahead to the right time stamp.

The video showed Patrick in front of the *koban* looking very nervous. An older Japanese woman talked to him. He held onto an overstuffed bag and shook his head. The officer fast-forwarded to the girls arriving. "The girls got lost. It happens more often than you'd think. You can see these two young women who found them, and I escorted them back to their father. If I'd known..."

"Any footage of where they went after that?"

"We found that too." The young officer checked his notepad for the time, rolled forward, and a different video showed Patrick and his daughters heading into the Keiyo Line, the girls looking up at their father and trying to help carry the bags as they got on the express train to Disneyland.

"We called ahead to the *koban* and train station by Disneyland. They'll have the video footage prepared when you arrive and stand ready to assist." The officer bowed deeply and apologized again.

As he hurried back to the car, Hiroshi's phone rang again. He listened, hung up, and ran to the car waving for Ishii to get the car started.

Chapter 38

"That was Osaki," Hiroshi told Ishii, buckling up as she pulled out of the circular drive in front of Tokyo Station faster than he expected. "How far to Akihabara?"

"Ten minutes." Ishii dodged through the last of morning rush hour. "Osaki's with Takamatsu?"

"He's waiting for him." Hiroshi wondered where Takamatsu found the energy to keep getting into trouble. Hiroshi wanted cases he could work from his office.

Ishii pulled along Suitengu Dori until it merged with Chuo Dori, and soon they were in Akihabara, once the central electronic goods shopping area of Tokyo. Once upon a time, everything from transformers to fuses, relays, switches, motors, and circuit breakers were sold from small stands. Larger stores catered to the latest models of consumer products.

But as tourism and online shopping exploded, the older buildings, and the industry they housed, were rooted up and fancier buildings with new goods plunked in their place. These new places catered not to the realities of electronics, but to the fantasy worlds of maid cafes, video games, manga, and anime.

Akihabara's windows and walls became covered in cutesy characters—big-eyed, round-shaped, bright-colored images to keep Tokyo's *otaku* entertained. The oddly alluring images pointed, in the psyches of some, to the real females working at predatory maid cafes, compensated dating, and porn films.

Hiroshi studied his cellphone app and stared ahead. "Osaki said there was a parking lot next to the gang headquarters."

"Gang headquarters? Here?" Ishii slowed the car in the back lanes.

"We need to cross the Kanda River." Hiroshi reached over and showed Ishii the old, unusual *kanji* character in the address. He wasn't sure how to pronounce it.

Ishii scrolled through the GPS list of *chome* blocks in the Akihabara area until she found it. The buildings were eight-story stacks of offices for small companies in what used to be the electronics industry. Hiroshi couldn't guess what most were now, IT or software companies, small companies to which all the real work was outsourced.

Ishii pulled onto a small lane with buildings rising up from the curb on both sides. The back lane was only big enough for one car at a time, though there were no one-way signs. "That's them, isn't it?"

Osaki stood by the entryway, a solid metal door, of a rectangular building. Next to the building was a small pay parking lot where Sugamo stood between parked cars.

Ishii looked around. "I wish there was somewhere else to park than here."

"We'll need you to help and we don't want to draw attention parking out of place."

Ishii backed into a parking spot. The tire lock barrier rose automatically from below, blocking the two back tires until they paid at the machine in the corner of the lot.

Ishii waited by the car and Hiroshi edged between the cars to Sugamo, who nodded at the building. Rust dripped down from the gutters of the balconies, staining the walls. The windows were painted black and there were no company name signs. There didn't seem to be any fire escape, either.

"Takamatsu's in there?"

Sugamo nodded. "We should have called you sooner."

"How long has he been up there?"

"Longer than we thought."

"Nozaki?"

"His old headquarters. Takamatsu said he'd staked it out thirty years ago."

"No back way out, it looks like. No fire escape, either?"

"Probably those rope ladder things. Takamatsu made us

promise to wait."

"He's been in there over an hour?"

Sugamo nodded. "Are we going in?"

"We'll have to."

Ishii walked down the lane to where Osaki was waiting, her baton open already.

Hiroshi called Takamatsu, holding his hand up for everyone to wait. Before he got an answer, the front door burst open and two men in all-black outfits with colored ties rushed out. The door slammed the wall by Osaki. Ishii rushed with baton drawn.

The taller man in a purple tie shouted, and the man with a dark orange tie sprinted to the parking payment machine. He tapped an IC card on the card reader pad and headed to a black van.

Sugamo and Hiroshi rushed him, but he pulled a gun, turned, and fired into the payment machine. Splintered pieces flew in all directions around the lot. Hiroshi and Sugamo ducked and covered their heads.

The man hopped into the driver's seat of the black van and started it up before they could get to him.

Osaki and Ishii circled the tall man who'd faced off with them by the door. Nozaki.

Sugamo pulled his baton out to smash the windshield of the van, but it wouldn't break. Hiroshi tried to think of a way to block him. Takamatsu always carried a knife, for tires among other things.

Nozaki hadn't budged staring down Osaki and Ishii.

When Osaki saw the van coming, he lunged at Nozaki, but Nozaki moved too quickly and Osaki only got an arm around his neck for a moment.

Ishii planted her legs and swung her baton hard into Nozaki's knee.

Nozaki hopped to the side, clutching his knee. Osaki grabbed his arm and tried to flip him, but Nozaki stayed balanced and pulled away.

Ishii cracked him on his shoulder. Nozaki kicked at Ishii. She dodged and hit his leg. Osaki grabbed him from the other direction.

Sugamo kept banging on the window of the black van. The driver twisted the wheel and rammed the van forward at Hiroshi. Hiroshi jumped out of the way.

The side door of the van popped open as it headed toward Nozaki.

Hiroshi saw the blur of Ishii's baton, but Nozaki ducked aside and the black van swung around, cutting Ishii off. Nozaki leapt into the van, sprawling on the floor.

Hiroshi ran close enough to grab Nozaki's ankle but Nozaki pulled a pistol and pointed it right at him, smiling calmly, waiting for Hiroshi to decide as the van kept moving.

Hiroshi let go and stepped back. It wasn't worth getting shot for. Nothing was. He thought of Ayana saying she was nervous when he went to work. He wouldn't tell her this.

The van sped off and Nozaki leaned out the side panel waving his gun and grinning at the detectives. The van turned left on the main wide road and was gone.

Ishii turned and ran for the car. "Let's go!"

Osaki hurried after her to the parking lot, but Sugamo stood in front of the payment machine. It was in pieces. Sugamo banged his fist on the box, and more pieces dropped off. The tire blocks were up on all of the cars in the lot, locking them in place.

Hiroshi leaned over to catch his breath. "We better find Takamatsu."

They gathered at the door. Hiroshi pulled the door back. Steep stairs ran straight up to the second floor. He looked back to see if everyone was ready to go. They braced themselves, and started up.

Before the second step, though, Takamatsu appeared at the top of the landing. He started down, clutching the railing and taking the stairs one by one.

Behind him were two young guys with scraggly hair and tight-fitting clothes. One had his hand under Takamatsu's arm, helping him.

Hiroshi hustled up to help.

Takamatsu, for once, let him. "Nozaki got the jump on me. Again." He clutched his stomach.

"At least he didn't break your nose." Hiroshi helped him but Takamatsu shrugged him off.

"Nozaki is in deeper on this one than I thought. And not just for his own money. He always seemed calm and collected before. But now, he's panicked."

"Why's that?" Hiroshi asked.

"From what I could tell, he screwed up with Nine Dragons. Maybe he's on the hook over this one."

When they got Takamatsu outside, Ishii checked him for injuries, following procedure, but Takamatsu waved her away and patted himself for his cigarettes and lighter. He pulled out a crushed pack and discovered a long tear in his camel hair coat. He held up the signs of his struggle and shook his head.

Osaki and Sugamo grabbed the two guys coming after Takamatsu and frisked them against the wall.

"We need to go." Ishii pointed after Nozaki and the van.

Takamatsu lit half a cigarette he managed to salvage and nodded to Ishii that it was OK to let them go.

Police from the nearby *koban* arrived and Hiroshi started explaining.

Ishii clicked her baton shut.

Takamatsu waved Osaki and Sugamo off the two guys who'd followed him down the stairs. "They're just renting this space from Nozaki for their business supplying outfits to the maid cafes around here. They have racks of every cosplay and holiday costume imaginable. Dry cleaning, stain removal, rental, storage. Quite the enterprise." Takamatsu smiled at the two young guys and Osaki and Sugamo let them go. "They told me they were moving. Nozaki kept raising the rent." Irritated at only half a smoke, Takamatsu flipped the butt into the gutter.

The local police called on their shoulder mics, and more police arrived on bicycles. Sugamo walked over with one of them to figure out how to get the payment machine to release the cars. The local cop called the parking lot company.

Ishii looked confused. "We should follow them. They're getting away."

Takamatsu pulled his cellphone out and handed it to her. The screen showed a tracking app with a pulsing dot moving east along the Shuto Expressway.

"How did you know which vehicle was theirs?" Ishii asked.

"I didn't." Takamatsu smiled. "I put a GPS on every one of the cars in the lot."

Ishii smiled.

Takamatsu showed her the app. "We shouldn't let them get too far away, though. Just far enough they won't see us coming."

"What are we going to do with these guys?" Osaki asked about the two guys who followed him down.

"Give them a reward. They got me out of the handcuffs Nozaki had me in. Universal key. The one guy tried to talk Nozaki into calming down. That's good enough for me."

The local police couldn't get the payment machine to work, so they grabbed the back bumper of the car Ishii drove, rocked it up and down on the tires, and lifted it over the immobilizing block. Osaki and Sugamo helped them with the other car.

Hiroshi took Takamatsu's cellphone and checked the app. "They're heading east along Route Nine."

Takamatsu took his cellphone back. "Can you call Sakaguchi and tell him to bring pistols. And that sharpshooter, what was her name? Made it to the Olympics. Sakaguchi will know. I wanted to do this one up close, but distance works too. Nozaki got away thirty years ago. He got away just now. But he won't get away next time."

"We'll get you some cigarettes on the way," Ishii said, heading for the car.

"Best thing for a broken rib." Takamatsu took a painful breath and smiled.

Chapter 39

Miyuki's body had taken over and she woke up from the deepest sleep she'd had since Patrick took the girls. She slept far longer than she planned.

After the police took the club hosts away, they offered to stay the night in the living room, but she sent them to wait outside. It wasn't that she felt safe, she just had to be by herself. She couldn't decide what to do as a victim, an account executive, a mother, or as a wife. She had to decide by herself.

She walked out to the kitchen she'd been so proud of. There was no one to feed. She wasn't even sure if there was any food in the fridge. She texted her boss and told him she was taking another day off. She almost told him it would be the week.

She was still processing what Patrick had told her the day before, but she couldn't wrap her mind around it. She was relieved about the girls, but she knew all along Patrick had them. She just wasn't sure what to do about it.

Maybe he was being truthful about the need to get out of Japan. His voice was more serious than she'd ever heard it before. Maybe they were leaving for good. Or maybe she should talk to the detectives, tell them where Patrick and the girls were waiting.

Neither option sounded good. If she could just see Patrick, she would know. And she had to be with the girls. The three of them were her world.

Until Jenna and Kiri arrived, Patrick took up every spare minute of her time. They spent days enjoying the city, the worn wood of temples, the exhibits of *sumi-e* and *ukiyoe*, the standing bars, and the endless choice of food. They went to every *matsuri* festival, to *kabuki*, *noh* and *kyogen*. When a Japanese film didn't have subtitles, she whispered translations to him in the dark and slipped her tongue in his ear. They ran in the Tokyo Marathon together.

Now, he was telling her they had to leave.

In their first apartment, she loved how the futon was never big enough to cushion all their positions. They slipped sideways onto the tatami, stood up in the kitchen, kneeled, and pushed against the table, the chairs, the walls. After, Patrick often had to lift her back onto the futon and hold her until she stopped shaking.

And then, their salaries climbed. Nine Dragons paid a lot—for longer hours and a lot more work. Her promotions at the bank took time and energy in trade for bonuses, perks, and pay. She was one of the first women to rise to a managerial position, but the bank was not mother friendly. Every day she considered quitting, but kept going instead. Their busy life became normal. It worked. Once they cut out sleep and sex and conversation.

Patrick paid cash for most of the apartment, and the remaining mortgage was still double what they paid for rent in their first place in Monzen-Nakacho. It was spacious and lovely, but she didn't know her neighbors' names. They had building meetings and no one introduced themselves. The area's shops were convenient, but they tried too hard to be hip or foreign, and were snobbishly overpriced.

Her mother moved in with them, souring things further. But what could she do? She couldn't leave her alone in the old house in the countryside. She couldn't even drive. She took over the room with tatami, which had been their secret love nest, their last little pleasure.

Her mother was the one who pushed her to file for divorce. She had never liked Patrick, barely talked to him. She never asked what he said or what he was doing, but she was fine to live at his expense while complaining about foreigners every chance she got.

Except for that, she'd never known how her mother felt about anything. Or even *if* she felt anything.

She called the funeral company and told them to postpone her mother's service and cremation. They explained the rescheduling and storage charges, and she said she understood, but another family matter had come up.

She wasn't sure she could trust Patrick, but to find out, she went to the kitchen and pulled out a huge cleaver. They'd bought it at Kappabashi-Dori, the kitchen supply street where they both loved shopping. She carried it to the tatami room, ignoring the stain from Taiga's blood in the woven threads. She pushed the cleaver between the mats and levered them up. It barely moved. The mats fit too tightly.

She went back to the kitchen and got a screwdriver and a bamboo spatula, laid them out on the tatami. She wedged the cleaver deeper down and got the screwdriver in beside it. She jimmied the spatula in, then moved down to repeat the process. The tatami was thick and heavy, and she started sweating. Finally, she got one hand under, and then the other. She braced herself, tugged, and the mat came free.

The underside of the mat was rough and dirty. The USB was inside several tight rounds of plastic wrap. When had Patrick done this? She peeled the plastic off and slipped the USB in her bra. She shoved the mat back in place and jumped on it to get it all the way in. She put all the tools in the sink on the way to Jenna's room.

Why had she never looked up inside the closet before? She dragged a chair over and pushed the ceiling panel aside to feel around. She got hold of a strap and dragged the bag toward her. The bag fell into her arms, and she tottered on the chair for a moment, then dropped the bag onto the carpet, hopped down and unzipped it.

She scratched the plastic from one tight-wrapped brick and found hundred-dollar bills. The next stack was ten-thousand-yen notes. It was a lot of cash.

She dragged the bag to the bedroom, found a rolling bag in her closet, and fit the money inside. Around it, she packed clothes, practical things easy to wash.

Was she really going to go? Hadn't she just filed for divorce? And now she was running to him like a schoolgirl? Was she going to fight him for the girls after they were safe? Call the police once she got the girls in sight? She wasn't sure yet. Once she held the girls and talked to him, she'd decide.

She put more clothes in her bag, and went to the bathroom, but took just a toothbrush.

Or maybe he was lying to her, setting her up for something that she couldn't even imagine? He wouldn't do that, would he? She was sure he wouldn't do that. She could trust him that far at least.

And maybe he didn't trust her. He was on the run, surely worried the police would follow her to get him. She wanted to slip away from them. She didn't mind Ota following her, but not the detectives.

At the front door, she grabbed an extra pair of shoes for the girls, slid two umbrellas in the side pouch, and slipped on running shoes. At the front control panel, she left one light on in the kitchen and one in the bedroom, lowered the thermostat setting, and set the timer for the other lights.

She moved the USB from her bra to her purse, then moved it back. Maybe it was safer where she could feel it. She glanced at the messages from her boss on the iPad and decided not to bring it. Either it'd be there when she got back, or she wouldn't be back. She had to be with the girls no matter what.

She hurried to the elevator, and through the lobby. She knew the hotel. They'd been there three times to take the girls to Disneyland and DisneySea. She was thankful Jenna and Kiri weren't as obsessed with Disney as some of their friends. They took it as the fun it was, but not the only fun there was.

She stopped by the front door to use her taxi app. Several circled nearby. She waited inside the lobby, looking out the window to be sure no one was there.

When the taxi came, she double-checked it was for her, and then ran to the opened door. She hoisted the rolling bag inside onto the seat and told the driver to hurry.

"Where are you going?" the driver asked.

"Disneyland."

"Ah, a nice vacation." He turned the satellite radio to the Disney Hits station.

She'd heard the songs so often from the girls she knew them all by heart, and started to hum along.

At the first turn, she looked through the back window to see if anyone was following. She couldn't see anything, so she settled in and texted Patrick she was on her way. It felt good to text him, just to know he'd read her text.

He sent her a thumbs-up emoji.

She wondered if she could believe it.

When Miyuki ran to the taxi, Ota came out from the side garden, texting Shibutani. He pulled his leather jacket tight around him in the cold and hurried to the street to take a photo of the car that pulled out after her taxi. The car was not the detectives.

He hadn't expected her to jump in a taxi so quickly, and he hadn't expected anyone to follow her, a single driver, it looked like. He looked around for the detectives supposed to be watching, but didn't see them anywhere.

Ota ordered a taxi on his taxi app but kept an eye on the busy street. An empty taxi came so he hopped in, typing a message to the driver to tell him where to go.

The old taxi driver had to change eyeglasses to be able to read the cellphone message. He held Ota's phone up, and Ota wanted to scream. He nodded that he understood, looked at Ota, maybe the first deaf person he'd ever met, changed to his driving glasses, and pulled out.

Ota leaned forward to look out the front windshield. He saw the same taxi, he thought, at the turn for the Shuto Expressway east. If so, the car would be easy to follow, even for this elderly driver. Ota didn't want to write another message. The old man would probably crash.

But once on the expressway, the old man took off his white gloves and put his foot down on the accelerator.

Ota sent a text to Shibutani. Shibutani could follow his coordinates the whole way from the tracking app Ota kept in his leather jacket. Shibutani would send Ota's position to Detective Takamatsu.

If not, he'd be on his own, and so would she.

Chapter 40

Patrick woke up tired from the late-night tour of Disneyland they squeezed in after checking in. The hotel was a short walk through a parking lot to the main gate. After arriving, they didn't even unpack, just washed their hands, bought discount tickets at reception, and went.

In the Disney Resort area, he and his daughters were invisible in the parade of jumpy kids, excited teenagers, and worn-thin parents. Those guys in black would stand out, though, even at night.

Inside the gates, it had been crowded and a bit cold in the early evening. He watched closely but saw no sign of the driver or the shovel-faced guy who followed them on the train.

He bought the girls sweatshirts and caps, and let them load up on Mickey Mouse sandwiches, Monsters melon bread, and churros slathered in tooth-melting layers of sugar. He stood right outside the door of the toilets when the girls went in.

Back in the hotel, he'd told them to brush their teeth twice, but they just giggled and dropped into a deep sleep before he could even open a whiskey from the mini-bar. He received a message from the Asian guy, Tim's replacement, telling him he'd lost them in Tokyo Station. He didn't write back. Patrick hoped he'd lost the guy in black too.

He pulled back the curtains a crack for sunlight without waking the girls. It was like they were born again every morning, re-emerging from that other world of sleep to reincarnate into themselves each day.

He'd almost missed Jenna's birth, the greatest day of his life. The idiots at his job at Pacific Investments had failed to call him out of a meeting to tell him that his wife had gone into labor. It was their policy never to interrupt a meeting, and that included a partner giving birth.

When the meeting was over, Patrick checked his messages, saw Miyuki was in labor, and raced out of the office. He made it to the hospital to find her screaming and sweating for the last pushes in the delivery room, her eyes wild. He tried to calm her down, but he had to laugh.

"What are you laughing at?" Miyuki screamed at him as she pulled on the handles of the birthing bed and pushed with all her might.

"I'm so happy." He kissed Miyuki's sweat-drenched face, wanting to help but knowing he couldn't do anything more than hold her hand, cheer her on, and watch Jenna emerge—a screaming blob of beauty dressed in blood and mucus. She was the most amazing thing he'd ever seen.

In the recovery room, when the nurses brought Jenna in, he realized again how beautiful Miyuki was. That first night he watched them, he felt he was in love twice more than he ever thought he would be. For the first time in his life, he had a home. He was home.

Kiri's birth was no less amazing, and much smoother. Miyuki had taken time off from the bank and worked from home for a couple of months. The second time, he was prepared to leave work right away and even took parental leave, rare for men in Japan. Kiri added another dimension, a fullness, and the family was complete, perfect.

Watching the girls through sleepless nights, messy meals, tantrums, and sicknesses had never bothered him. He finished their half-gnawed snacks, wiped their excretions, and held them like...well...they became the metaphor to compare everything else to. Now, they were the metaphor to protect.

He googled around and found a private jet company with an open slot and even a limousine shuttle to take them directly from the hotel to Haneda. They'd hide out at Disneyland through the day, and could leave anytime after three the next day. It was exorbitant, but it would avoid the departure lounge and surveillance cameras. He filled in the form and risked using his credit card to hold the reservation. They said they'd accept cash in payment before the flight.

Once they got to Honolulu, he and Miyuki would have their big argument and it would be over. Things would never be the same, but they would find a way through it. They had to.

Kiri sat up in bed. "Are we having pancakes this morning?"

"It's almost lunchtime, honey."

Kiri had on her new pink sweatshirt with princess characters all over it. Patrick knew better than to try to get her out of it, so she slept in it.

Jenna got up on her elbows, awake. "I'll share my pancakes."

"I don't want to share. I want my own." Kiri squirmed inside her oversized sweatshirt. Patrick caught a tone in her voice that he hoped was not crabbiness.

He changed into his newly bought clothes, and the girls got up and pulled on tights and sweatpants. He hadn't brought thick enough coats for them, so he got them to layer up. He thought of sending a message to Miyuki to bring warmer clothes, but it was too late and they'd be in Hawaii soon. She must be on her way.

When they were ready, except for needing their hair brushed, they put their shoes on by the door. Patrick checked the hallway in both directions. Nothing. He stepped out and the girls followed, still sleepy, with the excitement stirring inside them. The elevator arrived empty.

"When's Mom coming?" Jenna twisted away from him and checked herself in the elevator mirror.

"She'll be here soon."

The girls cheered and threw their little hands in the air.

The lobby was full of parents and children streaming over the tiled mosaic of Cinderella's Castle that covered the floor. Soft blue and pink tiles accented with sparkly gold formed the castle. Magical flying characters that Patrick recognized, but couldn't name, swooped and smiled below their feet.

Patrick dodged strollers loaded with babies and supplies for the day. Parents adjusted kids' outfits. Teenagers struggled to escape their parents and huddled with friends sharing plans on their cellphones.

Patrick took the girls' hands and headed to the restaurant, but halfway there, he stopped. There was already a line. A pleasant-looking young woman was taking names on a clipboard. Patrick hated lines, a constant aggravation in Tokyo, and wanted to give up right away.

Miyuki, though, could predict exactly how long a line would take with a single glance. Every Tokyo line looked too long to him, but he'd have missed out on half the films, art exhibits, and shows if she hadn't cajoled him into waiting.

A busload of Chinese tourists entered, pushing their rolling suitcases, looking at the mosaic tile, and talking loudly. They quickly filled the lobby with noise, vacation clothes, and erratic motion.

And then, there she was.

"Mom!" Jenna and Kiri raced to Miyuki. She stooped down to wrap them in her arms. The girls clung to her, and Miyuki wiped a tear from her eye.

He started toward them, wanting to tell her everything, but it didn't seem like a good idea to tell her they were being chased by violent, vengeful men. He didn't want her to know they'd be lucky not to be found by the men who probably killed Leung.

Halfway there, just as he stepped over the magic moat filled with toothy alligators and frogs who were really princes, he felt a ripping, burning pain in his back and fell forward like an axed tree trunk, slamming against the tiled floor. Above the ringing in his ears, he heard the girls shout, "Poppa!"

He tried to say something, but couldn't catch his breath. He twisted on the smooth tile and tried to kick at whoever and whatever it was. His eyes wouldn't focus and his back felt like he'd been slugged with a baseball bat, an electrified one.

He began to breathe again and looked up at a man in a black suit staring down at him. Patrick grabbed his foot and tried to tip him over, but the man hopped backwards and got away. Patrick dragged himself to his feet. The man backed off, stretching to see something by the front door.

Along with another busload of Chinese, in walked the man in the shiny dark orange tie from the pool. Beside him walked another man, taller, wearing a purple tie over a black outfit. They stood by the door searching the lobby.

The Chinese tourists swept in, some of them beelining for the free coffee table and others pulling discount coupons from a huge rack by the door. The second busload of Chinese had a tour guide giving explanations through a handsfree portable loudspeaker turned too loud. They looked for their luggage and pooled in groups taking photos of the ceiling and the mosaic.

Patrick looked through the flow of visitors. The man in black who had just tased him seemed to be the same one outside the hotel, the one who'd followed him on the train. How could he have gotten to this hotel? He was sure he'd lost him. Did he come with Miyuki?

Standing beside Miyuki and the girls was a short round man in a leather jacket with multiple zippers. Even stranger, Miyuki seemed to know him. The man started pushing Miyuki, Kiri, and Jenna out of the lobby and Miyuki followed reluctantly. Who was he?

Patrick looked for exits out of the lobby. There was another exit to the side of the lobby over which hung a big mouse glove sign: "Happiness This Way!" A line of life-size Disney character statues gestured in the same direction.

Another busload of what looked like retired Filipinos came in with their grandchildren. The swirl of colored shirts lit up the already brightly colored lobby. They jumped around taking photos at this most important stop on their once-in-a-lifetime

Japan tour.

Patrick sprinted to Miyuki, scooped Kiri into his arms, and took Jenna's hand. "We need to get out of here. Where's the—"

"I checked the bag already. And I put the other here." She patted her bra where the USB was nestled. Miyuki patted Ota on the shoulder. "This is Ota. He saved me."

"Saved you?" Patrick kept his eyes on Miyuki's and held the girls tight. "We need to get out of here *now*."

"Why did you fall over?" Miyuki's face tightened beneath her mask.

"We need to go."

Miyuki gave a single nod of OK.

Patrick leaned down and in a daddy voice said, "OK, girls, we need to hurry or we'll miss our entry time."

"What about breakfast?" Kiri said, but Jenna, sensing something wrong, shushed her.

Miyuki put her hand on Ota. "Ota's coming too."

Without looking at the men in black, Patrick turned Miyuki and the girls around, heading them toward the only idea of safety he could come up with—the huge happy crowd inside Disneyland.

Chapter 41

Ishii pulled off the expressway close to Maihama Station, Takamatsu checking his GPS and giving directions. "It looks like they're at a hotel near Disney. No, right at Disney. I'll call the local cops to meet us there."

Ishii could see where to go but not how to get there. She drove in the direction of the hotel, but the road curved away. She pulled a U-turn and headed back. The next turn looked like it would go through and she accelerated.

Takamatsu got a message from Shibutani. "Ota followed Miyuki to a hotel in the Disney resort area. Must be the same one. Let me see if Shibutani can contact Ota."

Ishii pulled the car into the hotel drop-off circle and angled it in front of a black van. "Is that Nozaki's van?"

Takamatsu checked his GPS app. "That's it." He got out and peered inside. He pulled out his multitool to try to the doors, but quickly put it away. "Enough with locks." He pulled out his knife and slashed the two rear tires, which dropped to the rims.

Hiroshi hopped out and headed into the hotel.

Inside the hotel was pandemonium. Tourists kneeled by overturned suitcases spilling their clothes over the floor. Two security guards squared off with men yelling in Chinese. Tourist pamphlets and discount coupons littered the floor mosaic. Elderly people huddled together by overturned benches. Hotel employees in blue uniforms raced in all directions trying to calm everyone and tour guides shouted into megaphones.

Hiroshi ignored the turmoil and looked for Patrick, Miyuki, and the girls. Three local police walked in, talking on walkie-talkies Velcroed to their bulletproof vests. Behind them came Ishii and Takamatsu.

At the far side of the lobby, under an overhead

sign "Happiness This Way!" A row of Disney character statues had been overturned. Hiroshi took off toward the exit with Ishii and a huffing Takamatsu behind.

Outside the exit, the entrance to Disneyland was several hundred meters across a bus parking lot. On the sidewalk, huge arrows and laughing faces pointed the way. In the distance, past the entry, the blue peaks of the huge central castle loomed.

Hiroshi stood on a bench to see through the buses from downtown hotels parked neatly in place. More buses from Kanagawa, Saitama, Chiba, and metropolitan Tokyo were waved in place by attendants in bright uniforms. Farther to the left, family cars pulled into dutiful rows.

He couldn't see Patrick and girls, or Miyuki, anywhere in the steady stream of visitors heading forward. Ota should be there too. Maybe they were already inside. Maybe Nozaki caught them already. Punctured tires or not, they could have another vehicle or get one easily enough.

Takamatsu caught up, reading his messages. "Ota's with them. He's inside the grounds."

"Did he see Nozaki?" Hiroshi kept watch on the entrance.

"He saw Nozaki in the hotel, with two men. Ota thinks maybe they lost Nozaki for now, but he won't be far behind."

Hiroshi wondered how Takamatsu was doing. He didn't want Takamatsu in another fight. "Write Sakaguchi to find out how close he is. Osaki and Sugamo should be here by now."

Takamatsu started on logistics. Hiroshi left him and jogged forward to the front gate with Ishii right behind.

Halfway there, three local police caught up on bicycles. Hiroshi slowed a moment to explain and they sped ahead to the entrance.

A brightly colored pedestrian fence separated the dawdling visitors from the parking area. The closer they got to the entrance, the more crowded the walkway became, bottlenecking the excited visitors. Hiroshi and Ishii dodged around strollers, wheeled bags, and wheelchairs. Ishii leaped over the fence and Hiroshi did the same. It was easier to run where the cars and buses ran.

Up ahead, the local police parked their bikes and breezed inside, disappearing in an unmarked door to the right of the gate. Hiroshi hoped that was the security office. If Nozaki and his men were carrying weapons, they needed all the backup they could get.

They flipped their badges at the gate personnel and charged ahead. Hordes of people streamed in all directions, pooling to take photos in front of a fountain with big-eyed elk, playing tag around plastic statues of goofy spacemen, strolling the faux streets of cutesy shops selling Disney merchandise. The seaweed smell of the bay mixed with the scent of melting sugar, fresh popcorn, and deep-fried food.

Schoolgirls in uniforms, college girls, and young couples sidestepped slower-moving family groups. Hiroshi tripped over a stroller, apologized, and stumbled forward through the ersatz streets. Benches were already full of grandparents. Every three or four shops, side streets with more shops curved away.

Everywhere, Disney guides held "End of the line" signs as tidy lines shuffled forward to the rides. If the family had gone inside any one of them, it would be impossible to find them. The rides swept them away from public view as soon as they loaded and left. They'd have to post a cop outside every ride, show, and shop on the grounds.

Draped in Disney-wear, the family would be as hidden here as anywhere in the world. Nozaki and his men's black outfits would stand out amid the cheery vacation clothes.

Hiroshi lost sight of Ishii. He stopped in a massive open plaza that spread out in front of Cinderella's Castle. It was harder to find someone in Disneyland than in the maze-like back streets of Tokyo.

Hiroshi had never been to Disneyland before and it was less

polished than he imagined. Here and there the pavement was unfinished and a few walls misaligned. The roofs over the arcades, cracked and brittle from the sun, looked like they leaked. No one cared about those rough edges in cartoon heaven.

He headed toward the central mountain and veered right to the back circle of the park. The shops started to repeat, selling the same goods. Signs pointed to places he just passed. Plastered with fanciful colors, people blurred together, everyone transcending their dreary day-to-day selves by turning into their happier cartoon selves.

Only the sunlight and the smell of the sea seemed natural. A cool breeze came in off the bay. Hiroshi wished it would blow him in the right direction. He couldn't see Ishii anywhere.

He checked his cellphone for messages but there was nothing.

When he looked up from his screen, Ota was standing under the overhead train tracks waving for Hiroshi to come over. Hiroshi skirted around an open electric car transporting those needing a ride.

Ota showed him the pulsing dot on his cellphone map and typed a quick message. He had put a tracker into Miyuki's purse. On his app, the pulsing dot was no longer inside Disneyland. It was in the neighboring DisneySea complex. Ota was confused.

"What's DisneySea?" Hiroshi typed to Ota.

On his cellphone map, Ota pointed at a monorail that ran around the outside of the two side-by-side resorts. Ota pulled Hiroshi's sleeve and they took off at a run for the exit.

They jogged around the outside of the massive resort area to the other entrance. Ota was short, round, and quick, like a mini sumo wrestler, fleshy outside, muscled inside. Hiroshi had a hard time keeping up.

Hiroshi stopped to text Sakaguchi where they were going. Sakaguchi wrote back that Osaki and Sugamo would follow them to DisneySea. Ishii called. She was riding the monorail and would be there in a minute.

Inside the gate, Ota checked his app and waved Hiroshi along. Long lines snaked back and forth in front of every ride. They crossed bridges over bright blue rivers, as artificially colored as everything else. The water stretched toward a gigantic volcano that rose on the other side of the water, "Mysterious Island."

Ota headed to the left of the volcano until they came to a bridge that led to a replica of an American waterfront. On one side a huge steamer was moored with kids and parents scrambling up the gangplank.

Hiroshi slowed for a moment, taking in the entire scene, letting Ota get ahead. Before he headed on, Nozaki burst through the crowd.

Ota rushed back and hustled Hiroshi out of sight behind an ice cream kiosk.

Nozaki stopped and looked both ways, his two henchmen beside him. Their suits shone in the sun. Black was the one color no one had on.

Ota waited a few seconds and then peeked around the side. He waved for Hiroshi to follow. Nozaki and his two men were striding down the walkway leading to the Lost River Delta, their black outfits parting the colorful crowd.

Takamatsu exited from the same side street Nozaki and his men had come from. Panting and wheezing, he had been following Nozaki more closely than Hiroshi had. Hiroshi pointed to where Nozaki went, and Takamatsu nodded.

Up ahead, the walkway narrowed to a large bridge made of railroad ties and thick wood posts that angled up to overhead struts. Cool air came from the bay in the distance and from the blue river below the bridge. People rested against the thick timbers taking pictures of the view and of themselves.

Nozaki started across the bridge.

From the opposite side of the bridge came Patrick, Miyuki, Kiri and Jenna. Patrick was looking behind him as they hurried onto the bridge's planks.

Nozaki barked an order and his two men pulled their pistols and fanned out, quickly surrounding the family.

Patrick saw them too late to turn back.

From the other side of the bridge, behind the family, came Ishii, Sugamo, and Osaki.

Nozaki held his pistol straight out at the family members and his men pointed theirs at the two sets of detectives.

A young boy next to Hiroshi pointed out the guns to his father. "I think it's a live performance."

The father asked, "What Disney movie is this from?"

Chapter 42

Hiroshi couldn't identify guns, but the two men had handguns with clips and Nozaki had a smaller, streamlined pistol. The black matte of the barrels absorbed the sunlight as they pointed them back and forth between the family and the detectives.

Patrick pulled Kiri and Jenna behind him, backing away. Miyuki moved next to Patrick to shield their daughters. They clasped hands.

Ishii, Sugamo, and Osaki spread across the bridge until Nozaki waved his gun for them to stop. Hiroshi stayed where he was.

People milled past from both directions, oblivious to what was happening, bowing apologetically as if interrupting a photograph. They kept walking by, chatting arm in arm, checking their cellphone maps.

The boy who thought it was an outdoor performance pulled his father forward, but his father didn't move.

The father took a step toward Hiroshi and leaned close. "Are those real guns?" he asked.

Hiroshi turned to him. "Yes. Get off the bridge."

The man grabbed his son's hand and started running. "They've got a gun," he shouted. No one moved. They just stared.

Hiroshi spread his arms and started waving people back. "Police. Move off the bridge. Move back."

Ishii did the same on the other side of the bridge.

A few people frowned at having their perfect Disney day interrupted, but when it clicked this was serious, they panicked and bolted from the bridge. From a short distance, some turned to watch, still wondering if this was some onsite filmmaking or free performance.

A half dozen Disney characters arrived and started herding the crowd off the bridge on both sides. They seemed to be trained in crowd control, Disney style, so Hiroshi let them take over and hurried back to the center of the bridge.

The three local police arrived, took in the situation, and spread out across the bridge. They had guns but kept them holstered. Two more arrived and helped move people away.

"Nozaki!" Takamatsu dashed out on the bridge, his breath rattling deep in his chest.

Nozaki pointed the gun at Takamatsu.

Takamatsu chuckled. "You never graduated from the Nanbu?"

Nozaki waved his gun. "This is the new one. Much improved. Just five shots, but that's all I ever need." He looked at his two men. "Of course, my men are not old-school like us. They like more rip and tear."

"Nozaki, there are a lot of people here." Takamatsu held his hands up and walked forward.

Nozaki laughed and aimed his gun at Patrick's chest. "I just need something from him and I'll be on my way."

Takamatsu took a few steps forward. "You can afford a lawyer to spring you and run back overseas. Toss the guns into the water and you're home free."

"Home? Free?"

Takamatsu gestured around. "By my count, there are five detectives here now, six policeman, and more on the way. You know how this ends. Make it better for yourself."

One of Nozaki's two men moved his gun from the family to Ishii, Sugamo, and Osaki. The other kept his gun directly at Patrick, Miyuki, and the girls.

Takamatsu took out his lighter and flipped it in his hand, his eyes on Nozaki.

Osaki and Sugamo moved toward Nozaki's men in subtle half steps.

Takamatsu flipped his lighter, edging forward. "Nozaki. What are your helpers' names?"

Nozaki smiled. "Takamatsu, those old tricks don't work. They won't listen to anyone but me. I just need the investing genius for a few minutes and then I'll be gone."

Takamatsu stepped closer. "You're good at killing cops so point your gun this way."

Nozaki kept the gun steady with two hands. "Still weeping over your partner all those years ago? Didn't know you were the type. Shibutani's cousin, wasn't it?"

Takamatsu's voice hardened. "Point your gun over here."

"I think I'll get what I came for. We can talk after. Or my lawyer can."

Osaki and Sugamo moved closer to the men. Ishii circled to Nozaki's blind side. The local cops, guns still holstered, angled for position for a clean shot with nothing but the river behind and the bay in the distance.

The further back the Disney staff pushed the crowd, however, the more people piled up. There were people at every angle watching what was happening on the bridge.

Patrick and Miyuki stood in place protecting their daughters behind them.

One of Nozaki's men, unsure where to point his gun, yelled, "Back off, all of you!"

Takamatsu took a step forward. "Nozaki, your men are getting nervous. For this kind of work, you need old-school guys. They don't get rattled."

Nozaki pointed the gun at Takamatsu.

Takamatsu kept playing with his lighter. "No one's hurt yet, so you can still get out of this."

"I'll definitely get out of this. Not sure about you." Nozaki stepped closer to Patrick and Miyuki. Hiroshi could see Kiri and Jenna cowering behind them.

In one quick motion, Takamatsu took his lighter and whipped it at the face of Nozaki's closest man. It landed squarely on his cheek with a crack as loud as a gunshot. The man reeled back, clutching his face.

Ishii whipped open her baton and lunged with it held between both hands. She landed full force on the side of his knee, and he dropped to the side. Ishii rained blows on his head until two local police dove on him. His gun clattered onto the wood and Ishii kicked it away.

Nozaki's other man turned to see what was happening, but Osaki had a running start. He landed on him with a rugby tackle that made the bridge shake. A gunshot blasted out and splinters of bridgework flew into the air.

Sugamo was right behind Osaki and latched his thick hands on the man's arm. Another shot rang out.

Hiroshi tried to see where it went, but Osaki bent the man's arm. Hiroshi thought he heard a bone break and the gun fell from his hands. Sugamo picked it up and tucked it in his waistband.

Nozaki bolted toward the family, grabbed Patrick, and pistol-whipped him with three quick blows. Patrick crumpled against the rails, his head bleeding.

"Poppa!" Kiri screamed. Jenna wrapped her arms around her sister. Miyuki leaped forward, clawing at Nozaki's face.

Nozaki slapped her to her knees and grabbed Kiri and Jenna by the hair. He yanked the two girls in front of him, smacked Miyuki on the back of the head again, and pointed the gun at Patrick's head.

Hiroshi stepped forward. "Let the girls go."

Takamatsu took a step forward. "The girls didn't steal your money. Let them go."

Nozaki laughed. "Here's what we're going to do instead." He reached inside his coat, took out a small tablet computer, and dropped it in Patrick's lap.

Patrick picked it up and tried to focus, wiping the sweat out of his eyes. He looked at his two girls, their faces terrified. "Leung's the one who took your money. It's Leung you want."

"He said he didn't know anything about it. We asked him twice. Once before I went to Wyoming, and again after. All he told us was he couldn't trust his employees." Nozaki turned to Takamatsu and spoke in a loud voice. "The whiz kid here will give my money back. I'll let my lawyers sort out the rest."

Sakaguchi burst through the crowd with three young detectives all with pistols drawn. Two of them flanked the sides and kneeled in firing position. One dropped to her stomach and set her elbows to brace her long-barreled markswoman pistol at Nozaki.

Nozaki pulled the girls tighter in front of him and kicked Patrick. "I thought we'd have a more intimate venue to discuss this. Start moving my money back. Now."

Patrick squinted at Nozaki. "You were in Wyoming, weren't you?"

Nozaki smiled. "This would have been so much easier to do there. But you left in such a hurry. We missed you in Honolulu too, by a few minutes at the hotel."

Takamatsu took a step closer. "He'll move the money. Let the girls go."

Nozaki lowered the gun toward Takamatsu's feet and squeezed off a round. Splinters flew in all directions.

Takamatsu didn't blink.

Patrick weighed the tablet computer in his hands. "I don't know what happened to your money."

Nozaki kneed him in the face. "You or Leung stole my fucking money. That's what happened. But that doesn't matter. Only you need to give it back. Now."

"Leung did all that. Not me."

Miyuki whispered. "Patrick, do what he says."

Nozaki kneed him again.

Without another word, Patrick picked up the tablet computer and tossed it behind him over the side of the bridge.

Nozaki swung his pistol at Patrick's head. Patrick thrust his arms up but the gun tore open a gash on his forehead. Blood spilled into his eyes. He reached for Nozaki, but couldn't see.

Nozaki picked Kiri up with one hand and grabbed Jenna by her shoulder. They screamed and tried to pull away. Miyuki ran for them but Nozaki pointed the pistol at her and she stopped where she was.

Hiroshi barreled straight into Nozaki. Patrick reached for Kiri and Jenna. Nozaki knocked Patrick's arm away but Hiroshi's momentum carried all five of them—three men and two little girls—into the wood rail. They teetered there for a moment. Nozaki pushed back and Hiroshi gave another shove, and they spilled backward off the bridge, the girls screaming until they hit the water.

The hard slap of the water disoriented Hiroshi and he clawed the water upward. Back to the surface, coughing and spitting, the first thing he saw was Ishii jumping in.

Patrick called out. "Kiri, Jenna, swim to the side. You know how." Jenna started stroking away, and Kiri did her best dog paddle, but the current of the river was strong and pulled them downstream.

Hiroshi raised himself above the surface looking for Nozaki. He wondered if guns worked when they were wet.

Patrick worked his way to the girls and got hold of Kiri. Ishii caught up with Jenna, who was swimming as hard as she could in the current.

Hiroshi looked back at the bridge and saw the sharpshooters balancing their weapons on the rail, waiting for a shot. He turned to swim downstream, but an arm wrapped around his neck and the hard barrel of a gun pressed into the back of his head.

Hiroshi stopped swimming and let himself float downstream with Nozaki cutting off his air and the gun jammed into his skull.

On the bridge, Sakaguchi and Takamatsu were helping the sharpshooters readjust their positions for a better shot. He saw Miyuki leaning over the rail, pointing and yelling.

Nozaki held the gun over Hiroshi's shoulder and fired off a shot at the bridge.

This would be his only chance. Hiroshi jammed a hand under Nozaki's elbow, grabbed his wrist, twisted, and broke free.

He tried to hold onto Nozaki's wrist but Nozaki twisted loose and shoved him under.

Hiroshi swallowed water and lost direction. He twisted, got oriented, and swam upward. When he broke the surface, he sucked in all the air he could.

Before he could see who was where, two sharp gunshots rang out, then two more. They fizzed when they hit the water.

He sank back under.

Chapter 43

Despite multiple scrubbings under a hot shower, blue dye from the fake water at Disneyland clung to his skin, stuck in the cracks of his fingers, and gave his face an eerie glow. He thought the water inside the park was from the bay, but it must have been processed and colored to create a brightened, animated idea of a river. The leather of his wallet turned an odd mix of blue and brown. His clothes had a creepy blue tinge. He threw them out.

After he toweled off, he found a thin robe in the cabinet by the showers, but no slippers, not even the throwaway kind. He'd gone barefoot often enough in Boston and nothing bad happened. The hallway floor of headquarters couldn't be worse than the dirt and grass along the Charles River. Or maybe it could.

Osaki and Sugamo waited by the vending machines in the hallway outside the shower locker room. Their pants and shoes were still damp from when they stepped into the water to drag everyone out. They stared at Hiroshi's bare feet but didn't say anything.

"Your skin doesn't look that blue," Sugamo said.

Osaki patted Hiroshi on the back. "Sakaguchi's waiting for you to interrogate the American guy."

Sugamo said, "We'll do Nozaki's guys. They'll break quickly. You can tell."

Hiroshi nodded. "Where are the girls?"

Osaki dumped his empty can in the recycle bin. "Ishii took them to the shower and got clothes from the child abuse section. The mother wasn't too happy about that, but they always have extras."

"I think I'll change before the interrogations." Hiroshi padded off to his office.

Akiko welcomed him back to his office with a double espresso and a deep bow. "Nice robe."

"Breezy."

"Ayana called."

"Did she send an address?"

"Back of the monitors." Akiko frowned at him. "You're blue."

"There was some kind of dye in the water."

"Didn't you wash it off?"

"I tried." Hiroshi checked the address on the sticky note on the back of his monitors. It was a wedding hall not too far away. He'd finish the interrogations quickly and go.

Two bright-colored tickets were taped among the notes. He peeled them off—two free tickets to DisneySea. He held them up.

"Someone left those for you." Akiko turned away, chuckling.

He taped them back to the monitor with a sigh. He was too tired and cold—and too undressed—to laugh.

"I'll let you change." Akiko shut down her computer. "Meet you at the interrogation rooms."

The warmth of the double espresso restored him. He pulled a change of clothes from his filing cabinet. Because he never slept in his office anymore, he barely remembered the button-down shirt and summer khakis in dry-cleaning wrap, wrinkled but serviceable. There were socks too. A pair of running shoes from a failed attempt at lunchtime jogging still waited by the coatrack.

He checked the sticky note for the exact time of the wedding. He had two hours. Ayana would meet him there. He buttoned his shirt, pulled an old jacket from the back of the coatrack, and walked off to the main building.

Sakaguchi was waiting in the hallway. "How did this case move from child abduction to murder to a shootout on the bridge at the most popular tourist site in the country? I see endless meetings."

Takamatsu reached up to pat him on his huge shoulder. "That's going to be your life from now on, *Chief* Sakaguchi. I like the sound of that."

Hiroshi turned to Takamatsu. "I see you stayed dry this time."

Takamatsu growled. "You should have let him drown."

Sakaguchi frowned. "If Hiroshi hadn't dragged him to the bank, we'd be on the hook for shooting him and letting him drown. You know how many meetings *that* would involve?" Sakaguchi dropped a hand on Hiroshi's shoulder. "It's good you brought him in. We've got a prize to show off."

"For the outgoing chief to take credit for." Takamatsu shook his head. "That's all the retirement gift he gets."

Hiroshi headed for the door. "Let's get this over with. I've got a wedding."

Takamatsu and Hiroshi stepped into the interrogation room.

Nozaki had his leg wrapped and splinted, propped on a chair. He hadn't had a shower, so the blue dye stuck to his skin even more than to Hiroshi's. His hands were cuffed through an eyebolt in the table.

Takamatsu peered at Nozaki's leg. "That's it? I told the markswoman to get a headshot."

Nozaki stared at him with dull eyes.

Takamatsu looked back at the observation room and made a gesture at his throat to cut the video. The red light turned off.

Takamatsu backhanded Nozaki across the face.

Nozaki took the blow and turned his face back ready for the next. The cuffs had a short chain, and unless he took his leg down, there was no way to move.

Takamatsu grabbed Nozaki's head and popped him square in the nose. And then did it again.

Nozaki shook his head and leaned back as far as he could in the cuffs. Blood flowed from his nose and he blinked the water from his eyes. He tried to wipe his nose but couldn't reach it. The blood dripped over the table, the cuffs, and his clothes, and splattered over his leg splint.

Nozaki turned his eyes back to Takamatsu's and reset himself in the chair. Hiroshi saw one shiver run through his body and then the soulless menace honed by years of brutality returned to his eyes.

Hiroshi held his hand up to Takamatsu. "Isn't that enough? Let's get this over with."

Blood trickled down Nozaki's upper lip. He licked it clean.

Takamatsu tucked his shirt in, straightened his jacket, and waved for the camera to be turned on. "I was just speaking his language. He's not going to give us anything."

Hiroshi turned to him. "Is that right, Nozaki? You've got nothing to say?"

Nozaki stared at Hiroshi, then focused his eyes on the tinted observation window on the back wall.

"So tell us about you and Nine Dragons. Did they handle your money?"

Nozaki stared dully at Hiroshi and Takamatsu in turn. It was not the first time he'd been interrogated. And it wouldn't be the last. Hiroshi knew Takamatsu, and whoever he enlisted to help, would be dragging Nozaki back for questioning over the next three weeks before they charged him. They wouldn't let him sleep.

Hiroshi turned to Takamatsu. "What did his little buddies have to say?"

Takamatsu let out a deep chuckle. "They'll start blabbering soon enough. Like I told you, Nozaki, you should have hired old-school guys. These young punks will say anything to save their own asses."

Hiroshi tapped the table. "If we work it that way, it'll be worse for you, Nozaki. It's better to talk a bit. Maybe the money wasn't yours? You were protecting someone? Give us something."

Takamatsu leaned forward and stared into Nozaki's eyes. "Just tell us who you were fronting. Just a couple of names. All that money wasn't yours, was it?"

Without dropping Takamatsu's gaze, Nozaki let his tongue move across his upper lip to wipe the blood dripping from his nose. He sucked in through his sinuses and Hiroshi pictured the blood flowing down the back of Nozaki's throat.

Takamatsu put his hands in front of him. "After the day you killed Shibutani's cousin, we searched for you everywhere. I found all the doctored photos, the blackmail letters, I even got into your office files and boxed up every bit of incriminating evidence. You had that set up pretty well, didn't you? Shakedowns were easier back then."

Nozaki's tongue snaked out to lick off the stream of blood. He turned his eyes to Takamatsu's.

"You were the big *sokaiya* back then, but now, you couldn't even get your money back from Nine Dragons. Sounds like they were extorting you! That'll happen. Be careful who you trust. You must have believed everything Leung said." Takamatsu laughed.

Hiroshi leaned forward. "Sounds like you made a big mistake. You didn't even know who to kill to get your money back, did you?"

Takamatsu laughed. "Those photos? That kind of thing doesn't work anymore. No one gets embarrassed like in the *sokaiya* days. You need to update your methods. Too bad you won't get the chance."

Nozaki kept staring without a word. The blood dripped along his lip.

Takamatsu pointed at Nozaki. "We've got you down for Leung's murder. And that grandmother? That'll be what keeps you inside for the rest of your life. Judges don't like grandmother killers. And we can add on extortion, blackmail, kidnapping, carrying weapons in a public area, and whatever else the prosecutors can find. Not sure what will happen to your money. We'll see if the kid can get into the accounts. "

Nozaki blinked slowly.

Takamatsu folded his arms. "So, why don't you tell us whose money you lost? We'll reduce the sentence for cooperation. And I'll toss in a bonus. The file about your stabbing Shibutani's cousin? Shibutani has it. It's why he was fired. Missing case file.

Lucky for you we didn't find you back then. We wouldn't have been so forgiving."

Nozaki licked off the blood dripping from his sinuses and raised his chin to look at Takamatsu.

Takamatsu leaned forward. "Think it over and see if you can't come up with a few names for us."

Hiroshi thought he heard something from the observation room and looked back to see the one-way mirror from the observation room turning the three of them into shadowy reflections.

Takamatsu stood and leaned over the table

Hiroshi tapped his arm to remind him the camera was on.

"Did you plan it? The big fight in the meeting hall? The chance to kill a cop? Something to brag about, boost your reputation? You were never man enough to do it face to face. Did you come up from behind him? Reach around for the abdominal aorta?"

Nozaki snuffled back more blood, swallowing it. He looked at his leg and shivered again. Blood was soaking the gauze.

Takamatsu slammed the table with both hands.

Hiroshi pulled on Takamatsu's sleeve to go, but Takamatsu kept his hands on the table and leaned toward Nozaki. "Shibutani's cousin was just twenty-five when you killed him. I used to think that was a weakness, to think about him and light incense at his grave. But it's a strength to remember, and remember well. He's still here as long as you are. You're keeping him alive." Hiroshi pulled Takamatsu toward the door. "Shibutani will come see you soon."

Nozaki kept his unflinching gaze on Takamatsu. Blood flowed from his nose, over his lip, and into his mouth, but he didn't bother to lick it off.

Hiroshi pulled on Takamatsu's arm. "Let's go."

Chapter 44

Sakaguchi was waiting in the hallway outside the interrogation room. "Takamatsu, we've got to cut back on that kind of thing."

Takamatsu nodded. "That one was thirty years coming. I've got no reason to hit the younger generation. They can't take it anyway."

Sakaguchi stretched his knee, balancing his huge frame on one leg. He breathed out slowly as he brought his leg down.

The in-use lights were on over all the doors. "Which room is Patrick in?"

Sakaguchi nodded at the room two doors down. "I'll leave you to the English."

"Where are you going?" Hiroshi was used to Sakaguchi always listening in.

"Meetings. And a press conference. We have a lot of explaining to do. Public safety disrupted is front page stuff." Sakaguchi ambled down the hall.

Takamatsu pulled out a fresh pack of cigarettes and a cheap disposable lighter. His lighter had dropped into the Disney river in the scuffle.

Ishii came down the hall in ill-fitting clothes. "Can I do anything?"

Takamatsu smiled. "You did enough already. You got those girls to shore."

Hiroshi looked at the room. "Want to help with the interrogation? Another English speaker would help."

Ishii frowned and looked down. "If you don't need me, actually, I have a meeting."

"Meeting?" Hiroshi asked.

Takamatsu packed his cigarettes in his palm. "You should take a day off."

"I should, but this is about a new task force." Ishii folded her arms. "Japan's always at the bottom of international surveys of women's equality, so a directive came down to make a task force on women's issues."

"Victims or police?" Hiroshi asked.

"Both. So, I won't be... I mean, I was looking forward to—"

Takamatsu stopped her with his hand. "Get that task force set up. It's about time they had one. You're the right person for it."

Hiroshi turned to Takamatsu. "Now you're a feminist?"

"Always have been. One way or another."

Ishii bowed. "You know, there's a good sake place in Shinbashi."

Takamatsu smiled. "Now you're talking."

Ishii smiled. "Next week?"

Takamatsu looked pleased. "I'll make sure Hiroshi comes too."

Ishii gave a curt nod to hide her smile, and walked off.

Hiroshi went into the interrogation room alone.

Patrick had been given a jumpsuit, not the kind of high-end clothing he was used to, but at least it was dry. He was handcuffed to the table. A bandage covered his head like a soft white skullcap. His skin was a little bluish as well.

Hiroshi told the guard at the door to undo the cuffs.

Patrick rubbed his wrists and resettled himself on the chair.

Hiroshi pointed at the light over the observation window. "This is being recorded. You can help us by getting right into it. If we have to double-check the recordings, verify the information, it takes time. Better to straighten things out from the start."

"Don't I get a lawyer?" Patrick squirmed in the chair.

"Do you need one?"

Patrick cleared his throat. "No."

"Then let's get to it."

Patrick nodded.

"Why did you take the girls?"

"They were being threatened. When I was transferred

overseas, to manage offshore investments—"

"In Wyoming?"

Patrick leaned forward. "Is there someone with Miyuki and the girls? Can I see them?"

"After this."

Patrick slumped back. "I can only tell you rough outlines."

"Start with who was threatening you."

"Nozaki. When I saw him, I recognized him from Wyoming. He wanted me to do the transfers there, but I rushed back here before he could corner me. I saw one of his guys at the hotel in Shinjuku."

"What can you tell me about the photographs of you and a blonde woman?"

Patrick sighed. "Not my proudest moment."

"Your wife showed them to us."

Patrick looked down. "Someone sent me photos of her too."

"Where are those?"

"On my cellphone."

"Which is at the bottom of the DisneySea river. No cloud backup? You seem like the kind of person who backs up everything."

"Not for this. I—" Patrick pointed to his head. "It'll be in this cloud storage forever."

"Why didn't you tell your wife about all this?"

"For one thing, she'd have freaked out. For another, the people helping advised me not to."

"What people?"

"The group of parents denied access to their children in Japan. They said it'd be easier not to tell her until I made sure my daughters were safe."

"That was Tim Branson?"

Patrick nodded.

"He was arrested on assault charges."

Patrick grimaced. "He's all right?"

"He assaulted officers."

Patrick shook his head. "And what about Kyle?"

"He's recovering. So, why did you take the girls?"

"I thought I could figure things out with Miyuki once we were all safe."

"Why didn't you go to the police?"

"And tell them what? I didn't know what Leung was doing."

"He must have sent you to Wyoming for a reason. I mean, you could have done everything from here, couldn't you?"

"It was easier to do it there, but that wasn't it. Leung wanted me out of the way."

"Out of the way of what?"

"Of ripping people off. Like with Nozaki's money, I guess Leung moved it, but was killed before he moved it back."

"Why would he move it at all?"

"Any number of reasons."

"If you can access the accounts, can you find that information?

"Most of it. But part of the security system is set up to keep me out."

"And you didn't know where the clients came from? Or where their money came from?"

"In wealth management, you don't ask that kind of thing. We set up accounts to make sure it earns what it deserves. But for Leung that wasn't enough."

"What more did he want?"

Patrick frowned, took a breath, and shook his head. "I'm still not quite sure. I think he was using client funds as collateral for short-term, high-risk investments. I never saw the whole picture. I was too busy. And I didn't look. Anyway, most ultra-wealthy clients wouldn't even notice."

"But Nozaki did?"

"And one other client."

"And what was your role in all this?"

"My role was making everything as airtight as possible. It's an art. And not easy."

"Maybe you did it too well. We need information on those accounts and how the bank transfers work. You want to help us out? Or do you want to miss seeing your daughters grow up?"

Patrick nodded. "Can I talk to my wife?"

Before Hiroshi could answer, an officer held the door open and Akiko ushered in Masaharu Watanabe, the head of the National Tax Agency, dapper and jaunty as always. Watanabe took off his jacket, folded it over the back of a chair, and snapped his suspenders. "Is this the kid?"

Hiroshi nodded. "This is Watanabe, in charge of income tax evasion."

Patrick sat up in his chair.

Watanabe loosened his tie, sat down, and set a list of people in front of Patrick. "Guess what I'd like to know." Watanabe spoke flawless English.

Patrick flipped through it and set it down. "I can guess. Can I talk to my wife?"

Hiroshi frowned, irritated. "There'll be time for that later, but now—"

"This client list is incomplete." He pushed the list back to Watanabe. "I have the full list. Or rather, my wife does."

"The full list of what?" Watanabe raised his eyebrows.

Patrick folded his hands. "Of clients and their shelter strategies. The rest I can explain. When you deal with *ultra*-high-net-worth individuals, you end up knowing a lot more secrets than you want to. Their portfolios are not just financial. It's how they live."

"What individuals are we talking about?"

Patrick cocked his head. "Look, you need someone to explain this from the inside. I need to get out of here."

Hiroshi and Watanabe exchanged glances.

Patrick continued. "I'll give the USB to you now, without any lawyerly negotiation, in good faith."

"Your wife was in on this?" Hiroshi had wondered about that since learning she worked at the largest bank in Japan.

"No. The first time she heard about it was yesterday. I made the list as insurance and kept it at home under the tatami. I only told her about it because I had no other choice."

"Insurance? So you suspected something wrong at Nine Dragons for a long time?"

Patrick nodded, admitting it to himself. "I didn't know what it was. Still don't exactly. But I didn't want it pinned on me. Maybe it will be anyway."

Watanabe smiled at Hiroshi. "I like this kid. He's kind of honest. You got to think ahead if you want to get ahead." He turned to Patrick. "You want a job?"

"I think I'm going to be convicted of abduction. After that maybe?"

Watanabe nodded. "After that."

A knock came on the door and a guard called Hiroshi out in the hallway where Akiko was standing with Miyuki.

Hiroshi held the door open and ushered Miyuki in.

Seeing Miyuki, Patrick blinked. "Did you bring it?"

Miyuki turned to the side and pulled out a USB flash drive from her bra.

Hiroshi took it from her. "Is there a password?"

Patrick smiled. "Just the girls' names and birthdates. Miyuki could figure it out in case something happened to me."

Watanabe and Hiroshi frowned.

"But I shift the date by six months, so I can always calculate it. Miyuki could too, if she needed to."

"Save us some calculating and write today's here." Hiroshi waved for paper and a pen from the guard by the door.

Patrick wrote it down.

Hiroshi held the chair for Miyuki. "We'll be back in a few minutes."

Hiroshi waved Watanabe and Akiko out of the interrogation

room. He nodded to the officer to let Miyuki sit down and stay.

In the hallway, Hiroshi told Akiko to take Watanabe to his office and have the tech guys download the files and make backups.

Akiko and Watanabe chatted cheerfully as they walked off, Akiko laughing at something Watanabe said while they waited for the elevator to take them upstairs.

The observation room smelled of smoke. Takamatsu stood watching. "Giving the lovebirds some private time?"

"They always sing. Something secret, something useful. You taught me that, to just listen."

Takamatsu smiled. "I didn't think you were paying attention."

"Why are you standing up?"

"My ribs hurt. Nozaki's guys punched me."

Miyuki and Patrick clasped hands on the table and Hiroshi turned up the volume.

"Are the girls OK?"

"They'll have a story about Disney for the rest of their lives."

"I think it's better if they forget this one."

"If you can't come to my mother's funeral, it's OK."

"I'm not sure how soon they'll release me. If at all."

"They will."

"The only way out of this is to help them. How's Taiga?"

Miyuki looked down. "I'll check on him after I leave. The police said he was all right."

"He can recover at our place. Give him the tatami room. We're going to need a good babysitter."

Miyuki sniffled. "I hired Ota to find Hello and Goodbye."

"He investigates cats?"

"Not investigates. Locates. He's done it before. Charges more for cats than people. Dogs are easier, he said." Miyuki laughed and wiped her eyes. "I told the girls they were at the pet hotel."

"They're going to stop believing us soon."

"I know." Miyuki looked in his eyes. "And I called the lawyer and stopped the divorce proceedings. I was so angry at you."

"I should have, I mean, I shouldn't have. It was a set-up, but it worked. I—"

Miyuki squeezed his hands. "The policewoman told me they were using us to get at Nine Dragons. The photo of me—?"

"Some guy with long hair and a stylish outfit—"

"Sato? He married one of my college friends. They divorced." Miyuki rubbed Patrick's hands. "OK, he was a college fling. Long before you and before he married my friend. But his family runs a funeral company. He was just helping with my mother."

Patrick searched her face and accepted what she said. "They were going to blackmail me in Wyoming, but I left too soon. When I figured it out, I had to come back and get the girls. Everyone was using someone."

"Not us. Not ever." Miyuki laughed and tears sprang out. "We can rewind, can't we? All of us on the sofa together?"

Patrick looked up at the observation window. The recording light was still on. "For now, you have the bag, right?"

"I checked it in at the Disney hotel. It'll be there until I retrieve it."

"I'll sort the rest out whenever they let me out." Patrick closed his eyes and took in a deep breathe. "People died."

"That was Leung, not you."

Patrick shook his head. "I'll give them what they need. Nine Dragons had a lot of clients. I was involved."

"Kiri and Jenna love you so much." Miyuki started crying, the tears falling on their hands.

"They'll be disappointed with me eventually."

"No, they won't." Miyuki clutched Patrick's hand. "And neither will I."

Chapter 45

After listening in on Patrick and Miyuki, Hiroshi left the rest to Takamatsu, Sugamo, and Osaki, and hurried back to his office. His cellphone was full of messages from Ayana, each with a rising sense of urgency. She sent him a copy of her speech five times. The last message told him to just show up.

It was six-thirty. The wedding banquet started at seven. He could maybe make it in time to hear her deliver her speech, but he was dressed like a slob. He'd have to risk it. He could at least sneak in and stand at the back, then escape and call her from outside.

He caught a taxi outside the station, told the driver the address, and asked him to hurry.

The driver looked in the rearview mirror. "Not your wedding, is it?"

Hiroshi looked up, startled. "My girlfriend's giving a speech. I was supposed to help her but was too busy with work."

When the light changed, the driver accelerated into traffic. "I'll get you there."

"And I forgot to get an envelope for the *goshugi*." To fail to congratulate the bride and groom with a gift of money in a special envelope would be worse than going in the wrong clothes, worse than not going at all.

"There's a convenience store up ahead." The driver changed lanes, pulled to the curb, and opened the automatic door.

Hiroshi ran inside and found the shelf of last-minute necessities. He grabbed a fancy envelope for weddings and a white tie, and dashed to the cashier. He realized he didn't have any clean bills to put inside the envelope. He asked the cashier if the store kept clean ten-thousand-yen notes, but the clerk just stared at him.

He paid and hurried back to the taxi.

"Do you have any clean bills?" Hiroshi asked the driver. Dirty used bills in a wedding envelope was taboo.

The driver handed his money bag back to Hiroshi. "Look in here."

"This is your money bag."

"You're a cop, aren't you? That's where I picked you up."

"Criminals exit there too. Not to mention lawyers."

"I'll remember that."

Hiroshi selected three crisp, clean ten-thousand-yen notes. "I can give you back a wrinkled ten- and one- and five-thousand-yen notes to replace them."

"I need the small ones for change anyway."

Hiroshi replaced the amount and slipped the ten-thousand-yen bills inside the inner envelope. "Do you have a pen?"

The driver laughed and handed him a pen kept in the visor. "Are all cops this disorganized?"

"Just before weddings." Hiroshi wrote his name on the inner envelope and tucked it inside the thick outer *washi* envelope. It took him a minute to replace the intricate bow tied with glitzy gold, red, and white string in the shape of a crane.

The taxi driver kept going at a swift pace. "A taxi driver friend of mine used to keep an extra white tie for weddings and a black tie for funerals."

"People forget ties that often?"

"Yeah. Not just cops."

"I haven't been to a wedding in a while."

"Neither have I, though my daughter just got married."

"Congratulations! Was it a big wedding?"

"There wasn't one."

"What?"

"She and her husband decided not to waste a lot of money on a lavish ceremony."

"Is that a trend now?"

"It should be."

"You raised her right. Sensible."

"She asked everyone to let her invest the five or six million yen a ceremony costs, and dropped it all into stocks and bonds. I don't understand it, but compound interest adds up over the years."

"It definitely does."

"She didn't want to end up having to drive a taxi after retirement like me."

"There are worse retirements. You get to help out rattled detectives."

The driver laughed. "You can help me if I end up with a speeding ticket."

When he got out at the wedding hall, Hiroshi offered him a tip, but the driver refused it. Hiroshi set the bill on the front passenger seat and hopped out before he could hand it back.

He ran down a graceful stone pathway to the elaborate white door. The name of the wedding hall, "Maison de Blanc," was done in curlicue metal and lit by soft spotlights. Ivy covered the white brick walls.

Hiroshi pulled open the door with a sense of dread. Was he really going in dressed like this? He hurried to the registration counter to sign in and hand over the envelope with the cash gift.

At the reception desk, two women, probably friends of the bride, smiled in welcome. They wore clingy, sheath dresses and sported sweeping hairdos pinned with flowers.

"Are you Hiroshi Shimizu?" One of the women asked, amused.

"Yes, I am. How—"

The other woman dug behind a curtain and pulled out a garment bag from a rack of coats.

"Your wife—"

"Girlfriend."

"—left it for you."

Hiroshi looked inside. She'd brought him wedding clothes. "Where can I change?"

"I'll show you." She walked him to a room with "Groom" on the outside.

Hiroshi slipped inside to change. Ayana brought him a dark-blue, almost black, jacket and navy slacks. The white wedding tie she'd bought was better than the one from the convenience store. He left the bag with his cruddy clothes at the coat check, and hurried to the double doors of the wedding hall.

Inside, one of the wait staff handed him a seating chart, menu, and schedule printed on thick paper. The banquet hall was cavernous. Fake stars covered the ceiling. Twenty-some round tables seated eight to ten people each.

Wait staff scurried around with plates of food and bottles of wine and beer. The room was dark with spotlights shining on the front podium where the newlyweds sat at a flower-draped table in front of a screen of glittering gold.

The couple, and everyone else, were listening to a woman at a small podium on the stage.

It was Ayana, in an indigo dress, her hair pinned up in thick swirls. She was talking into the microphone with all eyes on her. Hiroshi was too stunned to think of taking a photo.

Everyone in the hall was laughing at what she said. The newlyweds giggled and held hands, the groom in a tuxedo and the bride in a lavish white dress. They must have already changed from traditional Japanese wedding clothes.

One of the wait staff came over with the seating chart and offered to show him to his seat. Hiroshi told her he didn't want to sit down just yet, but he would love a beer. She came back with a glass of beer held in both white-gloved hands. Hiroshi drained it in one go. Another waiter refilled it immediately.

After another glass and refill, Hiroshi thought he might as well sneak to his chair while Ayana was still talking. Another of the wait staff led him to his seat at the front table.

He unfolded his thick cloth napkin and nodded politely at Ayana's colleagues. A waitress brought the first two courses for him. Everyone else was on the third course. Ayana's food sat untouched beside him. Hiroshi forked in the salad and scallop gratin. A waiter came over and poured champagne and red wine for him.

At the podium, Ayana delivered her speech like an actress, pausing at the right places to deliver the most important lines. The groom, red-faced with drink, took the hand of the bride, who touched a lacy white handkerchief to her misty eyes as the hall echoed with laughter and applause.

Ayana came to the end and walked over to give the bride a hug, tears streaming down both of their faces. Everyone let out a collective "Awww," before breaking into sustained applause.

Ayana bowed, pirouetted off the stage, and returned to her seat, giving Hiroshi a hard stare before joining in the continued applause.

Hiroshi knew he was in for it. He waved to the wait staff for more wine and put his arm around Ayana's bare shoulders, which had sparkles on them. He reached for her hand under the tablecloth, but couldn't find it. He touched her thigh but she pulled it aside.

The MC stepped to the podium, thanked Ayana, and introduced the next speaker, the best friend of the groom. As the handsome young man bounded to the dais, Ayana whispered, "Come with me."

When Ayana got up, one of the wait staff hurried to pull out her chair. Hiroshi followed her out of the hall. At the main door, a waiter cradling a bottle of wine circled to the side to hold the door open with a deep bow.

Ayana hurried toward the women's toilet without a word. She rushed in leaving him outside the door.

From inside, he heard Ayana vomiting, retching in loud heaves.

"Ayana? Are you OK?" He heard water running, Ayana rinsing her mouth, and spitting.

After a quiet minute, Ayana pulled the door open. "I will never forgive you for this."

Hiroshi braced himself for the worst. Before he could say anything, Ayana pulled him inside and threw her arms around him. She raised up on her high heels and kissed him hard, backing him against the wall.

Hiroshi kissed back. He had no choice. She turned so she could lean back and wrap her legs around him. The flower in her hair fell out. He leaned hard into her, stretching her sheer silk one-piece dress.

Ayana moaned, and he moved a hand to her breast and kissed her neck, but the door opened and a woman let out a startled, "Eh? *Gomen nasai.*"

The door slammed shut, and Ayana laughed, keeping her hands clasped behind his neck. "My dress is wrinkled."

Hiroshi put his hands around the small of her waist. "We better…" Hiroshi pointed at the door.

"Better what?" She kissed him again, pulling him closer with his white tie.

Hiroshi didn't want to pull away. "Ayana…?"

She pulled back. "What?"

"Does this mean you forgive me?"

"For now." She reset the straps on her dress and turned to the mirror to straighten her hair. Hiroshi tried to help get the flower back in her hair, but she waved him away and did it herself.

Hiroshi straightened his tie. "You remembered everything except my shoes."

Ayana looked down at Hiroshi's running shoes. "Oh, my." She laughed.

Hiroshi retucked his shirt and tightened his belt. He thought of the cold water of the river to dial his passion down, and straightened his pants.

Ayana surveyed him, brushed his clothes and hair, and rose for a kiss. She pulled back and touched his cheek. "What is that?

Blue dye?"

"I'll explain later."

They inspected themselves side by side in the mirror. Hiroshi felt like he could stand there forever.

They walked out acting dignified. Ayana offered a terse "*Sumimasen*" to the two women still waiting outside.

Hiroshi held the door for them, and they giggled and hurried in.

"I want you to meet my colleagues," Ayana said as they walked over the marble floor to the hall. "Is that OK?"

"That's why I'm here, isn't it?"

"No, you're here to be with me. The food's tasty too."

"You didn't eat anything." Hiroshi stopped at the door to the wedding hall and looked into Ayana's eyes. "Your nausea. Are you OK?"

"Just nervousness." Ayana took his hand as he pulled open the door. "I think."

Thanks to everyone who helped.

Allen Appel
Anne Brewer
Matt Kineen
Nancy LaFever
Marco Mancini
Richard Sheehan
BeauteBook

And thanks also to friends, family and students.
And always, to my miso and my mayonnaise, my wife.

Michael Pronko

If you enjoyed this book, please consider taking a minute to write a review on your favorite book-related site. Reviews really help indie writers like myself.

And if you're interested in future releases and news and insights from Tokyo, sign up for my newsletter here:

www.michaelpronko.com/newsletter

About the author

Michael Pronko is the author of three mystery novels and three collections of writings about Tokyo. He has written about Japanese culture, art, jazz, and politics for Newsweek Japan, The Japan Times, Artscape Japan, and other publications for over twenty years. He has appeared on NHK Public TV, Tokyo MXTV and Nippon Television. He also runs a website, Jazz in Japan, about the vibrant jazz scene in Japan.

Michael is a professor of American Literature and Culture at Meiji Gakuin University in Tokyo. He teaches courses in contemporary American novels, film adaptations, and American art and music. When not teaching, writing or listening to jazz, he wanders Tokyo contemplating its intensity and figuring out the stories to come.

His award-winning collections of essays about life in Tokyo are available at online retailers and from his website, as are the Japanese language versions. The novels in the Detective Hiroshi series have won numerous awards.

***

For more on the Hiroshi series: www.michaelpronko.com
Follow Michael on Twitter: @pronkomichael
Michael's Facebook page: www.facebook.com/pronkoauthor
For more about jazz in Japan: www.jazzinjapan.com.

Memoirs on Tokyo Life

Beauty and Chaos: Slices and Morsels of Tokyo Life (2014)
Tokyo's Mystery Deepens: Essays on Tokyo (2014)
Motions and Moments: More Essays on Tokyo (2015)

The Detective Hiroshi Series

The Last Train (2017)
The Moving Blade (2018)
Tokyo Traffic (2020)
Tokyo Zangyo (2021)

CPSIA information can be obtained
at www.ICGtesting.com
Printed in the USA
BVHW031116260223
659226BV00005B/99